DARK THE DREAMER'S SHADOW

Jennifer Bresnick

Aenetlif Press
Boston, MA
MMXV

ISBN 978-0692459195

Aenetlif Press
Printed in the United States of America

CHAPTER ONE

Megrithe took a deep breath, holding it in to steady herself as the empty room spun gently behind her eyes. The *callawif* had been right next to her, but now she was gone, her whispered injunction still ringing in Megrithe's ears. *He is trapped. He cannot be trusted. Find him. Find him before he shatters us all.*

She still felt ill from whatever the Siheldi had done to her – she shivered and sharply thrust the memory deep into the back of her mind – and she ached to stay tucked up in bed where she could rest and sleep. It was safe and secure at the Guild House, and she was surrounded by red iron that would protect her.

There was no place Megrithe would rather be, but the *callawif* had set conditions in exchange for saving her from the Siheldi Queen. The price for her favor was very heavy indeed.

Megrithe had agreed to leave her position as an inspector in the Guild of Miners – the position she had spent her whole life grappling away from richer, prettier, sharper girls – and the thought of doing so was nearly as bad as the death she had narrowly escaped.

Even though she knew she had to keep her word if she wanted to keep her life, she would fulfill the bargain on her own terms. She would not let the Guild Master expel her. Not in front of her superiors and her colleagues and the hopefuls who would trample over her to vie for her place before she could even leave the room. Not in front of the rows of spotty novices and the snickering enforcers and the entire building's curious, gossipy staff. She had done nothing wrong to deserve such treatment. She had only tried to do the duty she had sworn to do. It may not have worked out quite as she might have hoped, but she would accept no censure for it.

She would resign before they could oust her, and avoid the worst of all fates: a black cross next to her name in the record books; a stain upon her family's reputation for all eternity.

Getting out of bed took a bit of trial and error, but eventually she found her feet and staggered over to the writing desk. There was paper in the drawer, and an inkwell nestled in a snug hole in the corner. She sat down and smoothed a piece of the parchment in front of her, trying to think of what she could say that wouldn't make her sound utterly mad.

The words did not come quickly, and they were not written well. She was angry, and full of sadness, and she was probably about to vomit. Nothing she wrote would make much of a difference to anyone, anyway, so she folded the page over a few scribbled lines of regret and secured it with a shaky dribble of candle wax. It would have to do.

The only thing she had in her possession was her borrowed dress, and it had not fared well after being soaked in the ocean's brine after several weeks of sea and more than one rough handling of its owner. The silk was worse than spotted: it was shrunken, stiff, torn, and wrinkled, with ribbons of dye bleeding down the skirt, mimicking the tears that threatened to burst from her cracking heart at any moment.

She didn't want theft to be her last act within the walls she had loved so much, but she couldn't even get the blasted garment over her head again. There was no other choice besides wrapping a bed sheet around her shoulders before she slipped down the stairs with the letter in her hand to find an unattended closet and face the Guild Master, hopefully in that order.

The Master would give her any outstanding wages and let her have the balance of her accounts in gold coins. She could buy some decent clothes, and perhaps a hairbrush. She could find some lodgings in a quiet part of town. She could collect her wits, let her spirit settle, and allow her body to heal. She could find new employment in some commercial venture that might value her skills. In time, perhaps she could find a new purpose. In time, maybe she would learn to feel safe again.

Or she could go back to Niheba. She might no longer have the authority or the desire to arrest Arran for smuggling counterfeit red iron from Cantrid to Paderborn. She might no longer believe that he owned a false and criminal heart worthy of punishment, but the heart he did possess – a mystery to her in nearly all its actions – needed saving, and quickly.

Beneath the waves, she had seen the darkness of unnatural fire, and at the hands of the Siheldi, she had seen the damnation of her soul. The endless abyss had yawned open to swallow her, drag her screaming down through the fraying knot that held the demon underworld at bay. Arran had stopped the Siheldi from consuming her, and the decision had probably claimed his life.

There had been no reason for him to do it. He could

have let her die. He could have used those scant few moments to run, to flee, to save himself. But he had offered himself in exchange for her, unbidden and unexpected. She owed him for that, and she was not used to leaving debts unpaid.

The paper in her hand complained with a dull crinkle as her fist tightened, and she released her grip to smooth it out again. She could try to find a new life of quiet, anonymous contentment after leaving the Guild – or she could complete the task that had nearly driven her to death.

Find him before he shatters us all, the *callawif* had entreated her. Well, she would not be shattered, and she would let no one destroy her. Not with the sickening sorcery of the Siheldi or the honey-coated cunning of the *neneckt*. She would find Arran, wherever he was, as she had found him once before. She would put an end to this madness of seas and stones and nightmare spirits soaked in hate and shadow before anyone else had to suffer for it.

The Siheldi Queen had not defeated her. And if the *callawif* could be believed, it had not yet defeated Arran Swinn. But how long could he fight? It would take days upon days to ride the winds back to Niheba. It might take her several weeks more to gather the help she would need to find a way back under the drowning mountain. She wasn't even sure where she should begin.

With Faidal, most likely. The traitorous sea-dweller had offered to help Arran escape his predicament – right before shutting them into the stony peak's heart and leaving them to die. Certainly, he could not be trusted, but he *would* have the information she would need.

Hunting a *neneckt* who had gone to ground was no

easy task, however. Faidal would take extra precautions to keep himself quiet, and there were hundreds of places in Niheba where humans were forbidden to go.

Megrithe would need to enlist the aid of someone with experience in such matters, and that sort of specialized knowledge did not come cheaply or easily in Paderborn. She had a notion of where to look for it. She just had to get past the Guild Master first.

"I can't say I'm all that surprised, due to your recent erratic behavior," the Master said, adjusting the lenses of his spectacles as he read her letter of resignation. "But I am still disappointed, Miss Prinsthorpe. You have always shown great potential and capable service."

"I am disappointed too, sir. But I'm afraid I have no choice. I hope I have not lost the entirety of your good opinion."

"I think that rather depends on what you plan to do with yourself now."

"I thought that I'd like to travel and reconnect with my extended family. One of my father's old friends may be able to help me with that. Does your clerk have a recent address for Andrus Gunhilde, by any chance?"

The Master took off his spectacles entirely to peer at her with palpable disapprobation at the sound of Gunhilde's name. "I am well aware that we encourage lasting friendships with our colleagues, Miss Prinsthorpe, but I cannot in good conscience give you information that might put you in contact with someone like that man again. For your own good – and for ours – I must forbid it. I forbid it completely."

Megrithe was expecting the reaction. Gunhilde was well known to be a violent and dangerous fellow with little sense and even less self-control. The fire she had started in her dormitory had been nothing compared to the damage Gunhilde had inflicted during his time as an inspector, and he had been expelled unequivocally after nearly murdering a senior official with nothing more than a sharp pen.

Based on the tales he had left behind him, Megrithe certainly would not have held any love for such a man, nor any desire to extend her acquaintance with him, despite his close association with the father she had lost many years ago.

But Andrus had a brother, and that brother had a son. If the rumors were true, that son knew more about the *neneckt* and their peculiarities than any other man or woman who lived on dry land.

"I thank you for your concern, sir," she said. "But if I may be so bold as to remind you, you no longer have the grounds to forbid me anything."

"Neither do I have any obligation to help you."

"Yes, sir. I understand. I just thought I'd ask."

The Master sighed and cleaned his lenses against the hem of his robe. "What are you up to, my girl?" he asked in a much gentler tone.

She knew that voice. It was the voice that grown men used to entice secrets from children who hadn't yet learned the pain of false friendship. She had always had the utmost respect for Master Hawken as a shrewd leader, if a ruthless one, and so it didn't wound her that he was treating her like a babe in arms, but neither did it do much to foster any inclination to be transparent with him.

"It was just a passing thought, sir," she said with a warm smile. "There aren't many of my father's friends left. With my mother gone as well, I just assumed he might be able to put me in touch with some of my relatives. I will find him another way. He may be in the city directory."

"The hangman's directory, more likely."

"Perhaps so."

"Go on with you, then," he said. "On your own head be it. You can ask Parry for information when you settle up your accounts, though I don't think he'll know. I doubt there's anyone here who would rather remember than forget him."

"I assure you I feel the opposite about everyone here, sir. I have enjoyed myself immensely during my employment, and I wish you all the very best in luck."

"You will leave an address for yourself with Parry, please," he said pointedly. "I shouldn't like to lose track of you entirely."

"I certainly will when I have one to give."

"See that you do."

"Yes, sir. Thank you."

After a quick curtsey, she was practically trotting her way towards the head clerk's office. Under normal circumstances, a term in Parry's company was nothing to rush into. He was a dour fellow, self-important and achingly bland, but she didn't want to be caught in the halls by someone who might ask her why her eyes were blurring with tears.

The truth of her parting words was weighing heavily on her. She *had* enjoyed herself, and she would miss all of it most terribly. Even the slightly moldering smell of the ancient corridor leading to the clerk's room was making her nostalgic already, and she took a deep breath of it to keep as a memory before stepping through the door.

"All I need is the name of the street, Mister Parry," she said for the third time, her patience quickly waning as the man rummaged uselessly in some large and dusty books, trying to exasperate her so much that she would give up and leave. "And my money, please. Mostly my money, if we're being honest," she sighed when his stubbornness showed no sign of abating. "I can find the address on my own while you collect my funds."

"Not from my books, miss," he warned, holding the tome to his chest like a frightened child when she reached for it. "You might get soot on it. I'm sure there's still some under your fingernails."

Megrithe bit the inside of her cheek as the clerk grumbled off towards the vault to fetch her coins. She really was never going to live that down.

In the end, she left the Guild House for the last time with a great, heavy purse, a heavier heart, and no helpful information whatsoever. It had taken Parry an additional half hour to slowly count her coins, one by one, and then check the amount again before he released her earnings. It was mid-afternoon by the time she stepped out onto the street, and she put her hand to the wallet tucked tightly into the waistband of the undergarments supporting her newly pilfered dress, trying to smooth the ungainly lump it created. It would not do to attract the notice of pickpockets.

She hoped to leave for Niheba soon, but she certainly could not spend the rest of her time in Paderborn with a sack of gold hidden up her skirts. If nothing else, the chafing would be unbearable. She would have to spend the night at an inn, where she could find some relief, though everybody knew that the locks on the doors to guest rooms in public establishments were mainly for show. While she always tried to be generous to serving staff, she had no intention of gifting her life's savings to a nosy maid. The price of true peace of mind would be high, but she had no options other than to pay it.

"Mrs. Lanning, how kind of you to receive me," Megrithe said as graciously as she could while standing on the curb of the deserted road, facing down the old woman's mistrustful stare. "My name is Megrithe. I believe you knew my father, Gustin Prinsthorpe."

"Aye, I did," she replied shortly, showing little further interest at the mention of the name.

"Well, I was hoping that I might have a word with your husband about a business matter, if he's available."

"And what would my husband have to say to you, Inspector? You Guild pretties aren't much of a friend to our kind."

"Now, Mrs. Lanning, I know for a fact that you don't object to Guild patronage on principle."

"Principle? No. But practice is another matter entirely."

Megrithe smiled politely. "Yes, well. Perhaps I can change your mind if you'll give me just a moment."

"Steady on, girl," the old woman said, more than a little shocked as Megrithe turned aside, hiked up her skirt, and reached up under her dress. "This ain't that type of establishment."

"I have quite a bit of gold in my hand and no place to put it, Mrs. Lanning," she said, showing her the purse. "I should be very happy to leave some of it with you permanently, if I could come in off the street. I'm no beggar."

"No, apparently not," the woman agreed, eyeing the

coins with a slightly softer expression before she stepped aside.

Mrs. Lanning asked her guest to wait in the parlor while she found her husband, and Megrithe gratefully took a seat. It had barely been half a day since she awoke in her strange bed, and her head was still swimming. She closed her eyes for a moment to calm her nausea, but found herself jerking awake some time later as the sensation of falling through treacle alerted her hindbrain to the fact that she had nearly slipped off the chair.

"Rough morning, my dear?" Mister Lanning asked as she stood to greet him.

"Yes, sir. I'm so sorry, sir. That was very rude of me."

"Not at all. Sit down," he said, waving her back into her chair and ignoring her curtsey as he took a seat opposite. "How much rougher have these days been for Arran Swinn?"

"I – I beg your pardon?"

"You heard me."

"I didn't know you were acquainted with him," she said quietly, dropping her eyes as he stared intently at her.

"Swinn has been a valuable customer of mine for a long time. And you followed him to Niheba not much more than a week ago. So how come you are back here so impossibly quickly, Miss Prinsthorpe? And what have you done to our mutual friend?"

"I'm afraid I cannot discuss the matter."

"No? It was bad enough to make you resign from your post, though."

"That was less than an hour ago," she said sharply. "How could you know that?"

"Never you mind how I know. The fact is that I do. Swinn is a good man, and more importantly, I've made a lot of money off of him. You wouldn't come here trying to use your father's good name – God rest his soul – unless you wanted something from me, and you're smart enough to know what it means to do business here. So let's talk."

"I need Leofric Gunhilde," Megrithe said after a moment. "Andrus' nephew. If you can tell me where he is, I will tell you why I want him."

Lanning sat back in his chair and took out a handkerchief, which he used to mop a sheen of dewy perspiration off his head. "You don't want Andrus or Leofric," he said, tucking the cloth back into his pocket. "You want Nikko."

"Yes, sir. I do. But Andrus is much easier to find, the way he cuts up a scene. Leofric is too discreet."

"What are you driving at, Miss Prinsthorpe?"

"If you are interested in Arran's welfare, you will point me towards the pair of them," she told him. "I will tell you everything if you just give me a clue."

"Persimmon Street," he said after thinking hard for a while. "The house with the blue door."

"Thank you," she said, immensely relieved just to have a hint of something to build her plans upon.

"Don't thank me just yet. You have a lot more to say. Now, how about Mrs. Lanning fetches you a nice strong cup of tea to fortify you while you spin us your tale."

Megrithe got more than some tea out of the Lannings as she told them the story of her journey to the *neneckt* island. There was a hearty breakfast in it for her, too, which she hadn't realized she wanted until she had half cleaned her plate, and a nip of brandy at the bottom of her mug that helped clear out the cobwebs in her mind.

The banker had not given her much special treatment in regards to his holding fees for her money, although he had promised that the balance would be available in full whenever she wished. She had taken a healthy amount with her in case she needed to spread it about, because she didn't know what kind of man Leofric would turn out to be. She didn't know what kind of man Nikko would turn out to be, either, but there was never any telling what a *neneckt* was going to do from one moment to the next.

The blue door was easy enough to find now that she knew where to look for it. Persimmon Street ran through a quietly middling neighborhood, filled with the sort of people who filed dutifully from workplace to home every evening and stayed inside when they got there. Flashy décor was generally discouraged, and the sky-colored paint made the small house as distinct from its neighbors on the outside as its residents were in their beds.

"Can I help you with something, miss?" asked a slim young man with bare feet who came to the door upon hearing the bell.

"I was hoping to see Mister Gunhilde," she replied, trying not to stare at him. His eyes were a startling shade of emerald green, the pupils glimmering like polished silver. Their strangeness did not at all detract from his obvious, perfect, nearly maddening beauty, and he seemed very aware of it.

"Which Mister Gunhilde would that be?" Nikko asked, a smile playing on his lips.

"The younger," she said. "Both of the younger ones, actually."

"How good of you," he replied, the smile widening a

little. "And you are?"

"Inspector – that is...just Miss Prinsthorpe. I'm not an inspector. Not anymore."

"Perhaps you should come in, Miss Not-An-Inspector Prinsthorpe," he said, cocking his head curiously before ushering her inside.

"Thank you. Is your – is Leofric here now?"

"I'll get him. Won't you take a seat? I'll have Marius bring you some tea."

She knew she shouldn't be surprised at how ordinary the parlor looked. There was a pair of framed miniatures on the mantle, overseeing a pair of sedate rosewood chairs on either side, and there was clean, crisp cotton swooping decoratively across the windows. A few cushions were scattered on the floor in a corner next to a stack of half-read books, but the formal furniture seemed to get more use.

The only truly odd thing was the screen in front of the fireplace: an openwork mosaic of bright blue, green, and amber sea glass that would make the light of the flames shimmer across the walls at night like the moonlit waves danced above Emyer-Ekvori, the *neneckt* capital.

The thought of the beautiful, treacherous city, sparking like a jewel underwater, made her swallow hard to get rid of the lump in her throat. Its impression on her, during her brief visit, had not been a very nice one.

"Good afternoon," Leofric said from halfway down the stairs. In stark contrast to his lover's informality, he was rather stiffly starched and buttoned up in a dark, high-collared jacket and boots that must have been brand new from the way they squeaked. He appeared a bit older, with the beginnings of a gray streak in his neatly clipped beard, but there was an ornamented serviceman's sword on his hip and every indication in his movements that he knew exactly how to use it.

"I'm so sorry, but I'm just on my way out," he told her. "Normally I would be honored to help the Guild in any way possible, but..."

"This isn't about the Guild, sir," Megrithe said as Nikko took a seat while their serving boy brought in a tea tray. "I was hoping to speak to you about a personal matter."

"I'm afraid we don't speak to strangers about personal matters, miss," Leofric said. "Although they do seem to find out a great deal on their own."

"You are right, sir. And there is gossip enough on every corner to keep me entertained if that is what interested me. But it isn't. I need help with a very delicate issue, and more than gossip tells me that you're the right two men to speak to."

"Men, is it?" Nikko laughed, leaning forward to pluck a sweet from the tray, but frowning slightly as he sat back again.

She couldn't tell if she had offended him. Did *neneckt* dislike being referred to by the way they appeared? Nikko had chosen his face and form, after all, just as easily as he could choose to look like a woman or a child or anything in between.

"I need you to come with me to Niheba," she said, pushing on regardless. There was no point in tiptoeing around it. They would either say yes or no, and the way Nikko was now looking at her was starting to put her off.

She expected them to laugh at her, but they didn't. They just exchanged a glance, and then Leofric sat down.

"That is quite a thing to ask of a stranger," he said carefully. "What need would drive you to a question like that?"

"An urgent one, Mister Gunhilde. A man's life is at stake. Much more than one man. Everyone is in danger."

"You want help saving the world, do you?" Nikko asked, reaching for another confection. "No, thank you. Too hard to guarantee the chance of a hot bath."

"I'm rather of the same opinion," Leofric said, but he had met Megrithe's eye and was not looking away. "But I'd like to know why you should say such an extraordinary thing."

"Even aside from your choice in companionship, Mister Gunhilde, you know more about the *neneckt* than any human on this earth. I need to learn everything you can tell me about them. They have captured a friend of mine, and I must find him. I cannot tell you more than that without confirmation of your trust, but I will say that there is a rotten heart to Emyer-Ekvori, and I know that neither of you will stand for that."

"You know nothing about what we stand for, miss," Nikko said, growing very serious. "It is dangerous to presume that you do, no matter to whom you're speaking."

"I am well aware, sir, I assure you," she replied. "But you are both honorable men, and I –"

"What did I just say about presumptions?" Nikko asked, cutting her off sharply.

"Nikko, give her a bit of rope," Leofric said soothingly. "She isn't trying to upset you."

"No, I'm not," Megrithe agreed. "I'm sorry. Please give me the words you prefer and I will use them."

"Never mind," the *neneckt* muttered, slumping back in his seat at an admonishing look from his partner.

"I know you were both involved in creating the Treaty of Libourg," she said, trying to choose her words more carefully in order to stop Nikko's glower from deepening. "I know you both care very much about maintaining the peace between Niheba and Paderborn. I am only asking you to help me ensure that there will still be people left alive on the continent to appreciate your hard work."

"The Treaty of Libourg was some time ago," Leofric said. "We are both retired."

"And yet you appear to be dressed for court, Mister Gunhilde. Just a social call upon King Malveisin, I imagine?"

Leofric smiled briefly. "Naturally."

"What is the threat to us?" Nikko asked. "You must at least give us some clue."

"There is going to be a war. The *neneckt* are having dealings with the Siheldi. The Guild would be powerless to stop it, even if they had the faintest inkling about what is happening. I know no one else who would be able to muster up the strength to try. If I don't get my friend back soon, Tiaraku will murder us all."

"So to help you in this hopeless task, you turn to a pair of outcasts with no social standing, no political position, no money, and no armies, whose only power is to scandalize their enemies to death?" Leofric said.

"Speak for yourself, darling," Nikko said. "For me, it also works on my friends."

"I'm turning to someone who knows the *neneckt* better than the *neneckt* know themselves," she said. "Your power to scandalize is just a bonus. There is a person – a *neneckt* I need to find," she said, glancing quickly at Nikko as she corrected her choice of words. "He knows where my friend is, but I don't know where he's hiding. That's why I need you. Please. Just listen to me."

Leofric sighed and unhooked the buckle on his sword belt, placing it against the side of his chair. Nikko rolled his eyes, but poured out three cups of tea.

"We're willing to indulge you, apparently," the *neneckt* said, handing one to her. "Tell us more about this budding war of yours."

CHAPTER TWO

Nievfaya sat in the dark, her knees drawn up to her chin as she thought. Her rear end was starting to hurt from resting on the flat stone that had briefly served her as a bed, unencumbered by a soft mattress or sheets and pillows. There was nothing soft in that place: nothing warm, pleasant, or welcoming in the lightless underworld that lurked beneath the ocean's floor. The Siheldi had no need of comfort for themselves, and they didn't have guests often enough to understand the concept of hospitality. It was unlikely they would offer it even if they could.

The fact that Nievfaya had survived the passage through Sind Heofonne, the gateway between the world of the living and the realm of the dead, was a miracle in itself. The flesh she had worn as Faidal had been seared away during her passage, and she was not sorry for it.

She had always disliked being a man. Many *neneckt* felt equally comfortable as either human gender, and chose a form according to their whims or needs of the moment. Among the land-dwellers, they were famous for their flexibility, but she had always thought of herself as leaning towards the feminine in her own mind.

She had much preferred to be Elargwyd, with her red dresses and soft skin and her pleasing figure, than to suffer through the stinking companionship of other men on the *Celia*, or to endure the foreign feeling of that thing between Faidal's legs that seemed to have an inconveniently mobile life of its own.

She was not particularly proud of either of her recent incarnations. They had done terrible things for terrible reasons, and they had landed her in absolutely the last place she could ever wish to be. Everything was wrong in the darkness. Everything was crushingly close, with the weight of the entire world pressing down on her, trapping her into a little capsule of stuffy, suspended space sandwiched between miles of rock above and below.

While she could tolerate dry land with little discomfort, few *neneckt* strayed too far from the scent of the sea if they could help it. The ocean was her home, her birthright, and the only place where she felt safe – as safe as she ever could, at least. But here in the forsaken hell where she had found herself, there was no salt tang on the gently endless wind or tender swaying of friendly currents to bring her peace. There was no cool rushing of the tide to set the rhythm of her soul to the passing of the hours, or the shifting, freckled sands to anchor her to the gods of her kind.

But leaving those things behind was part of the choice the Siheldi had given her, and she had submitted to the demands of the situation. She had saved herself, for the moment – and more importantly, she had saved Arran Swinn.

The pendant she had stolen from Bartolo's pocket had red iron in it: just a thin wire, brittle enough to crumble into powder. She had made Arran swallow the iron dust, hoping she had ground it fine enough not to cut open his throat from the inside, and so had preserved the last precious drops of his life from the Siheldi Queen's thirst for as long as the mineral stayed in his body.

With any luck, that would be indefinitely. Every *ncneckt* knew that red iron did not pass through flesh in the same way as food and drink. The priests said that it stayed in the blood, and that sometimes the land-dwellers ate the metal to protect themselves from the night spirits without the risk of theft involved in carrying the material on their person.

She remembered being told, as a youngling, any number of gruesome tales about humans who were cut open by curious surgeons upon their deaths only to find that their livers and lungs were filled with huge lumps of black and grainy filings.

Nievfaya wasn't sure she believed all the stories, but she hadn't had much time to debate the issue. She hadn't even had time to think about what it would mean if the Siheldi could not put a hand to Arran's flesh without being burned.

Arran had plunged a blade deep into his own chest to prevent the Queen from supping on his spirit, and the Siheldi were not known for being well-versed in the arts of healing. Nievfaya had not been allowed to see or speak to him, nor had she even been told if he, too, had survived the journey through the molten gate.

The notion that it could have all been for naught had been plaguing her for hours – maybe days, for all she could tell about the passage of time in the lightless prison – and she had sunk into an anxious gloom, gnawing her fingernails down to the quick as she waited and waited for something to happen.

When something did happen, it surprised her enough to make her jump half way out of her brand new skin.

You will come, a voice said, suddenly close by her ear,

and she couldn't help flinching away. Normally, a *neneckt* had little to fear from the Siheldi, but Nievfaya was deep in their kingdom after betraying the tentative peace that had lasted between their two houses for millennia, and she hadn't exactly knocked nicely at the door when she asked to come in.

"Where will you take me?" she asked.

To the dying man.

She didn't need another word, but stood up swiftly and followed the faintest of firefly lights that bloomed in front of her. The Siheldi were the opposite of light, and they hated it with all the power within them, but the spirit seemed to know that she would need a guide. The glimmer was too weak to show much of her surroundings as it bobbed along in front of her, and she groped along uncertainly as she tried to keep it in view.

The tunnel was made of natural rock, she could tell by touch. It reminded her of an ant's nest, dug down into the living bones of the world like the tiny insects burrowed in the soft soil underfoot. There were winding corridors and bulbous chambers, little alcoves and goodly sized rooms, all devoid of recognizable furnishings. The spirits did not take solid form like the *neneckt* were forced to do when they left the protection of the water, and they had not acquired a taste for such things in their own dwellings.

"Where is he?" she asked after a long while of wandering.

Here.

The glow stopped, and Nievfaya did not take another step. It was difficult enough to walk through the lightless tunnels without feeling like she was going to tumble down into an endless void with every footfall, but now she really did think that there was some sort of pit in front of her.

Go down, the Siheldi said.

"How?" she asked.

Go down.

"Arran?" she called to the blankness in front of her. "Are you there?" Only silence answered. "I need light," she said.

There is light for you there. You must go down.

Nievfaya took a deep breath and stuck her foot out in front of her, gingerly sweeping it forward to see if maybe there was a ladder or a stair. There wasn't. It was just emptiness.

Jumping was not an enticing prospect, but the Siheldi could push her if it wanted to, and she would rather avoid that. Instead, she knelt down and felt for the edge, swinging herself over the lip of the chasm so her feet dangled down as far as they could go. She wished she had made her body a little taller.

The breathless fall ended much sooner than she had expected, jarring her bones as her ankles rolled under her, not three feet below her outstretched length. Such a short drop could not break her joints, but it certainly could hurt, and she stayed on her hands and knees for a moment to wait out the pain before feeling the bare stone floor for any sign of what she had been promised.

She couldn't suppress a yelp of relief when her hand closed on the sticky, pitch-covered end of a torch. A bit more sweeping with blind fingers led her to a pair of flints, and she struck the stones together so eagerly that it took her twice as long as was strictly proper to get a flame going.

When she did, she had to squeeze her eyes shut against the brightness of the flare. In the after-image on the back of her eyelids, she could see the shape of a man lying huddled in the corner of the pit, and she immediately crawled forward to find him.

"Arran? Talk to me," she said, resting the torch against the wall of the carven hollow, feeling thick, oozing blood nearly everywhere she put her hands. "Talk to me," she commanded again.

She could feel his breath, so very slow and shallow, but only because she had slipped knuckle-deep into a ragged gash under his ribs.

"I need bandages," she shouted upwards. A *neneckt* might survive an injury that serious, but she didn't think a land-dweller could. She had been kept too long from him, and she didn't know if anything she did now could help. "Please. And clean water and towels. I'll put out the torch for you."

Do it, the Siheldi told her, but it seemed farther away. It would not come down into an enclosed space with a fire burning. It couldn't.

Nievfaya ground the end of the torch under her heel while pressing as hard as she could with both her hands on what seemed like the worst of Arran's wound.

As soon as the light was extinguished, a soft thud near her leg made her reach out again. It was a bundle of cotton strips wrapped around something hard in the center. Surgeon's tools, she discovered when the light had been kindled again. Tools, a needle with thread, and a little vial of some liquid that glittered softly in the flickering light.

She wasn't a surgeon, and she didn't know what the cordial was, but she did know what to do with the needle. Or at least she would, if the edges of the gaping slash were firm enough to sew together. Corruption had already started to take root in the flesh, and every time she tried to make a stitch, the skin melted away and left the bloodied thread bare again.

"He's going to die," she said, giving up and simply binding everything together by winding the bandages around and around his chest as tightly as she could. "Do you hear me? There's nothing I can do. He's going to die."

He will not die.

"He's mostly there already," she argued. "I can't save him."

He will not die, the Siheldi voice repeated. *Nor will you, when you are in this place. It is protected.*

Nievfaya paused to consider the words for a moment before she reached out and touched the wall of the pit. There was a glassy smooth coating that was bitingly cold on her skin.

"*Bezhaka* stone," she said, surprised. She felt a little better with that information in hand, but not enough to slow the return to her anxious work, tightening another layer of bandages around Arran's middle as the gore started to seep through the first.

Bezhaka was nearly as valuable to the *neneckt* as red iron was to human men, though it had a different purpose. Shards of the milky stone could be found buried beside the scorching hot crevasses in the sea floor where the breath of the earth escaped into the ocean, and it was sacred to the sea people above all other things.

The *oughon* carved the crystals into secret shapes that channeled and amplified the shamans' power. The stones could be filled with magic like jars were filled with wine, so their spells for healing or luck or love could be sold, shared, and used by those without the same level of innate skill. It was a crucial part of *neneckt* rituals, too, for sealing promises and oaths, celebrating births, commemorating deaths, and binding the fealty of a vassal to his lord or a slave to his master.

Most of the common uses for the stone required pieces no bigger than the hollow of a child's hand, and finding a greater quantity through ordinary means was very difficult indeed. But every inch of the walls surrounding Nievfaya was lined with it. So much *bezhaka* would be immensely powerful, and it would allow the night spirits an untold influence over other living things. The Siheldi could keep Arran in a permanent twilight state if they wanted, preventing his death but holding his soul a helpless prisoner. He would dream for decades if they wanted him to. If they wanted, he would dream until the world came to an end.

During the frantic fight in the volcano's crater, Nievfaya had thought that the Siheldi Queen required Arran's death for whatever rite she hoped to perform, but it appeared she was wrong. It was clear enough now that the Queen wanted him alive. She wanted him pliable and suggestible; too weak to resist whatever she had in store for him, but still breathing. Nievfaya had given her exactly what she wanted, holding to the general belief that life was better than death, even for Arran Swinn.

She wondered, now, if she had been wrong to save him. She wondered if it would be better to sit back on her heels and let the pool of his blood on the ground slowly deepen – let him slip away into the darkness where he would know no more pain. It was no mercy to prolong his suffering. Not if the fate of all other lands was at stake.

The notion swam about in her head for only a moment before she pushed it aside. Death was no solution. The Queen may want him living, but so did the Siheldi's enemies. If Nievfaya kept him breathing, at least she would keep the chance of victory alive along with him.

And the *bezhaka* might end up being a gift she had not counted upon. Nievfaya herself knew little about the ways of the *oughon*, but she did know that the stone could work a bit like a speaking trumpet, lending strength to wishes and desires and funneling them upwards towards the gods. Perhaps they would be listening, she thought as she surveyed her handiwork, wondering if there was anything else she could do with the limited resources available to her.

If they were, then Tiaraku would be listening too, she reminded herself glumly. He could see many things with his far-sighted mirrors, and even the warded blackness of the Siheldi kingdom might not be beyond his sight. She hoped she was wrong. Keeping the sea king in ignorance of Arran's fate might be the only advantage she had at the moment, and she did not want to lose it.

Tiaraku would be watching the gateway of Sind Heofonne, but there had to be other entries and exits to the underground world, she mused. It was a prison to the Siheldi now, but it had been their rightful homeland for long, long centuries before the Queen was ever tamed.

The mechanisms of her captivity had been devised by the *nencckt*, the ancient legends said, and maybe her forbearers had been wise enough to anticipate a need for some communication, or some exchange of words or goods that necessitated flexibility in its design. Maybe she could use that wisdom to smuggle Arran away undetected. Failing that, maybe she could bring help down into the dark.

It would help to know how deep inside the earth she was, the less optimistic part of her pointed out, and it was clear that she would not be able to drag Arran's limp form up from the pit where she had found him. Neither could she see or track or fight the thousands of spirits that surrounded her if she decided that she had the inclination to try.

Reasoning her way out of her predicament seemed equally destined to fail – unless she could bring back something for the Siheldi that they couldn't get for themselves. But what did a soulless, deathless, formless entity desire from the mortal world, other than the massacre of innocent living things?

"I'm going to need more bandages," she said, tipping the little vial of medicine into Arran's mouth, trying not to let too much of it dribble wastefully down his chin as he sluggishly swallowed. She wasn't entirely sure what it was, exactly, but it smelled like it had *torodro* leaves in it, which were good for staunching bleeding. "And I need to stay with him to make sure he's all right. Give me something to make a proper fire. He's too cold."

No, the Siheldi said. *You will return to your place.*

"Are you going to come down here and make me?" she asked, gripping the torch in one hand and putting the other on Arran's shoulder. "I have flame and red iron. You will do as I say."

The sound of the Siheldi laughing felt like it was going to rip her stomach from her middle and wring its meager contents out onto the floor like sponge. It was not a sound that should exist, and yet it went on assaulting her ears for some time as the spirit expressed its scorn at her boldness.

You will do as I say, it repeated, mocking her words. It only took a moment for a gust of wind to sweep down into the hole and whip away the flame of the torch, plunging her into absolute darkness again.

You will go where we tell you, the creature said less than an inch from her ear, and she instinctively scuttled backwards into the wall, but she still kept her hand on Arran for what good the proximity to the iron in his body might do her.

"I will stay with him," she said firmly. "I am as much imprisoned here as anywhere."

The Siheldi laughed again, but this time the brutal assault on her ears was tempered by the dolorous scraping of stone on stone.

As you wish, the spirit said as she realized what was happening. The enormous lid that was slowly moving over the top of the pit didn't make the blackness any blacker, but the slight current of air from the long, open passageway above her faded as the slab of rock closed in.

Shouting did her no good, nor did jumping as high as she could to try to feel for any holes or cracks that might let the air in. There must be some way to breathe in the sealed cavern, or Arran would not still be alive, but the dense air was warm and clinging close and already crawling underneath her skin. She felt like a chicken that was about to be stewed in a cooking pot, and the chill of the *bezhaka* where it touched her did nothing to stop the nervous sweat from beading on her brow.

If anything, the cold stone amplified the horrible feeling. There was something flowing through the crackled craze of sooty veins already – the walls were humming with words of power that she couldn't quite hear, like the gentle breathing of a sleeping predator she dare not disturb for fear of becoming its next meal.

She settled back on her heels and took a deep breath, preparing to close her eyes and concentrate on a chant intended to calm distress, taught to her by her beloved *nienna*. Her great-grandmother had always been fond of telling tales that had been old when she was just a hatchling, and had spread them deeply again during her time as matriarch of the Black Salt Clan. Nievfaya hoped the words would bring back those pleasant memories of sitting by her elder's side, rapt and eager, soaking up the ancient wisdom of her heritage.

"Sea Father, Sun Mother, Brothers Sand and Sky," she whispered in the *neneckt* tongue. "Grant me your protection as I wander far from the shining waters. Lead me to the stillness past the breakers and preserve me from the anger of your brothers, your uncles, your foes. Sea Father, Sun Mother, help me..."

Help me, echoed something just on the edge of her ear, making her pause. It wasn't the voice of a Siheldi, with its ringing sharpness and concussive woe. It was softer, and farther away, and infinitely more desperately sad. It was the voice of a child, a little boy lost to everything it knew, wandering in the dark as its tiny heart churned with instinctive, primal fear.

She had heard that voice before. It had been her voice, the day the Kitefins came. The sea light had run ruddy as the raiders devastated her home: a cluster of cool, shady kelp farms far outside the glittering glamor of Emyer-Ekvori. The Kitefins were Tiaraku's clansmen, and a more vicious pack of cutthroats had never been born under the waves. Her *nienna* had died defending her land that day, along with eight of her half-brothers and half-sisters from her mother's latest brood, and twelve more of Nievfaya's own nest mates.

Someone had told her once that she had been lucky to survive it, but she had never been able to agree. There wasn't much luck in being sold into servitude, orphaned, wounded, and alone. Her injuries had healed, eventually, but her heart never had. There was no hope in slavery. There was no hope for her at all – until Bartolo had found her, and offered her a chance to change her fate.

Help me, the voice repeated, and she turned towards Arran, putting a hand in front of his mouth to feel for his breath. It was still there, if barely stirring, but there was no movement to form the words.

"Sea Father, Sun Mother, Daughters Sand and Sky," she said again, her voice shaking as the echo lingered on and on. "Grant me your protection as I wander far from the shining waters. Help me. Please, I beg all the gods. Help us all."

CHAPTER THREE

"Hurry up, you idiot," Bartolo hissed at Johan as the servant insisted on folding and smoothing each piece of clothing before packing it. Bartolo had already gathered everything that was important to him – mostly just his collection of ancient gold and silver coins – and now the manservant was lagging behind. "They'll be here any minute."

Tiaraku had a cavern full of far-seeing mirrors that he used to gaze upon his empire, and there was little doubt in Bartolo's mind that he had been using them to watch his servant very, very closely as the last critical moments of their plan had gone awry. The *neneckt* king would be sending his soldiers to demand an explanation, and Bartolo didn't particularly want to be part of that conversation.

"Just forget it," he snapped, snatching a tin of some sort of polish from Johan's hands and hurling it across the room. "I don't need any of that. Let's go."

Johan closed the knapsack, putting it over his shoulder and following Bartolo out of the room without stopping to put together anything for himself.

Bartolo scooped up his leather roll of jeweler's tools from the table and stuffed it into his pocket, one hand on the doorknob, before he froze under a wave of panic.

"Where's the pendant?" he said, rounding on Johan, who looked blank. "Swinn's pendant. Where is it?" he demanded again, thrusting his hand into every crevice of his coat, his eyes frantically scanning the room to see if the shell of tarnished silver had fallen into a corner.

"Did you take it? Did you think I wasn't going to notice if you try to make a tidy little profit off the iron? Answer me right now, you son of a bitch," he snarled, lunging towards his man, who took a step back and scooted around the table to safety, his face white and his wide eyes focused beyond his irate master at the doorway behind him.

"Is there a problem here, Bartolo?" asked Habur, who has silently found his way into the chamber with a trio of serious-looking soldiers at his back, their solid bulk blocking the door.

It was an unusual sight in Emyer-Ekvori. It took a lot of effort for a *neneckt* to fight its native element and hold together a physical form underwater. Tiaraku's captain took pride not only in doing so, but also in making his physical appearance match the caliber of his strength. Bartolo had to crane his neck upwards to look the warrior in the face.

"Lost something, perhaps?" Habur added, enjoying the discomfort he was causing.

"None of your damn business," Bartolo replied, trying to regain his composure as Johan silently glared at him from the other side of the room.

"Oh, I don't think that's true," Habur said. "It became my business the moment Tiaraku ordered me to mop up your mistakes. He'd like to see you, if you can spare the time. Derrol will be sure to watch your bags for you," he said, nodding for one of his subordinates to step forward. "We wouldn't want them to sneak away without you."

"How very kind," Bartolo said, trying not to let his tight smile shrink into a frown as Johan immediately poured a good measure of his master's wine for Derrol with a suspiciously respectful bow.

"Help yourselves," he muttered as Johan added a goblet for the second *neneckt*. A dwindling wine cellar would be the least of his problems now that Tiaraku knew he had been trying to flee. Bartolo would be lucky to escape with his skin intact, let alone have the opportunity to scold his servant for such unwarranted obsequiousness.

"Save some for me," Habur called over his shoulder, smirking as Bartolo's shoulders tightened under the hand he was using to steer him out of the room.

Tiaraku's seeing hall was large, cool, and dark. A hole in the very center of the domed roof let a single shaft of sunlight filter down through the water to touch a line of mosaic shell inlaid into the floor, dotted with colorful glass symbols that marked the hours at regular intervals which turned the entire chamber into a massive sundial.

In a wide circle stood Tiaraku's mirrors, each dedicated to the sight of a certain aspect of his realm. One showed the vast expanse of Emyer-Ekvori from far above the seabed, each path and road a brilliant white vein through the craggy skin of tumbled rock. Others peeked into the fine homes of his honored Kitefin clansmen, glimpsing into offices and studies, kitchens where serving staff gossiped, and bedrooms where couples sealed secret trysts, whispering love and treasons.

On land, too, Tiaraku kept his eye. A number of the enchanted portals were devoted to the palace of King

Malveisin, ruler of the human kind. The Guild House in Paderborn; a prosperous farm in Cantrid where a former minister had retreated for a retirement that was no such thing; Tiaraku's ironworks in the city of Niheba, where plain metal was transformed into fake red gold. Bartolo's own apartments; a heavy barge lumbering across a placid sea; the harbor in Port Ravenaught, where unlabeled crates were being hoisted onto the docks.

There was one blank mirror, pitch dark and slightly cloudy, as if a frost had crept over the image to obscure it from the king's vision. There was nothing to see, but it had nonetheless captured Tiaraku's whole attention.

The ruler of the *neneckt* rarely cloaked himself in fleshly form, but he didn't need to. The sheer force of his presence filled the room like an invisible, billowing smoke, making it clear even to the dullest understand that he was there – and that he was angry.

"Your Majesty," Bartolo said hesitantly, "I assure you that I am -"

"A complete and utter failure," Tiaraku rumbled, making Bartolo cringe. "Do not try to justify yourself to me. I have seen everything. You will be punished for your stupidity."

"Please, Majesty. I will fix it."

"Will you, now? And how will you fix this?" the king asked with a swirl of water towards the black mirror. "Swinn is down there, somewhere, and I have no sight. Will you brave the fires of the Siheldi yourself to bring him back?"

"I don't think it will be necessary for me to go personally, sire," Bartolo said carefully. "I did make plans in case the situation got away from us."

"You planned to run away and hope I could not find

you."

"No, sire. Of course not. I was merely hurrying to reach my contacts on Niheba to help me rectify the problem. They are nearly as well versed in the ways of the Siheldi as your own advisors."

"Children," Tiaraku scoffed. "Mewling babes toying with embers from the hearth. They have never proven themselves worth a clamshell."

"The Divided have grown strong in the time since you came to the throne, sire," Bartolo replied. "They brought my father to you. They brought me to you. There is no one else who has the knowledge we need."

"You thought *you* did. You have been shown a liar. I can no longer trust you."

"You must, sire. There is nothing else to be done. To leave Arran Swinn in the hands of the Siheldi is to doom your race and mine to extinction. The Queen will figure out how to get what she wants from him. I don't know why she hasn't done so already, but –"

Bartolo stopped mid-sentence as a memory jumped out at him. Faidal had knelt down next to Swinn's body and made him swallow something – Faidal had brushed himself against Bartolo's coat before taking Swinn and the Guild woman away. The pendant was gone, and the Siheldi Queen hadn't been able to complete her plans yet.

That crafty devil, he thought, his mind working at a furious pace. He couldn't even be angry at the *neneckt's* thieving betrayal. It might just have saved them all.

"But it's only a matter of time," he continued as smoothly as he could, suddenly feeling much more at ease. "Give me a chance, sire. A few days. Please. I will deliver Swinn to you, as I did before. And this time, there will be no unforeseen complications."

Tiaraku was silent, brooding in front of his blinded portal as he thought. "I will be watching you, Bartolo," he said eventually. "I will give you a chance to make amends before I take matters into my own hands. Be assured that if I must intervene myself, you will suffer greatly before you give up your last miserable breath."

Bartolo bowed low enough to touch his nose to his knees before backing out of the chamber, followed by Habur.

"I'm not in need of a nurse," he said to the *neneckt*, whose close proximity was making him uncomfortable.

"I'm not your nurse. A nurse wouldn't slice your throat down to the bone at the first hint of disobedience to your king. Get used to my shadow, land slug. You will be seeing it every waking moment and into your dreams."

"My nightmares, you mean," Bartolo said under his breath, and Habur laughed. "Take me to the surface," he demanded. "I have work to do."

Bartolo's ears popped painfully as he left behind the oddly crushing sensation of being deep under the sea. The open air was clean and sweet, with the faintest taste of salt stirring under a heavy green blanket of warm, moist vegetation, and he greedily took in the sight of the bright purple wood sorrel tucked away among the soothing rows of lavender and riotous spears of foxglove that lined the crunching gravel walkways of Tiaraku's pleasure grounds.

He would have to ask the head gardener where he had found that golden pale specimen, he thought absently as Habur trailed him through the rows of red ginger and fire lilies bobbing sagely in the breeze. The way the trumpet of blossoms faded to coral was really quite remarkable.

He would like to boast such plants on his own estates, but he would need to work very hard to find his way back into Tiaraku's favor if he wanted to enjoy the sight and scent of flowers in neatly tended exhibition beds instead of growing over his grave.

"You can't follow me where I'm going," he said to Habur when they had reached the limits of the palace complex. "They will not speak with me if you're flapping about like a wet dishcloth."

"I have no intention of boring myself with your black magic drivel," the warrior sneered, showing no sign of turning aside just yet. "I'm just making sure you're going to the right place. If you decide to play any tricks, you can be certain I will find out about it."

"I would expect no less," Bartolo said, hurrying through the streets as if he had half a hope of losing the *neneckt* before Habur decided to leave him.

The city of Niheba was a sharply segregated one. Each type of resident held strictly to his or her own quarter, all of which were more or less self-sufficient. The shabbier human laborers shopped in stores owned by their fellows, attended church schools run by their priests, drank in taverns that served the watery beer and razor sharp liquors popular among their kind in Paderborn, and laid glass jars of their ashes upon row after row of tiny shelves in tall, stone crypts, refusing to commit their bodies to the corruption of the sea.

While the *neneckt* had the luxury of owning most of the property and business in the metropolis, they too had their separate ways and exclusive neighborhoods. Traditionally, the major clans did not mix, and each had its own slightly different variation on how they presented their architecture, reared their young, and organized their lives.

Tiaraku's Kitefins held court in the center of the city, while their allies clustered around in a roughly-shaped spiral: the Redfin-Pike closest to their cousins, while the Wreckfish pushed in on their borders and the lesser Cuskeels flashily tried to emulate the richer, more powerful families. Merchant clans like the Bluegills and the Saltskins were relegated to the harbor side, shunned for their dealings with the distasteful humans even while they quietly built up enough wealth to rival the king.

Bartolo was not headed for the domains of the well-known tribes, nor even the hovels of the last war's losers: the Black Salts and the Box Claws, whose few unfortunate survivors – those that had not been sold into slavery or executed for treason – were forced to mix together in scrambling despair, crammed up against the land's edge or even spilling over into the areas of human habitation.

Those who had been pushed out of their homes in Emyer-Ekvori, yet could not bear the thought of mixing with the land-dwellers, had even taken refuge under the thin veneer of wood and brick that crusted the crowded island's face. Niheba's cliffs were peppered with caves underneath the waterline that served as homes for many of the disenfranchised *neneckt* too proud to abandon the ocean entirely, and there were caverns that peeped above surface, too.

On the western side of the island, where the green topsoil dropped away into sheer, dark basalt, there were grottos and tunnels that had been carved by the unceasing pounding of the waves. Generally, they did little more than provide excellent purchase for smugglers looking to bypass the Treaty of Libourg's harsh penalties, but some of the hollows held permanent residents with even darker secrets.

They called themselves the Divided, and claimed to live in two worlds, straddling the twilight between the mortal plane of men and the infinite darkness of the Siheldi. The caverns under Niheba were the closest they had ever gotten to Sind Heofonne, since its secrets were so carefully guarded by the *neneckt*, but proximity wasn't their primary goal.

The caves held many other benefits for them. The seeping warmth from the sleeping mountain upon which Niheba was built made the colder rainy seasons more tolerable, and brought with it venomous fumes from the core of the world for the priests to inhale as fuel for their nightmarish rituals. Their friendly relations with their smuggler neighbors gave them first choice of expensive goods too risky to sell in the city, not to mention that news to and from Paderborn traveled fastest and most quietly with those who had the most to lose from being exposed.

Niheba was the primary residence of the insular little society, but there were Divided strewn right across the continent, from Port Ravenaught to the Ivory Isles, working away like burrowing bees to uncover the haunted truths of the Siheldi.

To Bartolo, most of them seemed more than a little bit mad, even though he had been raised on their tales and taught his letters at the knees of the order's greatest men. He had only been a boy when his father had set the trap that mistakenly snared Giles Swinn and his pregnant wife wailing in her labor pains, but he remembered well how his father had done everything he could, from that point on, to rectify his errors. The effort had led to his early death, and Bartolo had made it his mission to succeed where his father had failed, even if it brought him into conflict with his own tutors.

The Divided were not a popular breed, due to the nature of their studies, and it was not uncommon for the humans on the island to invoke their name to curse their minor enemies in the same manner as they would call down the wrath of Kashni the Destroyer on an unscrupulous tradesman or wanton gossip. They were tolerated on Niheba, insofar as the *neneckt* authorities did not actively try to eliminate them, but it had always infuriated Bartolo that they let the prevailing public opinion dictate their actions rather than the other way around.

They slunk about in the night like beggars who skimmed the gutters for forgotten farthings and discarded meals, refusing to use any of the tools that Paderborn or Niheba could provide for them: the ancient libraries, the scholars of the old, withered religions, or the *neneckt oughon* who had mastered the mysteries of flesh and bone while the men of the land were still learning to pile brick upon brick. In Bartolo's mind, the obstinate secrecy of the Divided would be their downfall, and it remained his great pride that he had been the first to get the *neneckt* to cooperate with the cult rather than shun them.

The difference of opinion had made him somewhat unwelcome to the leaders of the unhappy brotherhood, but Bartolo was not truly a member of the Divided to begin with. He was more like a guest – a guest who had plans to make the castle his own – and he had no compunction or conflict of interest that would prevent him from pursuing a strategy that had, so far, reaped him great rewards.

He was looking forward to telling the High Warden that he had been among the first mortal men to gaze upon the forbidden gate to the Siheldi underworld, even if it had been from a distance. But he would need to do so without boasting, because in the next breath, he would have to ask the Warden for help to fix the disaster that had immediately followed.

"That's far enough," he told Habur when they had threaded their way through the respectable areas of the harbor side and come to the elderly, unwashed district where many of the illiterate human workers made their homes. It stank of the sewage that floated thick and oily on the surface of the stagnant canals, and Bartolo lifted a scented lace handkerchief to his nose to keep the pestilence away from him. "You'll shy away my boatman."

"Very well. But if you aren't back at this spot in two hours..." he said over his shoulder as he turned, knowing perfectly well that even a half-formed threat would give Bartolo the shivers.

Bartolo didn't move until the *neneckt* was completely out of sight, then he spun on his heel and hurried down towards the water with a spurt of anxiety as he tried to puzzle out the complicated formula for determining the day's passcode. The moon was just over quarter full, so the next neap tide was more than a fortnight away. That meant the boatman would be expecting three specific words instead of four. He hoped he remembered his festivals properly – and then there was the handshake, too, of course. That was easy enough, but he grimaced as he realized he hadn't brought any gloves. He would have to touch the man's bare skin during the ritual, and the gods only knew what kind of hideous scrofula the stranger might be carrying.

"Good day, sir," he called down to the ferryman when he found him, sitting in a rowboat and eating a pasty, looking bored.

"I ain't for hire," he replied, not bothering to look up as he spat a glob of greasy grizzle into the water.

"I'm not looking for hire," Bartolo said. "I just wanted to know if you had seen the white smoke in the sand."

The man did raise his head then. "Aye, but only at sunset on a feast day."

"The Feast of Green Waters is nearly upon us," said Bartolo, and the boatman nodded. "May I give you my best blessings on this day of peace?"

The man nodded again, and Bartolo carefully climbed down the narrow, steep steps cut into the rock that lined the canal. He was not accustomed to clambering around in boats, and it was with a complete lack of grace that he eventually managed to crawl into the vessel, having chosen the wrong step to use in order to properly launch himself forward.

"Steady on, sir," the man said, grabbing Bartolo's elbow to help him, leaving a streak of oil from his meal on the expensive cloth. "You ain't goin' nowhere if you tip us ought-side up first."

Bartolo did his best to refrain from looking too upset at the stained sleeve or too embarrassed at his lack of seagoing ease, and instead turned his attention to clasping the boatman's hands in just the right way in accordance with the day's appointed sequence.

Bartolo's gestures seemed to satisfy the waterman, and he picked up his oars as his passenger surreptitiously wiped his hand on his kerchief, holding on to the bench as the boat tipped slightly with the building momentum. Thankfully, the stranger didn't see a need to make conversation as he propelled them out of the turgid waterway, and Bartolo sank into his own thoughts, gazing sightlessly at the merchant traffic drifting across the bay as he ordered his words in his mind.

Before he even knew it, they had glided clear across the main harbor and out the other side, with nothing but blue ocean on the left hand and the leaden rock face of Niheba to the right. The island had been thrust upwards from the sea floor at an uneven angle during the fiery pangs of its birth, and millennia of soft, fertile ash had been blown to one side by the prevailing winds as the crater spewed and sputtered, eventually wearing itself down into a flattened hump. The layer of soil had helped to form the gently sloping harbor to the southeast, but had left the jagged cliffs of the northwest exposed to the corrosive bluster of salt and storms.

At their feet were heaps of stony spoil, knocked clear of the towering mass by the winter tempests or the occasional deep rumble of the earth. The wind-whipped waves crashed fiercely along the shore, cloaking rocky teeth ready to gnaw ships to pieces. Bartolo found himself gripping the sides of the rowboat as the man carefully maneuvered them through the spray.

"Are you sure you know what you're doing?" he asked, just a little breathless, as the edge of a hidden stone scraped loudly along the hull, sending a sharp spurt of panic up through the soles of his boots. He was nothing of a sailor, and being at the mercy of the pounding surf was all the worse for the echo of Tiaraku's irate voice that seemed to accompany it.

The ferryman just gave him a weary, condescending look and glanced over his shoulder as he pulled hard on the oars. *Sitting backwards, for the sake of all the gods,* Bartolo thought sourly as he wiped a droplet of foam from his face. How anyone ever got anywhere in such a state was beyond him. He clenched his teeth as the boat started to gain speed, aiming itself directly towards an arch of stone that seemed too low and tight to thread through.

The pilot snorted as Bartolo squeezed his eyes shut involuntarily, bracing himself to feel the crack of his skull on the rock overhead, ducking down as a brief shadow passed in front of his shuttered eyelids.

Almost immediately beyond the arch, everything was silent and smooth as a millpond. They had entered a rounded, sheltered cove that wandered invitingly into a grotto of dappled sun and crystalline sea: a natural dock where the boat's rail kissed gently against a lip of stone. Bartolo let out his breath and smoothed his hand through his hair, shaking off the droplets of water that had gathered like morning dew.

He didn't think the boatman deserved anything more than a quick nod in thanks, which he waited to dole out until he had navigated the tricky step up to the high ledge that led into the heart of the cave. One of the novices was waiting for him, leaning against the wall with his hands stuck deep into his pockets, the sleeves of his robe chronically creased from long repetition of the motion. He stood up straight and bowed appropriately when he saw Bartolo, however, his arms decently at his sides, before he turned and led his guest into the yellowing glow of the tunnel's torchlight length.

The acolyte was not allowed to speak to Bartolo during the long walk, but he didn't mind. Reverent silence was always an acceptable default when treading the sandy halls that led towards the Sanctum, especially when pacing through the tall, narrow door that separated the realm of the Divided from the common world. It was a fine example of stone craft, perfectly fitted into its frame so that it opened without the slightest sound, decorated only with an enormous eye carved into its ashen face, balefully staring down at any interlopers.

Bartolo kept his gaze away from the image. It had fueled his most secret nightmares for many years, with its stark, unceasing judgment. The Divided had made it their purpose to watch what no other men dared to witness; to see what no other men were capable of comprehending, and they did their job well.

Their sight bored even into the very souls of men who hoped to join their ranks, and the punishment for being found wanting was severe. Initiation was not a pleasant experience, and while Bartolo had never completed the process that led to the final, lifelong, binding vows, he had done enough to know that he was perfectly happy with having dropped off along the way.

The man who opened the ponderously heavy portal had not been such a shirker. He had finished his training years before Bartolo had ever come screaming into the world, and his long, gray hair hung over a face that had no use for the scarred and burned sockets where his eyes had been. The Divided looked deeply, but they used only their minds in order to see.

"Good day, Guthrin," Bartolo said, inclining his head in a gesture of respect anyway. The man had been blind for fifty years, and that was certainly long enough for his other senses to sharpen sufficiently to detect a lack of due deference. "I am here to see the Warden."

"I know why you're here," Guthrin replied. "And it is not just to see the Warden. You are a fool, Bartolo. There is no help we could give you for that, even if we wished to."

"I didn't know you spoke for him," he said. "Last I heard, you weren't even allowed to set foot in the council room anymore. Have things changed so much since I've been away?"

Guthrin's face darkened. He would be glaring daggers if he had eyes to throw them with, and Bartolo allowed himself a fraction of a smile. It helped to keep current with politics. They could always hurt.

"You will have to wait," Guthrin said tersely. "He is in the middle of his studies."

"Then get him out of his studies. I will give him something better to chew over."

"You're an arrogant prick, Bartolo," Guthrin muttered.

"Just bring me to him."

Accompanied by a string of displeased throat-clearing, Bartolo was led deeper into the earth, where the tangy scent of sea spray faded under the weight of ash, sulfur, and damp, moldering dust.

Bartolo was not quite as eager to see the Warden as he had indicated, and his breath was coming a little shorter than usual by the time they reached his study.

"You can go in, if you like," Guthrin said, his colorless lips working themselves into a mocking smile. It was impossible to hide the evidence of his discomfort from someone with hearing more acute than that of a white owl. "Or you could wait here while you work up the nerve."

Just to spite him, Bartolo didn't even hesitate before knocking, the rapping thump mimicking the uncertain rhythm of his blood.

"Come," called a strong voice from inside.

Bartolo did as he was told, leaving Guthrin in the hallway as he firmly closed the door, making sure it clicked shut to avoid as much eavesdropping as possible.

"Thank you for seeing me on such short notice, Warden," he said, placing his hands together in front of him in the cult's gesture of respect. The Warden couldn't see it, but he nodded his approval and indicated that Bartolo should take a seat in front of his desk, a purposely haphazard collection of cobbled-together driftwood that always made Bartolo think of the most unflattering stereotypes of blind men.

He had been told, as a boy, about the way that the Divided saw the world despite the fact that their mangled eyes had been burst by hot iron. It was like walking through a dream, one of his tutors had said, where objects could hazily appear and disappear without seeming to have any relationship to the laws of reality. The Divided existed half in that mercurial sphere of shifting reverie and half in the mundane world of their peers, carefully honing the foresight hidden in a mix of old memories and new senses, tumbled together with smells and fingertip touches and a sort of fluid awareness so highly developed that many of the brothers could defeat a trained, sighted man in a fight with hardly a second thought.

Bartolo couldn't beat anyone in a fight, blind or seeing, unless it was a contest of words. It seemed as if the Warden was up for the challenge as he steepled his hands in front of his chin and leaned forward slightly in his chair.

"You expect me to me angry with you, and I certainly am," the Warden said. "You have gone against my every wish, done everything wrong, and now you come to me to clean up your stinking filth. It does not please me to do so."

"I seek only your council, Warden. I am aware that I'm not entitled to anything else."

"Contrition doesn't suit you," the Warden replied, flicking his fingers in a gesture of dismissal. "Don't think that you can toy with me."

"Very well. I have lost my man to the Siheldi and I need him back," Bartolo said simply. "How do you propose I should accomplish this?"

"You gave Swinn to them on a silver plate. Now you want him back? Make up your mind."

"That wasn't how it was supposed to go," Bartolo replied, feeling a flush of blood rising into his cheeks. "The *callawif* interfered before Swinn could use the stones against the Queen. I didn't expect him to try to take his own life. What sort of simpleton would do that when he had the keys to his freedom sitting in his hand?"

"The sort of simpleton who can entirely outfox you, Bartolo. You completely underestimated him," the Warden said. "And the *callawif*, for that matter. Nor did you take Megrithe Prinsthorpe's role into account."

"She is irrelevant. The *callawif* took her away, but she was mostly dead already. It will be months before she even has the strength to sit up in her bed. And they will think her a raving madwoman if she so much as mentions what happened."

"That raving madwoman will be getting on a ship to Niheba tomorrow with a pair of dangerously mad men lured into her wake. And you are going to need her."

"For what?"

"For everything," the Warden told him.

"I don't understand."

"Of course you don't. Do you think you are the only force at work here? If you do not use the Prinsthorpe woman to take the Guild in hand, someone else will. And I doubt they will be as sweet-tempered and forgiving as Tiaraku," he added, standing up in an unmistakable signal that it was time for Bartolo to leave. "He is watching you closely, is he not? I suggest you find some quiet hole to burrow into while you wait for Megrithe to arrive."

"Can I -"

"I didn't mean here," the Warden said, cutting him short. "I will not risk everything I have built just to save you from your own foolish games."

"Foolish games? I've gotten closer to Sind Heofonne than any of you have ever dreamed in the past five hundred years. I think I deserve -"

"You deserve nothing," the Warden snapped. "Do not confuse proximity with progress. You've as good as ruined our chances to do things right. Sending Swinn to the Queen before you were sure of his intentions? With a woman in his care to stir up his honor? I cannot think of anything more amateurish.

"More shame on us that you ever left our halls as such an idiot. I would have you locked up and beaten every day if I thought anything could pound the least bit of sense into you."

"You just try it," Bartolo said, balling his fists by his

sides, but the Warden shook his head.

"I don't need any more attention from Tiaraku's cutthroats at the moment. Go run and hide, Bartolo. The woman will come to Niheba. Even you will be able to figure out what to do then."

Guthrin was looking maddeningly smug as he showed Bartolo out again. He didn't have to listen through the keyhole: the result of the conversation was written all over Bartolo's face, and in his hissing breath, and under his stomping feet as he followed the old man back through the twisting passageways.

He had been savaged, to be sure, and he would not be getting the aid he wanted. But the Warden had not demanded that Bartolo give up the matter to the Divided, which meant he still had the chance to rectify his errors *and* claim the credit when he succeeded. He was sure he would be grateful for the consolation at some point, but that didn't prevent a certain measure of rage at the Warden's scathing words from seething inside him.

"Get out of my way, you clumsy oaf," he nearly shouted at a younger man who had exited a doorway at the same time Bartolo was sweeping past.

"I beg your pardon, sir," the stranger said, nimbly stepping to the side before Bartolo could crash into him. "Aren't you –?"

"Aren't I what?" Bartolo growled, happy enough to use the hapless fellow as a scratching post. "How would you have any idea what the devil I am? You can shove your assumptions right up your –"

"Forgive me, sir," the man said quickly. "I thought I recognized your voice, that's all. Your brother Cederick and I are acquainted."

"My brother has more shiftless acquaintances than I care to count. Which one of them are you?" Bartolo asked, looking at the man a little more closely while Guthrin tapped his foot impatiently a short way down the corridor. The silvery film over his dark brown eyes made it clear that he could not see whom he was addressing, but he did not bear the mottled scars shared by his fellows.

"My name is Jairus Lanque, sir. Cederick and I shared lodgings for a few months in Paderborn before I came here. The Warden arranged it."

"I seem to recall something of the sort," Bartolo acknowledged gruffly.

"Perhaps I could see him out, Guthrin," Jairus called to the older man, who didn't put up much resistance before continuing down the hallway and turning out of sight. "In a manner of speaking, of course," he added with a little smile.

"You don't look like one of them," Bartolo said, still feeling too irritated to be entirely polite as they continued towards the exit. "They didn't blind you."

"No, sir," Jairus said. "A sickness took me as a boy and I lost my sight. I never thought I'd be grateful for it until I learned what the Divided did to themselves to achieve the same ends."

"Rather distasteful, the lot of it," Bartolo replied, clenching his hands again at the memory of the Warden's words.

"Yes, sir. But we seem to get on well enough."

"What do you do in this wretched place, then?" asked Bartolo after they had gone some way in silence.

"Provisions, sir."

"What?"

"I purchase and distribute provisions. The other humans on the island are somewhat wary of those of us with the more gruesome markings, but I don't frighten them so much."

"How do you count your coins? Don't they try to cheat you?"

Jairus smiled again. "I won last year's tourney, sir. And the one before that. No one tries to cheat me."

"Oh," Bartolo said, and took a little half-step away, nearly brushing his shoulder against the sloping wall. The nameless tourney was an annual dockyard tradition, completely unsanctioned either by Tiaraku or the loose association of lawmen that kept the human residents of Niheba in order. But for a hundred years at least, the sailors, stevedores, and foolhardy men of the city regularly battled for supremacy with fists, knives, and staves, the winners of each battle contesting the others until a single champion arose.

It was pure, bloody, often deadly violence, and the people loved it. If drunks and braggarts were going to fight anyway, they reasoned, it might as well be organized enough for the spectators to place some bets.

"And I can still feel the heft of the gold in my hand, sir. I know what a good coin should weigh," Jairus added as Bartolo considered exactly what it took to win such a competition two years running. Jairus showed little outward indication of any extraordinary strength or skill, aside from a bit of height and a broadness to his shoulders. He looked much more like the bookkeeping merchant he usually was than the twice-victor of a gory street war. But Barolo had dealt with *neneckt* for long enough to know that appearances were nearly always deceiving.

"Yes, of course," he said out loud. "Well done. You must have quite a reputation in the city."

"I try not to make too much of myself, sir. The Warden prefers that we don't kick up a fuss."

"Still, maybe you know someone who has some properly available to let? I find myself in need of some new lodgings. Something small and discreet."

"As a matter of fact, I think I might. I'm not sure it would be up to your standards, however."

"That's just what I need. Somewhere I wouldn't be expected to settle."

"I could make an enquiry, sir, if you're sure. I have a friend who owns quite a bit of property along the waterfront. He always seems to be looking for tenants to fill some new venture or another. No one will take any notice of another new face in the neighborhood, if that's what you're after."

"Can you do it today?" Bartolo asked, biting back a testy comment at the young man's easy tone. Bartolo might not hold official rank within the order of the Divided, but he was still Jairus' social superior, if nothing else. He shouldn't presume to know what Bartolo was or wasn't looking for. He should just do as he was told.

"I should really speak to the Warden, sir, now that I think of it."

"Go on, then," Bartolo said. "It was his idea," he added when Jairus suddenly looked unsure. "Pop into his offices and ask."

Tourney champion or no, there was a bit of nervousness on Jairus' face as he turned away, and Bartolo nodded in satisfaction. At least the boy wasn't completely daft.

He mused on daftness of all kinds, including his own,

as he waited. Panic made people do such stupid things. It had to have been panic that caused Arran to try to take his own life instead of seizing the power of the Siheldi when given the chance. There was no other explanation for failing to see how vital it was to collar the Queen properly and place her under the control of wiser authorities like Tiaraku – like Bartolo himself. It was simple common sense.

But perhaps he had been wrong to be so eager. If he was to be truly honest with himself, it had been that same fear and panic that had put Arran in a situation where he had the leeway to make the wrong choice. Bartolo didn't like to admit that he had indeed been too hasty, but Tiaraku was not a patient master, and he did not reward caution like he rewarded results.

Faidal was the only one who had had his wits about him, Bartolo conceded reluctantly. The *neneckt* had taken the only possible action to salvage the situation while Bartolo could do nothing but scream at a mirror from a hundred miles away. He did not enjoy the notion of being bested at anything by a bottom-feeding slave, but it did give him hope that Arran and the gemstones could yet be recovered. And when they were, Bartolo would not let anything cloud his judgment again.

"Sir?" Jairus said for what must have been the second time. "The Warden says I may take you into the city, if you wish."

"Good," Bartolo nodded. "Can we go by the overland route? I'll be damned if I entrust my bones to that bloody drunkard of a boatman again."

* * *

Megrithe was not looking forward to her fourth interview of the day. The Guild Master's disappointment, Lanning's cutting inquiries, and the careful skepticism of Leofric and Nikko would seem as sweet as roses compared to what Elspeth Swinn was likely to say to her once Megrithe managed to make herself turn the corner into the dead end of Archer Lane.

The last time she had come to the address, it had been in full pursuit of the woman's son, with a glossy black Guild carriage underneath her and a pair of thugs at her back to ensure that Elspeth would do as she was bidden. Now Megrithe had nothing – and she had to tell the widow that she, too, had nothing anymore, since her son was lost to the world, perhaps for good.

"What do you want?" Elspeth said flatly when she finally opened the door, a long minute after coming to the peephole.

"Mrs. Swinn, I'm afraid I have some – some rather bad news."

"You *are* bad news, girl," Elspeth said, but her shoulders sagged and she looked like she knew what was coming to her. She didn't say another word before turning around and walking into the house, clutching her shawl to her shoulders. Megrithe took the open door as an invitation to follow her.

"I would like to apologize if I frightened you the last time I was here, ma'am," she said when she had settled onto a gently frayed sofa in the parlor, every movement watched by Elspeth's hollow, glassy stare. "I was attempting to execute my duty in a hurry, and I may not have been very polite."

"If that is your news, Miss Prinsthorpe, it is already very stale. And if you are come here to tell me that you have captured my son, then you can take your arrogance elsewhere."

"That isn't why I'm here," she said. "I did find Arran in Niheba, but I didn't arrest him."

"Niheba? What was he doing in that heathen place?"

"Searching for something very important. But he couldn't – we couldn't find it. Or rather, we did find it, but it didn't go exactly as planned. I'm sorry. I don't know how to say this –"

"Is he dead, Miss Printhorpe?" Elspeth asked with a near complete lack of emotion.

"I don't know," Megrithe replied, slightly thrown off by the tone. "I don't think so."

"Then quit your mumbling. Tell me where he is and what you plan to do about it."

It wasn't easy for Megrithe to organize her thoughts in a manner that would be informative but not distressing. Part of the difficulty came from the fact that she couldn't exactly tell what, if anything, was actually getting through to Elspeth, who sat and listened to Megrithe's somewhat broken retelling without a single twitch, frown, or furrowed brow.

Megrithe was the only one fighting the flow of tears when she had finished, and Elspeth's seeming indifference was starting to get on her nerves. "He saved my life," she concluded, watching closely for any sign of acknowledgement, "and I am so grateful to him for it. So grateful that I intend to return the favor, if I can manage it. I will be leaving for Niheba tomorrow morning. I just thought you ought to know."

Megrithe stood up and was about to go when the tiniest ghost of a sob escaped from Elspeth's lips.

"I don't have a handkerchief," Megrithe said

apologetically when she saw a tear slipping down her cheek, looking around the parlor as if a substitute would somehow present itself.

"It was all a mistake," Elspeth whispered, taking one from her own pocket, but doing nothing more than twisting it in her hands as she silently wept.

"He thought he was doing the right thing," Megrithe said a little awkwardly. Being comforting was not a necessary skill in her line of work, and she was not very used to it. Usually when the crying started, it was because someone was about to tell Megrithe everything she wanted to know.

"I never thought I was doing the right thing. Even if I told myself – even when I convinced myself it was worth it," Elspeth said. "Even that night, when I looked into his little face the first time. The poor child. It was never right."

"You couldn't choose the time he would come into the world," Megrithe said. "It was an accident. Even Bartolo said that being there was an accident."

"But it wasn't," Elspeth cried, then she clapped a hand over her mouth to stifle her own secrets.

"What do you mean?"

"Don't tell him. You can never tell him," Elspeth said, practically begging. "He will never forgive me. I have done enough to him, gods help me."

"I'm sure he forgives you," she said, moving so she could sit next to Elspeth and hesitantly reach out to pat her hand. It was a lie, though. Megrithe had seen Arran's face collapse into a crumple of misery and confusion during Bartolo's recounting of his past, and she was certain that such a complicated knot of turmoil could not dissolve itself in anything short of a lifetime.

"But...what exactly does he have to forgive you for?"

"For choosing him," his mother said softly. "For bargaining away his future just so I could have his life."

"Bargaining? Who did you bargain –" she started to ask, but her stomach dropped when the quiet throbbing of the black rose on her arm began. "Oh. Oh, no. You couldn't have."

"I'm sorry," Elspeth sobbed, now completely undone. "I didn't know what she would take. I didn't know she would take so much."

Megrithe stood up and started pacing across the small room without entirely realizing what she was doing. Elspeth hadn't chosen the nighttime labor that had brought Giles Swinn to his death and Arran to the attention of the Siheldi. The *callawif* had.

It was a very dangerous thing to ask one of the deathless creatures for the gift of a child. The *callawif* nearly always demanded the life of the supplicant, or someone of great worth to them, in exchange. But for the infertile or the unlucky, for women who had been taught since their own first days that their only reason for living was to give a husband a handful of heirs, there was no price too high to secure a healthy infant, especially a male.

There were stories of such children – stories of the type Megrithe's grandmother would tell her little ones on cold, grim nights when they should be sleeping instead. Some called them changelings, and swore that the *callawif* switched the babes in their cradles with spirit children so the unwitting mothers would raise cuckold chicks. Others said they would grow to be great wielders of the deep magic, or deathless warriors, or evil sorcerers with curdled hearts that used the enchantment of their origins for unimaginable evil. They were the caul children, masked in blood and crowned with cobwebs: the symbol of a life chosen for greatness at its very inception in the dark, hidden warmth of the womb.

Arran was no sorcerer, as far as Megrithe was aware, and he wasn't all that much of a warrior. But he was lucky – at least, he used to think he was – and she could tell from Elspeth's anguish that his mother was not lying about her deed.

"They have him," she said eventually, the words squeaking out from the tightened cords in her throat. "The Siheldi have him now. What does that mean? Do they know? Who knows about this?"

"No one. Not Arran. Not even Giles knew. He would have killed me. As much as he wanted a son, he would have beat the life out of me for getting one that way."

"Don't say that," Megrithe tried, feeling uncomfortable at the mournful strength of her conviction. "I'm sure that's not true."

"You didn't know him. You should be glad you didn't. I tried everything to please him, and it never worked. Arran was always so angry with me, always so sad, but he never knew what would have happened to him if Giles had lived.

"I deserve the hell the Siheldi sent for me," Elspeth said dully, the handkerchief hopelessly creased as she wrung it tightly, over and over. "I have tried to be good, but I deserve that hell. I loved him too much. She said that if I loved him too much, she would take him away, and now she has. I tried not to show it. Please believe that I tried – for his sake, I tried to let him go. Gods have mercy, please I beg. Save my soul from the flames of *fyrendor*," she muttered, a long jumble of mismatched prayers tumbling into obscurity as her shoulders shook with sadness.

Megrithe had glossed over the descent into the depths of the volcano's heart, fearing it would sound even more absurd than the rest of it, and now she was glad she had. She had feared the consequences of coming face to face with hell when she had stared into the fiery pit of broken stone and boiling earth, and Elspeth's holy terror only stirred up those horrible feelings once again.

"I should probably go," she said. She was not yet done with unpleasant conversations for the day: she still needed to find a ship willing to take her to Niheba. But she didn't know if it would be right to leave Elspeth alone in her wretched melancholy, even if she had caused it herself some thirty years ago.

In some ways, the risk she had taken was hardly surprising. Megrithe knew well what women would do for their husbands, and what mothers would do for their children in times of desperation. She had seen the lies often enough, and how they tried to stand by their falsehoods even in the face of overwhelming evidence against them.

She had seen housewives and washer women take up weapons to fight off Guild-trained men three times their size just to give their spouses and sons a few extra moments to flee,. She had seen the street war widows of Sorrow's Walk gather all their courage to snitch on a brooding, violent neighbor for the merest hope of collecting a few pennies of reward money so they might put bread in their youngsters' mouths for one more day.

She had seen it all, and admired most of it, even when it led to her own frustration. But she wasn't sure if she could admire selfishness. Elspeth may have feared her husband, as plenty of wives did, but she must have known that Giles' death was not the kind of sacrifice an *callawif* demanded for the gift of life. Elspeth must have known something worse was waiting in the future. If nothing else, the *callawif* was bound by the rules of her kind to clearly state the terms she would accept in exchange for the safe and healthy birth of the infant boy. Elspeth must have known, and yet she did it anyway.

"Where do you keep your tea, Mrs. Swinn?" Megrithe asked, sighing to herself as the woman's tears showed no signs of abating. She wouldn't stay for long – just until Elspeth regained a sense of herself. There would be plenty of time to get to the docks and arrange her passage before the dark closed in. "I'll boil a kettle and we'll have a nice cup to calm your nerves."

CHAPTER FOUR

Nievfaya wrapped her arms around herself and hugged them tight, trying to stop herself from shivering. The motionless air in the pit wasn't cold, but she was shaking like a leaf all the same. The *bezhaka* stone that surrounded her was icy to the touch, and now that she was sitting still, it sucked the heat right out of her skin, never warming to her like an ordinary surface.

She reached out her hand again to feel the soft flutter of Arran's pulse ghosting through the veins on the side of his neck. The torch had burned out hours ago, and she kept accidentally brushing her fingertips against his cheek or his eyelids or his lips when she reached out towards him in the darkness, trying to reassure herself that he was still alive. Each time, she instantly snatched her hand back with a hindbrain abhorrence of such an unwarrantedly familiar gesture.

Touch did not form a great part of the intimacy between *neneckt*, who didn't typically wear bodies unless they had to, but she was aware that it meant much more to the land-dwellers. It both fascinated and slightly repulsed her when she saw human lovers taking every opportunity they could to hold hands, share a kiss, or place their heads on each other's shoulders, even in public where every passing stranger could see. It was odd and unsettling; a foreign craving she did not comprehend. Even as she feared deeply for his wellbeing, she had no right to do anything to Arran that he might misinterpret as affectionate, considering how many times she had betrayed and hurt him.

He hated her, and rightly so. She certainly hated herself for her part in the entire wretched affair. Her overwhelming sense of guilt had been building steadily as the uncountable hours wore on, touching her thoughts as often as she touched Arran's cool skin, and it was starting to get just a little bit unbearable.

At some point, when she thought she couldn't take it even one instant longer, she stood up and craned her neck upwards to the stone lid that locked her in.

"Hey," she shouted as loudly as she could, the sound falling back to her without penetrating the thick rock. "Siheldi! Where are you?" She waited for a long moment, but there was no reply.

"I'm talking to you," she screamed, and she kicked at the walls with a force her toes immediately regretted.

Silence, the Siheldi said, far away and muffled as it spoke through the coffin that encased her. She couldn't tell if it was the same individual as she had spoken to before – she didn't really know if the Siheldi were individuals at all, or if they were just pieces broken off from the Queen's central spirit that returned to their mother like drops of honey drizzled back into the pot.

"I need more supplies," Nievfaya said. "He's soaked the bandages through."

You will be satisfied with what you are given.

"I will be given what I need," she replied stubbornly. "Take me to the storeroom. I will collect what is necessary."

You will –

"Please," she cut over it. "You don't understand how

fragile they are. Not even the *bezhaka* can hold back his death forever. He needs to wake so his soul can return and his body can begin to heal. We both want him to live. We will both be out of luck if he doesn't. This is the one thing we have in common. Help me save him for you."

The Siheldi didn't speak for a long time, as if it was deciding, or perhaps conferring with its fellows. It was odd to think that she might be collaborating with them on something, but she thought it was a valid point. They might strive against each other again in whatever contest came next, but the game would be finished for both of them if Arran's body deteriorated too much to support his fading heartbeat. He needed to wake. Without his conscious mind guiding the reconstruction of his flesh, his shell would be nothing but an empty hearth without a fire inside to give it purpose.

The Siheldi seemed to agree, if grudgingly. The stone lid slowly scraped back, a puff of breeze prompting Nievfaya to inhale deeply of the comparatively fresh air.

"Thank you," she said when a thick rope lowered from nowhere to help her climb out. She grasped onto the line and tried to haul herself upward, surprised by the quivering of her arms that collapsed under her without any strength. She was very hungry, she realized. She had no idea how long she had been deprived of food and drink, but the lack of sustenance was starting to take its toll.

On the second attempt, she managed to compensate for her condition and clamber up the rope, catching sight of the Siheldi's guiding spark in the blackened corridor and following it forward through any number of twists and turns.

"Where in the five hells did you get all of this?" she exclaimed when the spirit stopped in front of the vast storage room. The space was filled – it was absolutely stuffed – with a jumble of items from the world above.

There were empty barrels and wooden boxes that may have been tossed from ships, tall piles of rotting sackcloth bags sorted carefully by the color of their markings, bales of raw cotton stiffened with seawater, frayed and soiled ropes straightened and hung with care, items of men's and women's clothing, splintered timbers from old houses with all the metal from nails, hinges, and handles meticulously removed and heaped into little piles by shape and size.

There were foodstuffs, too, again organized by the colors of their labels instead of anything meaningful to a cook. Rice and wheat flour from the continent's interior, stamped in blue by the coalition of merchants that shipped them outward to the coast, stood haphazardly in one corner. The green labels of oats, barley, and desiccated grape must from the Ivory Isles sat side by side with casks of expensive dried fruits from Niheba and strips of salted meat from the pastures behind Port Chardon, marked with the same verdant hue.

Nievfaya had never thought of the Siheldi as artistic – she didn't even know if they had eyes to see things like mortal creatures did – but she thought she could detect a method to the odd arrangement of their treasures.

"I'm going to light this," she said, picking up an unused torch from somewhere within the flotsam, feeling as if she should give the spirit a warning. It didn't say anything to the contrary, so she took the flints from her pockets and struck them together, the sparks jumping from the sharp edges to the pitch-covered rag. Wedging it firmly between some ceramic jars, she climbed up a stack of crates to survey the space from above.

What she saw made her gasp out loud. "Sun Mother preserve me," she whispered as her sight adjusted. There really was a pattern. The colors and tones had been pushed and piled to form the crude outline of an enormous human face with an imperious frown, the red and orange items clustered thickly around where the eyes should be, with shattered bits of wood standing up like spikes and scars. She knew that face. She had seen plenty like it before. It was the face of the Divided.

"Why would you do this?" she demanded as the flickering torch made the eerie image smirk and gibber. "What does it mean?"

Gather what you need, the Siheldi said, ignoring her questions.

"I need answers. Why is this here? What have they done? The Divided are the enemies of all right-thinking men."

Are we right-thinking men? the Siheldi asked, sounding amused. *Are you?*

Nievfaya didn't answer. As far as she was concerned, the Divided were almost as bad as the Kitefins. They kidnapped orphans to swell their ranks, blinding them as babes and secreting them away to learn black magic and the evil arts.

To those who were brave enough to seek them out, they offered protection from many terrible fates. But their words were false and their friendship traitorous. Few who ever entered the caves of Niheba ever returned – except as bloated, swimming corpses, tortured and hollow after being torn apart by the Siheldi in pursuit of the High Warden's studies.

"I don't need to be a human to know what the Divided do is wrong," she replied. "Or to know what you do is more wrong still."

As wrong as cooking a chicken or eating a fish, the Siheldi said as Nievfaya left her high spot and started to root among the objects for bandages, unspoiled food, skins of fresh water, and any herbs she could find that might help staunch Arran's impossible wound. *Livestock only exists to be culled.*

"Humans are not witless beasts to be slaughtered."

Neither are herds of cows and sheep. They are simply somewhat more witless than you are, which makes you think you have the right to decide their fate. Lesser things must be governed, and to be governed is to be used.

Look at your precious Guild. Do they not treat their own kind the same? The humans require it. They even crave it. All flocks must have a shepherd.

"I have no love for the Guild," she said absently, holding up a jar of musty, crushed leaves to the torchlight to peer inside.

We do, the Siheldi replied. *They make it so easy for us to tend to our larders.*

"You make me sick," Nievfaya muttered.

We do what is necessary to survive. As you are doing, too.

"I'm not doing anything," she said, sifting through the compartments of a surgeon's traveling case, most of its vials broken and its pockets filled with nothing but ancient, tasteless dust. "I'm just trying to save a life that you'd be happy enough to eat, given the choice."

This one is not for eating, the Siheldi hissed through its spitting, cracking excuse for laughter. *He would not be palatable to us.*

"Why not?"

He has our sisters' flesh. He stinks of them.

"Sisters? He isn't a *neneckt.*"

We have not counted you as our brethren for centuries, the spirit sneered. *You are nothing to us.*

"Then...the *callawif?*" She stopped her work and stared into the darkness, the clockwork in her mind ticking over. "He's a bargain child," she said eventually. "Of course. That's why you need him alive."

No one really knew where the *callawif* had come from. Like the Siheldi, they had just always been. There were many of them, but they were all one, linked somehow in thought and deed like the off-kilter reflections in a crazed mirror.

Nievfaya had dealt with the soulless creatures in the past, but the *neneckt* largely ignored them as a rule, and the icy-hearted sisterhood did not feature highly in their history or their tales. The sea folk had their own magic to rely upon, but the land-dwellers had not been given any such talents by the gods of their kind.

Bargain children, those humans born by the gift of the *callawif,* were special in ways that even the *oughon* didn't fully understand. The mark they left on their world, for good or ill, was unpredictable and often uncontrollable. Whatever Arran was, or whatever the Siheldi thought Arran could do, the incredible amount of *bezhaka* gathered around him would multiply it a hundredfold.

Yes. We want him alive, the Siheldi confirmed. *A flute without a reed does not play music.*

"Nor does a flute that refuses to be played."

You ascribe great strength to this broken man.

"Apparently, so do you. Have you not yet learned

that he won't help you?"

Perhaps he wishes to revenge himself upon his enemies. We can help him.

"You are his enemies."

We are the ones letting you save him.

"I have what I need," she said, stuffing her bounty into one of the empty sacks and slinging it over her shoulder. She didn't want to talk anymore. She needed to think before she said the wrong thing. "Take me back."

The Siheldi's spot of light rekindled itself, and she followed it away from the storeroom, doing her best to remember how many turns she took. The room contained more useful things than she could carry at once, and she hoped she would be allowed to find her way back there. But in case she couldn't, she had been sure to slip an extra torch into her waistband.

The surgeon's case hadn't been a total disappointment. She had found the herbs needed, crumbly dry but hopefully still potent enough. She suspected that the Siheldi hardly knew what most of the things in their possession really were, as they had no particular use in their strange, barren society. If the talkative spirit had been just a bit more knowledgeable, she might not have had the chance to do what she now intended.

"Here, now. Just drink a little," she whispered to Arran when the Siheldi had departed and she had crushed the mixture of leaves into a bit of water. The pit had been sealed again, but the seclusion would work in her favor this time.

"Only a little more," she coaxed, trying to prevent the potion from dribbling out the corner of his mouth. "Please let this work. Please, please let this work."

It was the second time she was poisoning him, she thought with a wry smile as she patiently dripped in the last few drops. She had given him far, far too much *ychauyad* before taking him down to Emyer-Ekvori, and she was lucky it hadn't done him any serious harm. She had needed him to sleep heavily through that night, to give her time to arrange things, but now she needed him to do just the opposite. All she could do was hope against hope that she wouldn't be killing him in the process.

As the last of the liquid slipped down his throat, she took a piece of smooth wood from her trove and planted it firmly between his teeth. She turned him onto his side and drew him close and tight to her chest, one hand over his gaping wound and the other over his heart, which would begin beating too furiously for comfort in just a few moments.

"Wake up, Arran Swinn," she said, trying to push the words into the stones that lined the walls, imagining the sounds bouncing back into her ears, back into the earth, gaining speed and power each time they ricocheted, building like a tidal wave that ghosted through the depths until it crashed with unimaginable fury when it reached the tempting sands. "Wake up. There is work to do."

* * *

Jairus tried to ignore the heavy jingling in Bartolo's pockets as they walked up to the surface together. *He must have three pounds of gold weight in there*, he thought. *How can he even walk straight?*

Bartolo probably imagined he had wrapped the coins so well in thick leather rolls that no one could hear them, but he had come to the wrong place for dull senses. He had come to the wrong place for everything he wanted. The Warden was not one to be bullied into solving other people's problems, especially someone with a reputation for arrogance as rank as Bartolo's. Jairus hated arrogance. It was sloppy. Sloppiness got people killed.

He spent the next few turns idly entertaining thoughts of knocking Bartolo down and running off with the hoard like a street urchin scrimping an apple, but quickly put the notion aside. It would easy, but a very foolish thing to do. Bartolo was a notorious lover of rare monies, and he had likely filled his pockets with the dearest items in his collection. Even if he made it more than a few steps without Bartolo screeching for help like a stuck pig, there would be no way to unload those unusual treasures without getting caught.

Besides, he didn't really need any more gold, but he did need Bartolo to like him. The Warden had told him to make a good impression, and even though it seemed like it would be heavy going, he was determined to give it a try.

"How is your brother faring, sir?" he asked out loud when Bartolo gave no indication of wanting to continue their former conversation. "I haven't heard from him since I left Paderborn."

"I really wouldn't know," Bartolo said. "I do my best to stay clear of anything that dribbles out of his mouth these days."

Jairus smiled politely. "Would you prefer, perhaps, to wait in the library near the north gate while I try to make arrangements for you in town? It may take some time for me to find the owner of the property."

"No, I'll come with you. The sooner I get away from this horrible place, the better. I don't know how you stand it down here."

"I find I can get used to nearly anything with a little bit of work, if I must."

"Being unambitious is nothing to brag about," Bartolo said quietly. He probably thought that Jairus wouldn't be able to hear him, but he was wrong.

"The lodgings I have in mind are rather small," he said instead of responding to the jab. "The sitting room is really more of a corner. But Basset – that's the owner, sir – he says there's an excellent harbor view, as I may have mentioned. I can't think of a better place to be if you're interested in departures. Or maybe in arrivals."

"What makes you think that arrivals would be any of my concern?" Bartolo asked sharply.

"Nothing, sir. Nothing at all. I just know some people like to watch the ship traffic to pass the time. My sister was very fond of it in Paderborn. She knew the name of every licensed –"

"Yes, yes," Bartolo said peevishly. "I'm sure. It's this way, isn't it?"

Jairus let him walk ahead briskly, putting some distance between them as he muttered to himself about something or other. There was no point in pressing the issue when Jairus already knew all about it. The Warden had said that Bartolo would be waiting for a woman named Megrithe Prinsthorpe to find her way to Niheba. He had stressed the name, because Jairus was supposed to find her first.

He didn't know who she was or why she was important, but neither was he much accustomed to questioning his orders. Loyalty and obedience were qualities that the Divided stressed highly, and Jairus had always found that obedience, at least, could serve him quite well.

"This way, sir, if you please," Jairus called. Bartolo had taken a turn towards the service tunnel that ran further inland, sloping upward to deposit carts and wagons into a yard at the back of a warehouse owned by the Warden's friends. It would be locked at this time of day, and he wouldn't put it past Bartolo to throw a bit of a fit if stymied by something so trivial. "We can use the small gate."

"This is new," Bartolo said as Jairus opened the grating.

"Relatively, sir. I'm not sure if we used it when you were here more commonly."

"Well, that's why I went the other way," he said, pushing ahead as they climbed the steps to leave the sea caves.

It was always a bit of a challenge for Jairus to reacclimatize to the city's noise after the velvety quiet of his underground home, and while Bartolo lifted his chin to feel the warmth of the brilliant sunshine on his face, Jairus just shook his head a bit in a nearly unconscious gesture that helped him clear his ears.

"I expect Basset will be in his offices on Cloud Clam Street," he said when he could once again distinguish the one-horse carts from those drawn by two, and the cloddish footsteps of the lazy, clay-like *neneckt* from those who passed for nearly human. "May I presume that taking a shortcut through the palace grounds would be unwelcome?"

"Have you been listening at keyholes?" Bartolo asked stiffly.

"The Warden mentioned a few things to me before we left, sir. He has placed me at your service entirely, and I am to do everything and anything that would help you, including protecting you if any of your errands take you to places that are somewhat less than savory. I should like to have your trust, sir, and I am a very good listener, but I don't expect to be given your confidence until I have earned it."

"Start with the lodgings, boy," Bartolo said after a moment. "We will move on from there."

"Of course. After you, sir."

Cloud Clam Street was nearly halfway across the city, and the necessity of circumnavigating the central bulk of the palace made the walk even longer than usual. Normally, Jairus would be perfectly happy with an afternoon above ground for whatever reason, but Bartolo was making him anxious.

The man held his breath and hesitated each time they crossed a street, looking each and every way as carefully as an old crone, as if Jairus couldn't be trusted to put one foot in front of the other without a sweeping cane and a warning bell. At any moment, he was expecting Bartolo to reach out and take his elbow, and he wasn't sure that he would be able to contain himself if such an insult was presented to him.

It was irritating, and it was making it harder for him to concentrate on the things that really would keep him safe from the trundling carriages and careless pedestrians. The vehicles could be heard – they could be sensed through his boots, too, as they rumbled along the cobbles – and he could apologize to the people on the pavements if he did, in fact, brush a shoulder or step on a toe, but he almost never did. He had made all his mistakes when he was just a boy, clumsy and uncertain in the face of a blank and frightening new reality, and the many years since had taught him all the lessons he needed to function in a sighted world.

It had been difficult, of course. The red rash fever that had taken his sight had left him burning long after his young body had healed: not with anger or blame directed at the gods for allowing such injury, but with the smoldering knowledge that his path had shifted irrevocably into the darkness, and that it would be very, very easy to fall into the waiting abyss of despair if he lost his resolve for even a moment.

Naturally, his youthful determination had wavered at times, as it did at some point for most men. His twin brother had not survived the disease, and that was a loss that constantly haunted him like the unquenchable pain of a phantom limb. The quick and brutal sickness had also taken two of his sisters, a newborn boy, and his favorite aunt during the long, impossible winter.

The Lanque family had been devastated by the losses. Death hit the poor doubly hard in Paderborn: along with the pain of grief and the uncertainty of lost wages, it had cost them dearly to purchase and fill so many gravesites. Until he had come to Niheba, Jairus had never missed an opportunity to clean and attend to each of one them during the Black Moon festival, leaving his offerings of pomegranates, rice, and sweet wine in front of the tall, narrow stones etched with generations of names from his father's line.

The sorrowful experience had eventually led him to the Divided, and now the Divided had led him to Bartolo. Jairus had a very strong suspicion that Bartolo would lead him exactly to the place he had wanted to be for a very long time – if he managed to worm his way into the cantankerous fellow's good opinion first.

Despite his human nickname, Basset was a *neneckt*, and not a very genial one. The face he favored came with a built-in frown that rarely shifted out of place unless he was presented with a suitable sum of money.

He had made a good living off the Cuskeel tribe in the years since Tiaraku had come to the throne, taking quick advantage of their sudden desperation to become intimates of his newly formed court. The Cuskeels, hoping to adopt the fashions of the older, more settled families, had sold off most of their less desirable lands in exchange for a tightly packed complex in the city center, and they hadn't been all that particular about who scooped up the valuable commodity in their wake.

Basset was now the lord of a dozen human slums, to which he owed his social status, but a rather large portion of his wealth came from an entirely different source: the blind man now standing in front of him. Jairus had inspired more jeers than wise wagers during his first surprise victory in the lucrative yearly tourney, and Basset had not been slow to take advantage of that, either.

"It's still empty," the *neneckt* confirmed when Jairus had explained his request. "And I suppose you'll be wanting it for free," he continued, looking Bartolo up and down without much pleasure.

"I am fully aware that nothing is free, sir," Bartolo said, putting a handful of gold on the desk. "Especially not silence."

"Indeed," Basset said as Bartolo added a few more coins to the pile with a meaningful look. "I'll get you the keys."

He went to the back of his office, where there was a large cupboard, and selected a ring from one of the dozens of rows of hooks jingling inside. "You certainly have a lot of interesting friends, Jairus," he said as he handed Bartolo a bit of card with the address.

"None of them greater than you," he replied, and Basset snorted at the perfunctory flattery.

"You can have it for a month, but then I'll be coming a-calling," he said. "You want it any longer, you pay double what you gave me today. It's a good spot that I can sell in a trice, when it's ready, to someone a lot more respectable than you."

"Of course. Thank you."

Bartolo seemed satisfied enough as they headed towards the waterfront buildings, and even regained enough of his equanimity to start shifting from his dour, defensive attitude to a more solicitous and probing stance as they threaded through the avenues of Niheba.

"Interesting friends, indeed," he remarked, trying to sound friendly. "Do you have any other acquaintances that I might be interested to know about?"

"I really wouldn't know what interests you, sir. Perhaps if you see fit to tell me what this is all about, I can be more useful to you."

"Is this the right building?" Bartolo asked, looking upwards at a tall brick construction with its entrances facing away from the harbor.

"I'm afraid you'll have to tell me, sir," Jairus said. He was fairly certain they were on the right street, but it wasn't an area he knew intimately. Besides, Bartolo seemed to like to be in charge. It wouldn't hurt to let him be right about a few things now and again.

"Yes," Bartolo said, matching the number on the paper to the placard screwed to the rail, which wobbled slightly under his hand as he climbed the steps. "But it could be a bit less shabby."

"When Basset said it was not quite ready to sell, sir, he meant that there may be a few...inconveniences," Jairus thought it prudent to say as Bartolo put the key into the lock.

"Inconveniences?   Oh," he said when the door opened.

"Yes, sir."

Jairus could smell the dried blood that had seeped into the floorboards, but that probably wasn't as bad as having to see it without much of a warning. Basset took his rent rolls seriously, and occasionally he was required to defend his reasoning to those who believed differently.

"Well, I'll just have to walk around it," Bartolo said briskly. "And this one, too."

"I'm glad you feel you can make do with less than perfect circumstances, sir," Jairus said, unable to stop himself.

"Careful, boy," Bartolo warned. "You give me lip and I'll tell the Warden you're not as useful as he thinks you are."

"I very much doubt he would believe you, sir. He didn't seem too pleased at your visit. I gathered that something involving Tiaraku might not have gone exactly as planned?"

Jairus could practically hear Bartolo thinking in the silence that followed. That was a good sign.

"Tiaraku and I had a disagreement," he said carefully. "I have been responsible for certain aspects of his trade with the mainland. Due to circumstances beyond my control, that trade has been compromised."

"I am assuming this trade was of a delicate nature," Jairus replied, feeling his pulse quicken a bit.

"You could say that. There are some people who have poked their noses into my business, and it has upset the balance of things. One person in particular, actually. I may ask for your assistance with finding him. A *neneckt*. It calls itself Faidal."

"A *neneckt* may call itself many things, sir. I should need some more details about the nature of this business if I am to help you."

Bartolo paused again. "Red iron," he said after a while. "False red iron, to be more exact. This Faidal fellow was dealing in it, and he has associates here on the island. I need them uncovered so I can learn more of his plans."

"Is he the arrival you may or may not be waiting for?"

"No. That is a private matter. If you wish to prove your loyalty, you will chase down this *neneckt* and anyone he may have contacted in the past few weeks. I need to know what he thinks he knows, if you take my meaning."

"I understand, sir. May I enlist the help of a few of my brothers among the Divided?"

"You may not. This is strictly between you and me. If I hear a word of indiscretion, you will not live to face the Warden's disappointment. Are we clear?"

"As the grotto pool, sir."

"Good. Now, you can do me another favor. I need you to go to the palace. Someone there has to know where my blasted manservant has gotten to."

Jairus was dismissed and sent on his way, smiling broadly as he skipped down the steps two at a time. It was anything but an unwelcome departure, since Bartolo had just told him more than enough to crack open a mystery that had been plaguing him for years.

Everyone knew false iron was being made in Niheba, but no one had been able to prove it, much less stop the counterfeit from flooding the shores of the mainland. It was driving down prices and stretching the Guild's resources very thin, making it impossible to put a finger in every leak.

The Guild of Miners got the worst from both ends of the situation: smugglers and counterfeiters made sure that the inspectors couldn't stop the fake product from getting into the hands of hopeful peasants, but when the goods didn't work to repel the Siheldi, they got an earful from bereaved families for allowing the deceased to put his or her faith in the useless metal.

It was deeply unfair to all of the parties involved, but while Jairus' sympathies lay with the poor, his duty placed him on the side of the indomitable Guild. He has sworn himself to them as a child, ever since his frantic mother begged the Guild's physicians do to what they could to save the sight of her surviving son.

They hadn't succeeded, of course, but they had been kind enough to let him recover in the Guild House's sick ward. There he gathered a taste of what it meant to belong to the institution, listening in silent fascination as inspectors and knock-about enforcers shared the stories and adventures that had led to their wounds.

Tales and dreams were his only companions during his recovery until one of the physicians, sons and daughters all long dead, took to reading to Jairus after his world had gone dark. The bland appeasement of children's stories soon lost their charm, and the doctor soon moved him on to the same classic texts the finer schools in Paderborn used to instruct their pupils. Jairus had striven to store as many facts as he could into the corners of his memory before he had to return home, losing access to the Guild's copious collection of books.

His new breadth of knowledge had led to some rather interesting encounters with the parish schoolteacher, whom he had first shocked and then astonished with his determination not to let the one currency that mattered slip through his fingers.

An education was better than gold for a stricken child, who would otherwise be pawned off as a useless burden on the church's coffers or consigned to a short, brutal life in a plague-ridden workhouse. Jairus knew perfectly well that no one else would ever bother to make something of him if he didn't do it himself.

In the years that followed, he never failed to seize an opportunity to listen to anyone with wisdom to tell, soaking up knowledge like a sea sponge while he simultaneously trained his body not just to avoid the pitfalls of his condition, but to far outstrip any one of his peers.

He had put his skills to use as he grew old enough to seek employment, securing his first income as a warehouse errand boy by the time he was ten. But the Guild remained his ultimate ambition, and he had argued his case before the selection board with such conviction and vigor that the admissions clerk had been forced to put him on the list of untrained hopefuls angling for a place in the inspectors' academy.

Despite the honor of being awarded a spot in the queue, it was very, very difficult to come out of it again. He had no money to pay the tuition, and charity sponsors were few and far between. He had languished on the list for years, taking odd jobs to support himself and his family while he waited and waited, wondering each morning when he woke if that was the day he would give up hope.

But he hadn't had to face that day. Seeking to ferret out the source of the Guild's distress, and wary of the *neneckt* response to the Treaty of Libourg, the Master had started sending feelers out to Niheba. When his agents returned with tales of the secretive cult that thrived under the waterline, the Guild's board of elders agreed that something would have to be done about it. The Divided were an unknown variable in a complicated puzzle that couldn't be solved from hundreds of miles away, and the brotherhood could only be penetrated by someone with very specific qualifications.

Jairus had been more than happy to leap at the chance, even if failure meant certain death at the hands of the seers. They had been hesitant to accept him at first, as was only natural, but once he had proved he was willing to learn from them – and he had indeed learned a great deal – he had become as one of their own. He had quickly ruled out the Divided as the source of the false red iron, but the Guild had asked him to stay, entrenched in the doings of the island, in case he uncovered anything else worthwhile.

Today was the day that he had succeeded. The link was a tenuous one: Bartolo had certainly been lying to him about some or all of what he asked – but it was there, and it would only get stronger as he dug into the affairs of the *neneckt* that called itself Faidal.

"Good afternoon, miss," Jairus said, sliding into a seat at a table in an empty pub. His errand to seek out Bartolo's manservant could wait half an hour or so.

"You don't have any juniper beer today, do you?"

"Not today, love," said the barmaid with perfume so strong Jairus would have known her anywhere.

"That's the third time this week," he complained.

"Ain't my fault. You should talk to the owner if that's what you like."

"I think I will. Would you fetch her for me?"

"In a tick, dear. Have something on the house for your troubles." It was a well-rehearsed conversation, but the barmaid did a very good job of acting like it was all perfectly natural as she filled a tin mug and plunked it in front of him.

"I wish you'd stop your bellyaching," Agnise said after he had sat for a short time on his own, sipping the very acceptable substitute for his request. "You're my most difficult customer."

"I get a free drink every time you run dry of what I want," he told her. "Why would I stop?"

"You get free beer because I like you, not because it's part of the arrangement," Agnise said, pulling the mug out of his hand and taking a drink of it for herself. Jairus smiled.

"I think I can make up for the trouble this time."

"Do you?"

"Have you ever heard of a man named Bartolo? A particular favorite of Tiaraku – up until today."

"Maybe I have," Agnise said carefully. "Shifty fellow. Fancies himself a lord, or close enough to it. Been underwater a few times, too, from what they tell me."

"They're not wrong. I made his acquaintance today. I think you might find it very interesting if you got to know him, too, in your own special way."

"Would I, now?"

"Just a hunch. He's a friend of the Warden. Well, I say friend..."

"I see."

"Bartolo asked me to work on some things for him. I hope to have more details soon, but I probably won't be able to come back to share them for a while. I just wanted to get you started on what I think is a promising path."

"I appreciate it," Agnise told him. "I confess that he's been of some interest for a while, but I haven't been able to find a way in. Is there somewhere I can start?"

"Yes. You can help me find a *neneckt* called Faidal."

CHAPTER FIVE

The insistent drumbeat that ran though every one of Arran's nightmares had become a comfort to him: an anchor in the chalky blankness of terror and tears that galloped through his feverish mind. His dreams were scattered and slippery, but his mother was always woven among them, crying out for him, alone and afraid; waiting for him somewhere with open arms. He longed for her, but though he ran and ran to say he was sorry, to console and hold her, the rhythm of the drums quickening its pace as he panted for breaths he couldn't take, she never seemed anything but impossibly far away.

More than just distance separated them. There was something that always seemed to come between them, but he couldn't tell what it was. It was beautiful. It was coy and charming and intoxicating, as soft as the whisper of silk when a woman dropped the shield of her garments for his pleasure. It might have been a woman. It might have been something more. He ached for it, even as he cursed it – strained for it, shouted and screamed and begged for it, and railed against it for keeping him from the only person he had ever tried to love.

The beautiful thing consumed him. It sang to him, froze his blood and breathed promises into his ears that obscured the pained, lonely weeping of Elspeth's ghost, and it was everything he ever wanted just to lose sight of that confusing, depressing, endless obligation in favor of his own selfish satisfaction.

But there were other evils, too, that stalked him in the midnight of his distress. Faceless shapes with shapeless, scar-filled eyes breathing fire at his feet, taunting him as he fled their searing heat. The Siheldi, shredding his flesh with their invisible talons, scooping and sucking him dry as they howled in triumph at the shell of his desiccated corpse. The thunderous ocean under a stormier sky, no lanterns in the world big enough or bright enough to scour away the shadow of what was coming for him.

A terrible, terrible pain in his middle that made the drumbeats sing wildly whenever it touched the surface of his turgid thoughts, echoed by the brush of skin against his lips or cheek or the ashen parchment of his neck. It was an important touch – somehow he knew that. But he shrank away from the understanding of the gesture, since it brought such great agony swimming up to drown him.

Help me, he thought, but he knew no one could hear him. He was alone, and he was frightened, and he wanted his mother to be chasing him instead. He wanted her to catch him, to comfort him and hold him close, to say it was going to be all right. He knew she never would. She never could. He had just betrayed her trust in a way that had changed everything forever, and she did not forgive easily.

What had he done? He couldn't quite remember. It had something to do with the pain. But didn't everything?

The beautiful thing had caused it. The beautiful thing had made him think that his suffering was necessary. It was probably right. He was starting to get the impression that leaving this mad place, with its lurid visions that pressed upon his ribcage like the evil hags of legend, would only bring him to something worse.

But something worse was coming, whether he willed it or not. He was floating again, a disembodied soul with little sense of up or down, right or wrong, and he thought maybe, finally, it was the beautiful thing that had him wrapped tightly and firmly in its arms.

Wake up, Arran, it said. Like the sputtering of the volcano that had led him to his fate, and the liquid rock that had burned its light into his unseeing eyes, it called to him. And like a moth helpless against the golden glory of the flame, he drew closer to the curious sound.

Gently as the current of an ancient river longing to rest its drying bones, the thing that wasn't really beautiful at all reached out its fingers to ensnare him. It was the darkness that was singing to him: a lightless, hopeless place lined in shining ice, and he cried out in dismay as it solidified around him. He didn't want to go. He didn't want to leave his mother sobbing in the twilight. He didn't want to leave the lovely thing that kept him from her. He didn't want to feel the pain.

But he had no choice. An explosion of iron shards dug into his brain as the agony slammed him into a wall of cold stone and miserable night. His teeth ground hard against something that splintered and cracked, and he couldn't breathe. He couldn't breathe, and the drums had stopped, and he was shaking, shaking, convulsing with tremor after tremor of sickening agony as the nightmare hags squeezed his faltering heart and laughed, and laughed, and laughed.

"It's all right, it's all right," repeated a murmur on the edge of his hearing. "It's all right, Arran. Just breathe."

He didn't know the voice. Maybe he did. Maybe he

had, but he didn't anymore. He didn't care. There was blood in his mouth, and blood bubbling up his throat, and the taste of bile and copper and the rare green lightning of the sea. He couldn't breathe.

A hand stroked his hair as he vomited, holding him securely on his side so he wouldn't choke on the filth, but he just wanted it to stop. A false comfort. A meaningless nod towards what could never be: someone who cared. He couldn't move his arm to bat the hand away, though, so he endured it as he endured everything else: in wretched silence as he retched up black blood and putrid phlegm from the rotten core of his wounded chest. He was going to die.

"You're going to be all right," the voice soothed, wiping his mouth with a cloth when he had finished, laying his head gently across its lap and trickling a stream of blessedly clean water down his throat. "Lie still."

He didn't have the strength to ask who the stranger was. He could barely see the face that loomed above him through the tears that had gathered in his eyes, and he had no memory that would help him piece together the shreds of his uncooperative, cloudy thoughts.

There were things he had to recall. He knew that. Big things. Big, important things to remember, and the stranger was probably one of them. There had been a mountain, and a trap, and fire, and a woman. A real woman. And something nice about her knees.

"I can't -" he tried to say, but the stranger hushed him.

"Go to sleep," she said softly. "Real sleep. You must rest."

There was something about her voice that made it hard to disobey. She had been the one to haul him back into wakefulness, he realized as his eyes started to drop closed. He didn't want to listen, but now her hand was warm and soft as it rested lightly on his brow. It felt nice, and the pain was ebbing, and he couldn't stop himself from giving up the fight as his consciousness slipped away into lesser dreams.

Something was angry when he next woke up. There were voices above him. They were quarreling with each other, and he just wanted them to shut up. His head was hurting. Every breath felt like he was drawing molten gold into his lungs. He didn't really understand how he wasn't dead yet. The angry voices were making him wish he were.

Was that what he had to remember? He had done something very, very wrong. He had been trying to stop something from happening, and he had been afraid it would make his mother cry.

"Oh," he breathed, a flat and strangled sound that grated against his eardrums as a sudden flood of remembrance rushed in swirl around his empty head like a swarm of stinging bees. The voices stopped their bickering.

"Arran?" the woman asked, bringing a torch closer to his face. He was still lying across her knees, and the angle from which she looked down at him confuse him again as he tried to puzzle out why she looked familiar. "It's Faidal," she said. "Do you remember what happened?"

Arran blinked a few times, but the features didn't change. Faidal had been a man. Faidal had been a *neneckt.* Faidal had been Elargwyd first, and they had both tried to kill him.

"I remember," he tried to say, but he wasn't sure what actually came out.

"The Siheldi have us," Faidal told him. "But you're safe from them here. You need to rest."

"It's cold," he whispered, and she reached over to pull a blanket up to his chin. The wool smelled of stale mold and dry rot, but it helped lessen the chill.

"I'm going to get help for you," she said.

"You did this," he murmured, the slurring of the words making him cringe, which in turn made a shudder of pain dart through him. "You brought me here."

"You can be angry at me later. But you have to hold on. You have to get better, Arran. You have to."

It was an absurd request, and he hoped she knew it, but he still felt compelled to try. More than ordinarily compelled, even under the circumstances, but he didn't have the wherewithal to figure out why.

"How?" he managed.

"If there's one thing the *neneckt* know better than anyone, it's the secrets of building flesh from nothing. There are *oughon* who make a study of it all their lives. Perhaps they know how to rebuild you, too."

"I'm not a *neneckt*," Arran said, the struggle to form each new word and push it out of his mouth making his head chime with a unique, exquisite agony.

"I can't think of anything else to do."

"Why haven't we been eaten?" he asked, feeling rather pleased with himself for identifying what seemed like a pressing concern.

"The Queen wants you alive."

"She tried to eat me."

"And I tried to kill you a few times, but that doesn't mean I really wanted you dead."

Arran closed his eyes again. "You lost me."

"Go to sleep," she sighed. "I'll figure it out by myself. I always do."

He didn't need to be told twice. He barely finished listening to being told once before he had plummeted headfirst into slumber again. When he awoke some indeterminate time later, Faidal, as Faidal was wont to do, had disappeared.

His lap – her lap – had been replaced with a rolled up blanket placed carefully under his neck, and he was actually quite comfortably cocooned in the musty wool, as long as he didn't try to move. The torch had gone out, and it was utterly, completely dark, but it didn't bother him.

He felt strangely, completely calm, like the time he had gone to Port Ravenaught with Durville, years ago. They had visited an ancient temple of the Namarja, and the priests had let them inhale the acrid, intoxicating smoke from a sacred plant they used in their rituals. They had stayed in the gardens for hours, looking up at the clouds as they drifted by, sharing rude jokes and pointless stories, and sipping at honeyed wine. There had been little in the way of religious epiphany for either of them, but it had been a great deal of fun.

There was no sharp scent of smoke in the blackness in front of him. There was no scent of anything at all. The air wasn't moving, and though he couldn't stand up to investigate, his more nebulous senses told him that he was somewhere enclosed.

A prison, then. He always seemed to end up in prison when Faidal was involved. And if Faidal was in league with the Siheldi, then he was in impossible trouble.

There were too many questions for him to easily

order in his weary, half-shuttered brain. What did the Siheldi want with him? Why had they kept him alive? Where had Bartolo gotten to? And more importantly, where was Megrithe?

"The *callawif*," he whispered, the tiny action of his throat prompting a coughing fit that lasted for terrible, uncountable minutes as his shredded flesh squealed in protest.

"Oh, bloody hell," he gasped as his breath slowly returned. The words wilted into the thick air as soon as they came out of his mouth, and for a long time there was no other sound than the hiss of breath in and out, in and out of his nostrils as he tried to quiet himself.

Megrithe was safe, somewhere, if the *callawif* had honored her agreement. But that bastard Bartolo had probably run to ground. Tiaraku would be sheltering him, and he might never be found. The *neneckt* were too clever, their allies were too powerful, and their secrets ran far beyond the understanding of their human neighbors.

Faidal had even been talking to a Siheldi. No one had ever heard of such a thing – no one even knew if they had voices – but then again, Arran didn't think many people had ever had much interest in striking up a conversation.

He had been told that there were wild prophets of the outland fells who claimed to be able to understand the demons, predict their strikes, and even turn them away without the use of red iron, but he wasn't sure he believed the tall tales. Perhaps he should start. He had been surrounded by madness for so long that anything could be true.

He would have to learn to get along without red iron

from now on, in any case, since Bartolo had destroyed his pendant. "Spiteful little sod," he muttered, gently flexing his fingers to try to work the cold out of them. His feet felt numb and each breath was a battle he wasn't sure he could win. He was so thirsty.

"Is anyone there?" he called.

He waited for a while, but there was no response. Eventually, he disentangled one of his arms from the blankets and reached out to see if Faidal had left a cup or a pitcher nearby. He was happy to encounter a tin canteen with his questing hand, but his stiff fingers knocked the container on its side. The cap had been left open for his convenience, but it was now letting the liquid spill onto the stones.

The only small consolation was that he was able to stop himself from reflexively trying to right the bottle, which would have been disastrous. He would rather be a bit parched than tear himself open and bleed his veins dry by accident, alone in the dark.

The jolt of surprise that shook him when he heard the grinding of stone on stone from above nearly accomplished that fate for him, however, and he grasped at his chest, moaning, until a speck of light hovering on the rim of the round pit distracted him.

"Faidal?"

The neneckt *is gone*, said a voice that was blank, toneless, and frighteningly familiar.

"What did you do with him? Her. I don't know. What happened?"

She has seen your death, the voice said, *and she thinks she can stop it.*

Arran swallowed hard. "Can she?"

No.

"Then why did you bother letting her go?"

By the ancient pacts of our brethren, we have no right to keep her. But neither do we have an obligation to let her back in.

"Why are you keeping me, then? You were going to kill me before the *callawif* came. Why won't you finish the job?"

Your life is more valuable than your death, the Siheldi said. *That balance may change if you do not do as you are told.*

Arran couldn't help laughing a little. "That isn't much of a threat. How could you think I value my life after doing this to myself? I will finish the job if I have to. I will not help you kill more innocents."

He really would do it. The Siheldi was promising him death, but he already expected to be dead. These moments, as confusing and painful as they were, seemed like nothing more than an unanticipated bonus. Maybe that's why he felt so calm, he thought as he did his best to shift his weight onto his shoulders. One sharp arch of his back and he would rip the delicate wound wide open. One quick movement and he would never see the sun again.

Your neneckt *knows your value better than you do,* the Siheldi said. *You are a man hunted by many, Arran Swinn. But few know what you really are. If they did, they would not pursue you. They would fear you.*

"Like you fear me?" he guessed.

The Siheldi hissed like a spitting cat, which Arran supposed passed as laughter in such a harsh and hostile place. *Those with power need not know such things.*

"But my people should be afraid?"

If they are wise. Ask your friend Faidal why the sea

king sleeps uneasy, and the iron men tremble in their beds. Ask her why your mother cries inside your dreams.

"I don't understand."

The Siheldi did not reply, but a small skin of water landed near his feet and bounced into the nested blankets around his knees. It was followed by the ear-splitting shriek of stone as the boulder rolled over him, sealing him back into velvety silence.

Arran sank back to the ground, feeling certain he was going to throw up again. The calmness might have just been an illusion, because his heart was howling at furious speed and he was fairly sure his head was going to burst. He didn't want to move an inch ever again – he just wanted to think about what had just happened. He wanted to sleep, and not think at all. But his dry mouth had only gotten worse during the unhelpful exchange, and he needed the water.

He hoped it was water, he thought as he tried to work the container closer to his hand without straining himself. Poison seemed like a very roundabout way of killing him. The Siheldi had said it wanted him alive – but also that he wasn't going to live. Was he to be some kind of experiment, then? Some caged animal in a menagerie intended only for study and observation until he collapsed into a fatal fever on his own?

It would happen soon enough, whether they wanted it to or not. He only had to wait for it. At some point in the blind timelessness, he would close his eyes to sleep. At some point, he simply wouldn't wake up again, and it would all be over. He could feel it approaching. He knew he shouldn't fight it. It would do him no good in the end.

He was so cold and so thirsty, even after he drained the waterskin dry, alone in a grave where no one would ever find him, dead already to anyone who might have cared. At some point, he wouldn't care either. He only had to wait.

* * *

Genedi had always enjoyed watching the sun rise in Niheba, heaving itself up from under the sea like a whale breaching to splash on the surface with the pure joy of being alive. The best way to see it was from the top of one of the high towers of Tiaraku's palace, where nothing could obstruct the clear, clean bowl of the warming sky. It took a lot of effort to get there – stairs did not come cheaply when one was unused to the creaking joints and uncooperative, swinging weight of even the slimmest, most fragile human shell – but if he was going to be forced onto the land for any length of time, he was going to enjoy himself.

Dawn was his favorite part of the day. No one but human servants and human merchants were abroad at such an hour, and Genedi could ignore those like he ignored the ants that scuttled beneath his feet. He didn't dislike them, nor did he actively hate them, as some of his kind had taken to doing. They just weren't interesting enough, on the whole, for him to pay much attention.

As one of the Tiaraku's liaisons with the land-dwelling populace, however, he did occasionally have to consider them as legitimate residents of his island, no matter how irritating. The position was not a desirable one, nor one he had ever coveted. But Genedi was not a particularly desirable personage in Tiaraku's new world, and his options were few. As an offshoot of the lowly, mercantile Bluegills, he had been lucky enough to take whatever court position he could get, and he had learned to be relatively happy with it.

Still, he started his day with the sunrise for the same reason that the wealthy ladies of Paderborn started theirs with a dip in a scented soaking tub: as a ritual act of cleansing before facing the soiling effect of other people during the long hours to come. The very thought made him spend a few extra moments letting the sun's rays warm the awkward prison of his earthy flesh before he made his way back down the tight spiral of the tower's steps, one hand running lightly along the smooth, curving wall as he spun around and around during his descent.

The tower door led directly into one of the city's main thoroughfares, which was handy enough. His first rendezvous of the morning would not be taking place on the palace grounds, and he didn't particularly want his whereabouts known to the general public. Not everyone who flitted in and out of the gardens and between the administration rooms was interested in minding their own business. There were plenty of prying eyes scattered among the lush greenery and cloudless pools that rippled quietly with the pounding of nearby feet.

To combat the ever-present threat of inconvenient gossip, Genedi had the habit of choosing different faces for different occasions, and today he was using one he had never used before. Catching sight of his unfamiliar features in the reflections of the water was always somewhat jarring, but he savored the little thrill of intrigue as he led his mild eyes and bulbous nose towards a highly unofficial assignation.

"Do you have any juniper beer?" he asked a passing

server at a tavern near the water's edge.

"I'm sorry, sir. We're fresh out," she replied.

"That's a pity. It happens quite frequently in this place. Third time this week, I reckon."

"I can fetch the owner for you if you have a complaint, sir," the girl said after hesitating for a fraction of a second, his strange face making her wary.

"I would be much obliged if you could, miss."

The young woman nodded and disappeared into the back, leaving Genedi to wait for some time, rubbing his fingernail absently along a deep groove in the wood.

"Is there something I can do for you?" Agnise asked when she emerged from the kitchens, her hair done up in a kerchief and her hands wrinkly and clean from scrubbing dishes. "My girl said you had a problem."

"The juniper beer, Agnise," he said. "You're always out. And I wish you would start serving that sesame cake again. The one with the lemon blossom honey drizzled on top."

"Oh," she said, sitting down. That was their private code for when she didn't know his face, and it seemed to satisfy her. "Well, the man who sells me the honey has been on the mainland these past six months. I don't like to buy it from anyone but him."

"Adventuring, is he? I wonder what he will learn."

"Some very interesting things, I'm sure," she replied, undoing the kerchief and running her hands through her hair, now fading from blonde to coarse gray. "But there are plenty of stories to be had right here."

"I am with child to hear them," Genedi said.

"I thought you might be. Do you know a personage who goes by the name of Faidal?"

"No, I do not."

"He's one of yours. One of Tiaraku's own, in fact. A Black Salt."

"Ah."

"Yes. A Black Salt with a very strong will for his freedom. You might even say he has an iron will," she added, stressing the second to last word. "It has led him into all sorts of trouble."

"Such as?"

"You might want to ask his new comrade, a Paderborn smuggler called Arran Swinn. They were both last seen in the company of our friend Bartolo, and neither of them has been seen again. It's been a week at least."

"I see. And where are these stories originating, if I might ask?"

"You may ask, but I won't answer," she replied. "A reliable compatriot gave me the tip. The rest is just due to digging."

"What is this reliable compatriot's agenda?"

"The same as mine," said Agnise. "He thinks this Faidal may give up Bartolo. If Bartolo killed the smuggler from Paderborn, that's grounds for the Guild to hold him. We haven't been able to find any other way in."

Genedi sighed and flicked a speck of dirt from the table. "The Black Salts just want revenge against Tiaraku. No one will believe this Faidal creature is telling anything other than a lie. I cannot bring this to anyone of note. You don't have any proof about the smuggler?"

"I have some details," she said, and he felt the corner of a piece of paper bump gently against his knee under the table. He quickly folded it into his palm and slipped it into a pocket with a practiced motion, the whole transaction taking less than the blink of an eye. "If he's under-island, that's your domain, not mine," Agnise added.

"True enough," Genedi nodded. "I will see what I can do."

Agnise smiled. "Thank you. Now, will you stay and take some breakfast? I've got a lovely ham come from the market just this morning."

"I suppose I ought to, if only for the look of things," he said. "But you know human cooking does nothing for me. Especially yours."

"Oh, aye," she laughed. "I'll bring you a double portion then."

A meal at Agnise's table was ample compensation for the inconvenience of walking all the way out into the slums, and Genedi left the tavern more or less satisfied with the morning's work. He would have to wait until he was in a private place to look at the note, but he was in no hurry. Agnise was not a frivolous person, and she would not have signaled his attention unless she thought she has something worthwhile for him, but his initial inclination was that the case was going to be a waste of his time.

The Bluegills had never liked the Black Salts, and perhaps that's why he was reluctant to believe that this Faidal person was of any real importance. Black Salts were notorious for being little more than thieves and fraudsters, skulking at the heels of the better tribes to snap at their scraps and leavings. He would not stake so much as a penny on the word of one, and if he was to follow up with Agnise's cryptic assertions, he would be gambling with so much more: not only with his life, but with hers as well.

"Would you excuse me for a moment, Poeling?" he

asked his human assistant, who was doing something with the papers on his desk in an office that rarely needed any additional tidying. Genedi was a fastidious soul by nature and delegated few of his affairs to the attention of others, especially humans. He had been asked to take on the young man's services in the spirit of unity, but he suspected that much of what Poeling did with his day was simply try to look busy.

When the young man had gone, Genedi locked the door behind him and settled into a chair to read Agnise's letter. He was glad to see that it was coded into neat, vertical rows of numerals. Not only was it important to keep up the Guild's practices, but it was nice to have a puzzle to work on for a few moments.

A novice would need a separate page, a pen, a special code book, and a great deal of patience to read the missive, but Genedi was not as young or naive as he liked his bodies to appear. Long practice had made the cypher second nature to him, even when the entire sequence had been turned inside out to add extra difficulty, as Agnise always made sure to do. She was a bit of a genius when it came to the mathematics of it, and his respect for her talent was one of the reasons he was doing his due diligence for her.

"Oh, dear," he murmured when he had finished reading. He scanned it again for good measure, then carefully folded the letter, placing it on his desk and pushing it away a bit, as if it was a snake that might leap to strike its venom at him. If even a fraction of the information was true, then he had been wrong to misjudge Agnise, and even more wrong to dismiss the Black Salt slave as irrelevant.

Despite what he would like Agnise to believe, Genedi

did not work for the Guild of Miners in any capacity. Nor did he really work for Tiaraku – at least, not entirely. He worked for crown of the *neneckt* nation, which was not the same thing. The king who sat on the throne at any given moment quite often had the best interests of his unwieldy realm in mind, but he equally often did not, and it was up to relatively anonymous ministers like Genedi to decide which was which.

The Guild was a useful ally in the endeavor, if only to gauge the desires of the humans who had colonized the *neneckt* homeland. While the land-dwellers themselves held little attraction for him, he had rather a soft spot for their most famous institution. The Guild had no need to play nicely with those who crossed them, and made no pretense at it. He admired their efficiency, their complete disregard for their detractors, and the way they always paid like with like, for good or ill.

Agnise had found a *neneckt* called Mikkal, a family relation of the mysterious person of interest. After some persuading, Mikkal had seen the wisdom of cooperating with Agnise, and it was his words that she had reported in the letter.

If they were true, Mikkal's testimony would lead Agnise and the Guild directly to Tiaraku's enormous cache of plain pig iron that was shaped, sanded, dyed red, and delivered to eager underhanded markets on the mainland for more than ten times its actual price.

That presented Genedi with a quandary. He knew about the counterfeiting operation, of course. Nearly anyone with half a brain and a diplomatic pass had figured it out ages ago. While he found it somewhat morally repugnant to cheat helpless peasants out of their silver and their lives, he was a practical fellow at heart.

The more that Tiaraku's wealth increased, the more his own crept upwards, too. Fastidiousness about such things had never done a politician any favors, and he had no particular desire to try bucking the trend.

Besides, even if he hadn't been profiting off the situation, the *neneckt* king was not someone to trifle with. The Black Salts had learned that lesson years ago, but it could just have easily been the Bluegills who were ravaged, destroyed, and scattered beyond the limits of the Sea Father's sights. It could easily be the Bluegills next time.

The choice he was about to make, therefore, wasn't really a choice at all. He may value the Guild, and he may value Agnise as a colleague as well as a cook, but he valued his own welfare just a little bit more than any of those things.

Agnise would have to be taken care of. Mikkal would have to be silenced, and Genedi would need to find where Faidal and Arran Swinn had gone before the Guild's network of informants had time to spread the information where it ought not to be. Fortunately for him, there was a very simple way to accomplish all of those things without even leaving the room.

"Poeling? Can you come here for a moment?" he called, unfolding the letter again and drawing a fresh piece of paper from his writing desk, placing the two pages side by side so he could translate the code for an uneducated reader. "I would like you to get Habur for me."

Genedi had finished his task and made it half way through some unrelated paperwork by the time Habur decided to grace him with his presence. The warrior was in his usual foul mood when he arrived, and had no interest in formalities like the mid-morning nibbles that were considered the bare minimum of hospitality among the *neneckt*, so Genedi saved the last of his favorite spiced, crispy kelp for his own enjoyment later that day. He would be in need of some consolation after betraying a woman who likely considered him a friend, and the treat would go some way towards cheering him up again.

"What do you want?" Habur said bluntly when Poeling had shown him in. He was unused to being summoned, and Genedi was not someone who typically had enough authority to do so. Poeling must have been very persuasive.

"Can I offer you anyth–"

"No."

"Very well," Genedi said, indicating that Habur should have a seat. He did so, dwarfing the chair as he crossed his arms and settled in.

"Speak."

Genedi pushed his other papers away and placed Agnise's letter in front of him, trying not to fidget with the edge of the parchment as Habur glowered in front of him.

"As you know, I sometimes have dealing with land-dwellers who are not always interested in the peace and harmony of our great King Tiaraku's rule."

"I know what your duty is. What of it?" Habur asked when Genedi paused, choosing his words carefully.

"Sometimes I must extend the appearance of my friendship to them," he continued slowly. "Sometimes it appears as if I am involved in their affairs, when really I am just encouraging them to be forthcoming."

"But you have always been a loyal servant of the great

and wonderful master and would never betray him," Habur said in a high-pitched, mocking tone. "Yes, I hear that a lot. What pile of parrotfish dung do you want me to dig you out of?"

Genedi sighed and pushed the translated page towards him. "This one."

"Who sent this?" Habur asked sharply when he had finished reading. It didn't take nearly as long as Genedi suspected it might.

"A Guild agent called Agnise. She keeps a bar by the harbor. I think it might be beneficial if she stopped being so knowledgeable about this particular issue."

"And what issue is that?" Habur asked, looking sternly at him.

"I'm sure I don't know," Genedi replied automatically. "I don't really know anything."

"Like hell you don't."

"I'm coming to you in good faith," he said nervously as Habur stood up, a hand on the hilt of the ornate coral glass knife he always kept in his belt.

"Good faith? I think there has been plenty of snooping where that nose of yours doesn't belong."

"It's my job," Genedi protested.

"What else do you know about Swinn?"

"Nothing. I swear. I had never heard of him before today. Everything I know, I learned from the letter you're holding. There is nothing more."

"Where is the original?"

"Right here," Genedi said quickly, handing it over.

"Who has seen this?"

"No one but you and me."

"And the woman who wrote it," Habur said. "And whoever gave her the information. Give me a name."

"I don't have one. She doesn't share her sources with me. It's better that way. It keeps us quiet. Very quiet," he stressed again.

"Not as quiet as I can keep you," Habur replied, a fleeting glint of light the only warning Genedi had before the blade was out of Habur's belt and deep between his ribs.

It was difficult to kill a *neneckt*, and even more difficult above water when there was an extra layer of flesh to rip away from the core. But Habur had long practice, a sharp eye, and the cold-forged coral glass to aid him.

The part of Genedi that was not reeling in shock from the foreign sensation couldn't help but approve of the efficiency of motion and immense strength required to drive the knife so very cleanly into his gut. He had always taken pleasure in a job well done, and even in the absurdity of his final thoughts, he couldn't help but be satisfied.

The rest of him was screaming, his mouth silently gaping open as his breath failed him, a cold, cold burning spreading like treacle from his innards as the body and what was beneath it faded from the world.

Habur dropped him behind the desk, where no one could see the corpse unless they were looking for it. Poeling wouldn't come in without being called, and speech was no longer in Genedi's power. It might take until the following morning for anyone to realize he was missing, and by then Habur would be well on his way to discovering who was spreading rumors about red iron and Arran Swinn.

Genedi had no doubt that Agnise would be next on Habur's agenda. The only question was what she would reveal before the end. It was deeply frustrating that he would never be able to figure out what he had uncovered that was dangerous enough to lead to his own murder. Nor did he like having to die on the land instead of under the waves, as was proper. The Sea Father would have to search to find him. The Sun Mother had clearly already turned a blind eye. He hoped there would be a nice a funeral. He hoped someone other than Poeling would show up.

Habur was long gone by the time Genedi died. The full-throated cries of the while gulls perched on the top of the high, sharp towers went unheeded as Tiaraku's palace bustled and hummed with the activity of just another busy day, his empty shell staring outwards into the angry red glare of the sunset as the island sailed peacefully into the darkening skies.

* * *

Bartolo had never done well with anonymity, and his inconspicuous lodgings were starting to rub on his nerves. He had been cooped up in the tiny suite for days, with no company and barely an inch to move, and he felt too nervous about his unsavory neighbors to even think about soothing himself by examining and polishing the few coins he had been able to bring with him.

Johan had joined him, which was a small comfort. At least he wasn't being forced to make his own meals – or worse yet, dine in a public house with dock workers, shopkeepers, laborers, and their assorted diseases. His manservant was sleeping in the storage closet at the moment, due to the lack of space, but his sullen attitude about the whole thing led Bartolo to think he probably deserved it. It would teach him a lesson about doing his duty cheerfully if he expected to be paid for it.

Luckily, Johan wasn't the only one who had found him. Certain well-informed persons, most of whom were quite a bit more eager than his servant to benefit from Bartolo's generosity, had gravitated towards him, as they always did. Their tales of the outside world had been his only source of entertainment and information during the long evenings, and what they said to him was worth far more than the gold he doled out in small but steady amounts.

The Siheldi had never been very active on Niheba, as a rule, but his informants had been bewildered to report that there had not been a single attack for more than a week. They seemed distracted and uncoordinated, unwilling or unable to strike at their usual victims. Sometimes their presence couldn't be felt after sundown at all, which was practically unheard of.

Bartolo wasn't entirely sure if this was cause for celebration or not. If the Siheldi were still musing over the value of their new capture, he might still have a chance to somehow steal Swinn away from them again. But if they were simply preoccupied with putting their plans into action, he had little luxury to be sitting idle.

Faidal must be found, Megrithe must be captured, and Swinn must be recovered, and his time to do so was quickly running out.

"What's the news, then?" he asked a young woman whose name he had forgotten. There had been clusters of people whispering under his windows all morning, and his curiosity had gotten the best of him. He had risked a short walk down to the corner to speak with her, since no flower-seller would ever enter someone's home to hawk her wares.

"Murder, m'lud," she said with a wicked gap-toothed smile. "And a pair of right good ones, at that."

"Go on," he encouraged, dropping a coin between the plant stalks as he pretended to pick over the blooms.

"A lady of the Guild, they say, though don't she'd of wished no one knew it," the woman replied, digging out the shilling with nimble fingers. "Been selling secrets to the fish men and got her gullet good and gone for it."

Bartolo was intrigued. The Guild had no official presence in Niheba, by the laws of the Treaty of Libourg, but its agents were everywhere. They mostly kept their eyes on the flow of trade, but those in higher places sometimes acted as intermediaries for humans who felt mistreated by the *neneckt* in authority.

Despite Tiaraku's appearance of indifference to the working classes that swarmed his lands, he had more or less accepted the arrangement, and even devoted a handful of his staff to heeding such concerns.

The informal take on diplomacy usually worked quite well, but without the oversight of the official Houses on the mainland, it wasn't unusual to hear that a Guild representative was quietly amassing a tidy little fortune by charging unsanctioned fees to promote someone's cause or turn a blind eye to some unsavory dealing. But murder was an unusual end to such petty scheming, and in light of Bartolo's own illicit activities, it was a bright red flag waving in front of his nose.

"What was the woman's name?" he asked.

"Don't know, guv," the flower girl shrugged. "Happened in a tavern last night. Blood everywhere, they told me. A real splasher."

"You said a pair of murders," Bartolo said, trying to

block out the image.

"Aye. The fish man copped it, too."

"A *neneckt* was killed?"

"Coral knife, they said. One of 'is own kind, in all liking hood. Stuck the bugger and left him to bleed."

"Shit."

"That too, I suppose," she said, showing her blackened teeth as she laughed.

"Who knows about this?"

"Nearly everyone by now, I'd suspect," she told him. "Got some of 'em real upset, too. Can't say the Guild ain't encouraging it, but it got the chance to turn right sour. Folk here ain't stupid. We won't be having the guppies cutting Guild throats. We ain't safe if we don't even got that anymore."

"I'll take half a dozen of the lilies," Bartolo said, paying triple their value before she wrapped the stems in a bit of twine and passed over his bouquet.

"Very grateful for your patroning, m'lud," the woman said, and he nodded distractedly at her as he hurried away, scowling.

Habur was an idiot. He was worse than an idiot. He was a typhoon of thoughtless, stupid, impulsive, clueless lunacy stumping around on clumsy feet bigger than his infinitesimal brain.

It must have been him. There was no one else capable of that degree of mindless violence in defense of a cause he had no hope of truly understanding.

Not only had he just exposed Tiaraku's counterfeiting activity to the whole of Niheba, but he had gifted the constables of Paderborn an ironclad reason to come to the island and investigate the murder. But it wouldn't be city constables who would demand access to Tiaraku's hidden forges. It would be Guild inspectors in those uniforms instead.

The massive operation would be uncovered in a matter of days, and the *neneckt* would lose all of their trading rights with the powers of Rhior-Adril. Tiaraku would be forced to pay the heavy penalties involved with violating the Libourg Treaty. And if the *neneckt* refused to abide by the reparations agreement, there would be open war.

"Johan, where is that blind bastard?" he snapped when he had returned to his lodgings, tossing the lilies into the canal before galloping up the steps and locking the door firmly behind him. "I need Jairus here immediately."

"You are in luck, sir," Jairus said, standing up from a tall-backed armchair that had hidden him. "I thought I would come give you the news, but I see that someone has already done you the favor."

"I was getting some flowers," Bartolo said, shooting an annoyed look at Johan, who had just come in from the galley. Bartolo could have been dead if the surprise guest was anyone other than a friend, and the servant hadn't been there to warn him.

"It's too bad you didn't bring them with you, then," Jairus replied, wrinkling his nose slightly. "Lilies are much nicer on the table than in the gutter."

"The canal, actually. What business is it of yours?"

Jairus shrugged. "Marcie is a good girl, if a bit easily taken with the bloodlust. She'll have told you everything I was going to say already."

"Then what good are you?"

"I can protect you if you're next."

Bartolo slumped onto a chair and rubbed the sweat

off his brow. "Who was this Guild woman? Was she important?"

"Everyone is important, sir," Jairus said mildly.

"You know what I mean."

"Her name was Agnise," he said after a moment, sitting down opposite Bartolo. "I frequented her establishment on occasion. Her mincemeat was worth the trip."

"What was she involved with?"

"I'm sure I don't know, sir. I wasn't even aware she was a Guild contact until this morning."

Bartolo looked at the young man carefully as he spoke, but it was hard to divine an expression in those peculiar, blank eyes of his. They were silvered over more completely than most *neneckt* – more like the clouded eyes of a poached fish, filmy and pearly from the inside – and it was impossible to tell if he was lying just by looking at him.

"Who was the *neneckt* that was killed?" he tried.

"His name was Genedi, sir. A liaison with some of the human trade associations, ostensibly, but I think it's fair to say that he had other interests."

"I have never met him," Bartolo said. "But I *have* met the witless oaf who killed him. While it would give me great satisfaction to ream him out for it, I'd rather not come in contact with him again at the moment, if you take my meaning."

"I understand, sir. Is this tied in any way to the *neneckt* you asked me to find? The one who was dealing in counterfeit?"

"Yes," he said after a while, an idea forming in the back of his head. "In fact, Faidal is the killer I just mentioned. A nasty soul all around. I suspect he wanted to cover up his tracks so the Guild couldn't investigate him."

He was about to make a terrible gamble. Bartolo knew that he could not find Faidal on his own. Even his spider's web of informants could only reach so far, and it would not be far enough to dig him out.

However, if the humans were really as upset about the murders as Marcie had indicated, the entire populace of Niheba would soon be on the lookout for the killer as soon as his name was known. If that name was Faidal...well, Bartolo would be very happy to see the *neneckt* torn apart by a vengeful mob before he could spill his secrets to anyone.

But there was a risk. If Faidal died and Megrithe Prinsthorpe somehow eluded him after her return to the island, Bartolo could be losing his only connection with the lost Arran Swinn.

There were too many boiling cauldrons and not enough lids. If Faidal was eliminated, Tiaraku might grudgingly thank Bartolo for saving his trade with the mainland, but that wouldn't be enough to absolve him of the mistakes he made with Swinn. He would have to start over again in the hunt to recover the gemstones, control the Siheldi Queen, and regain the sea king's favor. It would be doubly difficult, now that he had turned all his former friends against him...but there were worse things to work with than a blank slate.

"I need to get a message to the palace," he said out loud after thinking for a while. "To someone named Habur. Can you do that for me?"

"Tiaraku's clansman?" asked Jairus.

"Yes. He is absolutely not to know where I am. Under no circumstances. Do you understand?"

"Yes, sir. I can go right away."

"Not you. You're too conspicuous. I will write a letter for you to give to Marcie. Tell her to hire a messenger boy. I will watch from the window as you do so," he said pointedly, only realizing after he said it that the blind man was unlikely to sneak a look at the missive himself before handing it off.

"As you say, sir," Jairus replied.

Bartolo took some time to carefully word his message before scratching it down on a piece of parchment. Habur was a touchy soul, and there was no telling what he might take from the letter should Bartolo leave an opening for misinterpretation. The written word carried less weight than a face-to-face scolding, but he had to make sure Habur understood that he must disavow all involvement with the killings and blame Faidal instead.

"Here," he said eventually, sanding the wet ink and folding it securely. He had no sealing wax, but a dripping candle did just as well in a pinch, and he pressed his thumb deeply into the warm little puddle, holding it there as the heat faded into his skin.

He did indeed watch Jairus from the window as long as he stayed in view, craning his neck and pushing his nose against the glass, which kept him in sight until just before he reached the corner.

Bartolo had asked Habur to capture Faidal alive if it was possible, and kill him as quickly as he could if it wasn't. Knowing Habur, the latter was significantly more likely than anything else.

Bartolo rarely questioned his decisions, but he was pinning his life on this one. He couldn't just wait for the Prinsthorpe woman to arrive and hope that the Warden's cryptic predictions would work in his favor. He would have to use all the tools that remained at his disposal, as meager as they were.

"Johan," he called, sitting down at his writing desk again with a fresh sheet of paper. "Make sure Jairus has gone his way, then go back to Marcie and give her this, for what good it'll do me," he commanded, scrawling a short message that he sealed as before. "I want her to bring me everything and anything she learns, no matter where from. Nothing is too small, do you hear me? Someone has got to know *something* I can use."

CHAPTER SIX

For the second time in as many weeks, Megrithe was making the long and uncomfortable journey to Niheba. After more than seven days at sea, delayed in the Bay of Burlera by a squalling storm that wouldn't quit, she was incredibly eager to make landfall again.

She had been horribly seasick, her lingering weakness combining with the tossing waves to disastrous effect. She had kept to her cabin, which was more than a little short of being a palace, but at least it had kept her from having to deal with Durville too much.

The embarrassment had been overwhelming. Despite the lack of any evidence against him, Megrithe had put Durville in prison for attempting to murder her while colluding with Arran during their foray into smuggling. The *Tortoise's* sailing master had not been very pleased to see her when she showed up at the Old Gaol, not even after she paid his fees and signed her name to his release, a clean shirt and a flagon of good wine in her hands to serve as a peace offering.

But when she had explained Arran's troubled situation, Durville had slowly come round. He had taken her to the dry docks to see the *Tortoise,* levered up on her side to expose the shocking gash that had nearly doomed her.

The shipwrights had taken Arran's money and put it to good use, however, and the hole had been neatly patched over with clean, bright oak, shaved and smoothed to perfection. Durville explained to her that there was still plenty of work to be done if the little ship was to withstand a long journey, but at her insistence – and with a great many of her coins – he had spoken to the workers and refocused their attention on the essentials. She had no interest in making sure everything was pretty. She just needed it to float.

They had soon left Paderborn's dismal shores behind them, the bows pointed north and west towards Niheba. Megrithe had purchased a new red iron medallion with some of her Guild earnings, and she kept it curled tightly in her hands when she wasn't clutching the edges of a basin and losing the few bits of dry bread she had been able to force down.

The unpleasantness of illness was compounded by her mounting trepidation, creeping deeper into the crevasses of her mind with every passing night. She was keenly, constantly aware that there was nothing but the thin skin of the ocean's surface between her and the watery underworld that haunted her splintered dreams. She could get no proper sleep, but spent the nights tense and wakeful, staring at the thick, gnarled timber overhead as the moon crept silently across the dim marble of the sky, expecting at any moment for the Siheldi to take advantage of their exposed, helpless prey.

She knew very well that a building on land offered no more protection from the spirits than the wooden planks that surrounded her, but there was something a lot more comforting about the quiet solidity of a brick-lined room than the swinging, creaking canvas hammock-bed that was such a trouble to get into and so very hard to leave.

"Do you mind if I come in?" Nikko called quietly

through the door, unsure if she had managed to fall asleep.

"Not at all," she said, pushing back a bedraggled lock of hair and tucking it behind her ear, as if that would do anything to make her seem more presentable. There were no bathing facilities on the ship, other than a bucket of brackish water on the forecastle once a week if she was feeling adventurous, and even though she thought she was getting better, she was quite sure she didn't look it.

"I thought you might like to take a turn on deck," Nikko said. "The fresh air will be good for you."

"Must I?"

"Yes indeed," he nodded briskly, steadying her as she climbed out of the swinging contraption, scattering her pillows on the floor as she did so. "And I'll thank you not to kick me in the face in the process," Nikko laughed, leaning down to pick up the cushions.

"I'm so sorry," she replied, her face going a little pinker than it really ought to have. He had such an intoxicating smile, and she had to keep reminding herself that there wasn't the slightest bit of interest in her behind it.

They had been spending a lot of time together, after managing to overcome their rough introduction with a little intermediary help from Leofric's cooler head, and she was starting to enjoy his company a great deal.

He was engaging and entertaining, quick with his wit and quick to laugh at hers when she could muster it, which made her brutal days pass more easily. He did not relish being her nursemaid when the seas kicked up – she certainly did not blame him for that – but endured the close and somewhat smelly confines for his own good as much as hers, because everything about Nikko made

Durville's crew very uncomfortable.

Many of them had sailed on the *Tortoise's* maiden voyage, where Elargwyd had so violently put an end to their cruise, and they were deeply displeased to find a *neneckt* among their company again. Many more were simply unable to accept the nature of Nikko's relationship with Leofric, despite the fact that the two of them had been quite careful to keep their distance from each other. The evidence didn't need to be exhibited to be understood, and though Durville kept a tight rein on his crew's discipline, it was starting to fray some of their more delicate nerves.

Nikko had taken the hint, and turned to Megrithe in her private cabin for company and to keep out of view. He filled their hours with stories from his homeland, regaling her with his chatty descriptions of the workings of his native isle. Her short time on Niheba had not prepared her for how complex its society was, with its long histories of rival clans who could barely even agree on how much they disliked the humans who served their needs.

Far from being a stable, unifying force, Nikko painted Tiaraku as a divisive and disputed ruler, his throne built not just on rock and coral but on blood debts and violence and shifting alliances that occasionally erupted into death and vengeance, just as the cracks in the deep earth's crust spilled scalding gasses and ashes into the sea.

Tiaraku wasn't only using the Siheldi to try to snare the humans in his net of fear and pain. He was trying to control his own people: the Bluegills, growing rich and fat and discontent with the limits on their business interests; the Black Salts gathering their strength again after decades of oppression and slavery; the Cuskeels jockeying for position with the king's own Kitefins, rubbing up against each other in quarters of the city too small to contain both.

"Which one are you?" she had asked, and Nikko had laughed.

"I'm a Daggertooth," he had told her. "And don't I wish we were as fearsome as that sounds. We are masons and miners, for the most part. Nothing but a minor branch of the Green Stone Crabs, who have dropped far below the station they enjoyed when they built most of Emyer-Ekvori, long ago in the Sunset Days."

She had thought that sounded romantic, in its way, but speaking of his own past seemed to put Nikko on edge, and she hadn't pursued the matter much further. Instead, she had asked about Leofric, a subject Nikko had been more than willing to pursue. With his wide smile, he boasted about his lover's achievements in King Malveisin's service, wooing the neneckt into the Treaty of Libourg that now held such sway over all their dealings and helping to quell the bloody Ravenaught Rebellion that had swept along the eastern coast of Rhior-Adril twenty years ago, when King Malveisin had been nothing more than a novice princeling sent by his father to sort out the starving peasants who had made such a mess of his trade routes.

Leofric was far more accomplished than most people knew, she was pleased to learn, though Nikko's conversation almost always wandered away into meaningless anecdotes about their life together that held little interest for anyone who wasn't in love with the man.

She didn't really mind it. She just liked to hear him talk. It distracted her from her troubles and made her forget her anxieties, if only temporarily. Remnants of his initial prickliness could still rise to the surface, if she spoke about aspects of Niheba that he didn't think she could really understand, but more often than not, as the miles slipped by, there was something about Nikko that made her feel very comfortable.

He was a confident soul who had clearly decided that he would simply pay no mind to anyone who expressed disapproval of his choices, and that was fascinating to her. It seemed impossible that she could ever approach that level of certainty within herself, and she envied him for it.

Despite winning all of the battles that had stood between her relatively humble beginnings and the bright iron prize of an inspector's badge, even her Guild-given authority had never felt wholly natural to her. She had spent the entirety of her adult life telling other people what to do, but when she blew out her candles at the end of most days and settled into bed, she still felt as if she was that half-grown girl parading around in her father's shadow with a crossbow she didn't know how to use.

Megrithe had been told, at times when her doubts slithered away from her and into the ears of her confidantes, that everyone felt that way. Everyone was unsure of their choices, and everyone faltered from time to time. When she was younger, she hadn't been able to believe it. She had been convinced that everyone other than her had all their affairs well in hand. But they just told her that everyone at her age felt like that, too.

Her work had soon taught her what false courage really looked like, and she had stopped fretting so very much once she learned how prevalent it was. But being in the rare presence of real conviction could still shake the foundations of her surety, driving her into private despair. It was in those moments, she found, that she most craved what Nikko and Leofric gave to each other: the love and trust of someone who exuded quiet assurance wherever they went.

Leofric kept to himself as well, fully aware of his part in the sailors' discomfort, but she watched the two of them together as often as she could. His domestic choices may have ended his more public ambitions, and cut short his ability to gather the accolades which his partner recounted with such pride, but Megrithe had the feeling that he didn't regret it.

Every time he caught Nikko's eye, she was struck by the depth of feeling he could exchange in nothing more than a glance. It always made her look away and blush, as if she had intercepted a very private letter than no one else was ever meant to see.

It shamed her to think of how she had always assumed that such unorthodox relations were based on nothing more than a peculiar sort of lust that she could never really understand; some powerful attraction of flesh to flesh that pulled two people together more strongly than the mores of the earthly world or the admonishments of heaven.

She knew she must be wrong. She had never seen the same look between a tavern floozy and a licentious drunk, but only between husband and wife, whose bonds were deep and patience strong and lives long lived in tight unison. A *neneckt* could make itself into anything, but she did not think even a sea-dweller could falsify something like that.

The hurried journey was no time to start longing for secret glances of her own, flinging herself as she was into deathly danger and unknown peril. But it made her think, while she lay in bed with green skin and a stomach full of heaving vinegar, how nice it must be to draw such strength from a love that outweighed the fear of a world that hated them for it.

She mused often about such acts of true courage, and those thoughts frequently turned to contemplations about Arran Swinn. He had thrown glances towards her, to be sure, but they were of the ordinary, fleeting kind – a perfunctory ogling that held no malice but little meaning. She had done the same to him, when he wasn't looking. It was only natural, really.

Megrithe hoped with all her heart that he was still alive. She thought he must be. The *callawif* wouldn't lie to her, would she? Could she? *Find him before he shatters us all,* she had whispered, and the words still made Megrithe shiver even though they had been running through her head a thousand times since they were first spoken, each repetition strengthening her conviction that she must obey them, regardless of what it would cost her.

"Megrithe?"

"What?"

"You're staring into nothing again," Nikko said.

"Oh? Yes. Of course. I'm so sorry," she stammered. "You wanted to go for a walk."

She wasn't sure if the benefits of the fresh air compensated for the nuisance of the buffeting breeze snatching at her clothing and raking through her shamefully greasy hair, but once she was settled on the little bench nestled into the transom rail, the shade and protection made it less of a bother. The sun was gently warm on the nape of her neck, and she smiled to thank Nikko for persuading her out of her burrow.

"You look like you're on the way to recovering your health, Miss Prinsthorpe," Leofric said, bowing somewhat formally before sitting down next to her.

"I certainly hope I am," she replied. "Durville says we will arrive in a day or so. I'd like to be strong enough to leave the ship on my own two feet."

"And after you accomplish that?"

"I rather thought you might be the one to tell me," she said.

"You want us to find a *neneckt* that doesn't want to be found," Nikko said. "That is not easy. I'm not even sure I would know where to begin, and I have experience being on both sides of the equation."

"I know where we can start," she told him.

"And where would that be?"

"With his true name," she said quietly.

She wasn't entirely sure how Nikko would react to that news, especially since she had been keeping the information to herself so far. She hadn't been sure when would be the right time to bring it out. "The *callawif* gave it to me," she added, as if that would help absolve her of the serious breach of *neneckt* propriety.

Leofric and Nikko exchanged one of their looks – not such a pleasant one this time – and Megrithe suddenly got very studious about the state of her fingernails.

"That is not knowledge you should have," Nikko said eventually. "Why would an *callawif* tell you something like that?"

"She wanted me to help her fulfill a bargain. I would not have asked unless it was absolutely necessary," she continued, but she thought that was probably a lie. She had just wanted to make her job easier.

"Be that as it may," Leofric said, possibly even less

pleased than his partner. "It seems like a foul trick to use that against him."

"I know. But it is the only leverage I have."

"No, it isn't," Leofric said. "I know of this Bartolo character you mentioned. He would be nothing but a petty street swiller if it wasn't for his ties to the Divided. They are a force not to be ignored."

"The night-fire cult?" she asked. She had heard of them, but not as anything more than a strange offshoot of a long-dead religion devoted to worshiping the Siheldi as gods.

"They are more than that on Niheba," Nikko said. "They are dangerous. It will be extremely problematic if they are working with Tiaraku."

"What would we do then?" she asked.

"Lose your phantom war," Leofric said with his wry smile. "Without any doubt."

"But we can get help from the Guild," she said. "Even on Niheba, there is always the Guild."

"And what makes you think they will aid someone who has broken with their ranks?" asked Nikko.

"They don't know I resigned," Megrithe said. "Not yet. There isn't a ship that could have gotten there before us – nor one that would have any interest in spreading news about me. And...and I may have taken some of my cards with me," she added in a low voice. "Just in case."

"So that you can find yourself in even more trouble once someone discovers that you're lying?" Leofric asked.

"I am unlikely to escape a prison sentence no matter what I'm caught for," she replied. "What's an extra few years for impersonation?"

Nikko laughed. "That's the spirit," he said, patting her hand. "We can only hope prison will be the worst thing that happens to us."

Leofric was not as amused. "Maybe we can turn to something more or less legitimate first. I still have friends in Tiaraku's palace. I worked with a fellow called Genedi for several years on the trade agreements. He's always had a finger in the right pies, and he's been favorable towards the Guild. Maybe he can help."

"What type of fool puts his trust in a Bluegill?" Nikko muttered, but Leofric didn't hear him.

"Very well," Megrithe said. "That sounds like a good place to start – if you think he'll be a better friend to you than he is to Tiaraku."

"His friends are largely negotiable," Leofric said, "and I am very persuasive. Isn't that why I'm here?"

After dodging Durville on her way back below, Megrithe spent the rest of the day and most of the following morning dozing quietly, trying to shake her weakness. It wasn't easy, especially as they drew nearer to the island and her nerves started to fray again, leaving her shoulders twanging with anxiety at how slowly the wind could carry her.

Eventually, however, the bellowing cry of the lookout shook her from a nodding sleep, and she sat bolt upright in her hammock, the excitement of the long-awaited moment practically throwing her out of the bed with its insistent force.

She managed not to hang herself in the tightly twisting ropes and dressed herself properly, slipping her feet into her shoes and pattering out of her cabin before Nikko could come to fetch her.

"I don't see it," she said, craning towards the horizon when she found the *neneckt* leaning on the rail, gazing down into the water instead.

"Not yet," he replied. "You'd have to be higher up. And don't think I'll let you go climbing the rigging. We'll be there sooner than you think."

"What's down there?" she asked, following his stare into the depths.

"Nothing. Not anymore," he said. "Do you have all your things together?" he asked, raising his head and smiling brightly.

"Yes, I packed up earlier – is that smoke?" she said suddenly, pointing towards the horizon where a haze of dark cloud was hanging ominously in the north.

"It looks like it," Nikko replied, frowning as he followed her finger. "Old smoke. I wonder if another warehouse went up by the dockside. It's rather common, unfortunately."

Even in Paderborn, fires started by homeless squatters or careless tenants in the slums could decimate huge swaths of the crowded city. It happened to some degree at least once or twice a year, bringing a high death toll and a great deal of misery for the suddenly dispossessed. For an unattended storeroom to burn to the ground was nothing unusual at all, but the breezy blemish in the sky made her feel more than ordinarily uneasy.

"It still makes my skin crawl," she said.

"Me too," Leofric said, coming up behind them to stand next to Nikko, searching out the *neneckt's* hand to hold, hidden between their bodies and the rail. "I lost a house to fire once. I can't say it's an experience I would ever wish to repeat."

"Nor I," Megrithe said, recalling her brush with death

in the Paderborn Guild House. The burn on her arm had stopped being painful, but she suspected she would carry the mottled red mark of it forever. "Hopefully it's nothing."

They talked idly about other things for a while, trying to pass the time, all three of them glancing occasionally at the lingering smudge in the sky until a distant bank of clouds marched in to obscure it. The wind began to shift as they drew closer to the island, backing to blow southerly into their faces.

Durville was muttering to himself on the quarterdeck as the helmsman tried to steady their course against the strengthening breeze. His face darkened as the line of clouds deepened into an unpleasantly purplish hue, charging towards them on the wind and bringing along the scent of charred wood and ashes.

"There will be a right old storm tonight," Nikko said after a while, pulling his collar up against the growing chill. "A proper typhoon."

Durville seemed to be of the same opinion, and started shouting orders to his men to strike the sails and secure the empty barrels and other items they had started to bring on deck in preparation for landing and replenishing their supplies. It was work wasted, and the men couldn't help but grumble a little as they undid everything they had spent the morning doing, but no one tarried as the sky closed over and the first cold, fat drops of rain began to splatter on the planks.

"Time to go below," Leofric told Megrithe, catching her arm as the backstay beside them suddenly stretched taught with a peculiar, half-heard twang. "And get your bucket ready. We'll be tossing around all night."

"No need to remind me," she grimaced. Her stomach

was already lurching again as the *Tortoise* fought the kicking swell, and she held onto Leofric's hand as he guided her towards her quarters. "Will we not make land today, then?"

"No, I shouldn't think so. It's impossible to tell how long the storm will last."

"Can't Nikko - I don't know. Can't he do something?"

Leofric smiled. "Ten miles from Tiaraku's throne? As much as I love the fellow, I am under no illusion that he is powerful enough to control the weather under the nose of such influence."

"Tiaraku brought the storm," she said with sudden, leaden certainty. "He must know we're coming. Is he going to sink us?"

"Tiaraku sees many things. I would not be surprised if he has kept his eye on you. There is nothing on his island that escapes his notice."

"The mirrors. Bartolo had one."

"Tiaraku has more. But there are ways to avoid him," Leofric said. "He is good at making enemies, and those enemies are good at making sure they don't fall into his clutches. He can only see what he is looking for, just like anyone else. We can find help, but the first step is to make it ashore."

"That may not be so easy," Megrithe said as a howling wall of wind slammed into the little ship, causing it to careen sideways into an oncoming wave. "Oh - are you all right?"

"Fine, fine," Leofric said, rubbing his forehead where he had smacked it into a beam, taken off balance by the sudden motion. "Nikko always says my skull is as thick as a ram's. For once, I'm glad he's right."

Megrithe smiled, and assured Leofric that she would be fine as long as she had a basin and a glass of water nearby. When he had left for the safety of his own dry quarters, she curled up in her hammock and drew the blanket right up over her head, trying to block out the whistling wail of the wind while a few stray tears found their way down her face.

She was deeply frustrated by the delay, which she could do absolutely nothing to rectify, and Leofric's innocent comment was making her feel inexplicably lonely.

She was an independent person by nature, and the notion of living alone had never scared her. But dying alone was a different matter – one she never really thought she would have to consider. She was still young, and her career was just blooming, and there had always seemed to be plenty of time to settle down to the business of sorting out the rest of her life.

But after the terror of the Siheldi and the shock of waking up half way around the world with no one but the coldly mercurial *callawif* to anchor her to a strange new reality in which everyone was an enemy, time didn't seem so much on her side any longer, and the tenderness with which her two companions spoke about each other was like a jabbing needle ripping out seams she had always thought to be entirely secure.

It had nothing to do with Arran Swinn, she told herself as her breath collected hot and damp around her cheeks. And she was certainly not using his distress to mask the urgency of her own. If anything, she should be furious with him. She should hate him for ruining her career, nearly ending her life, exposing her to the madness of the mountain under the ocean and the predatory spirits that lurked within its rotten core.

She should be livid. So why couldn't she help wishing that he was there to take her hand again to reassure her, like he had done as they wandered the tunnels under Sind Heofonne?

It was just an illusion, she told herself as she turned over and drew her knees up to her chin, trying to stop her insides from quaking. It wasn't Arran Swinn she wished for. It was anyone. It just so happened that he had been the last one to be close to her, in whatever small way. If she died on Niheba seeking his fate, she would never be close to anyone again, and that thought made her weary soul whimper in despair.

A galloping lurch started her bed swinging, and she found herself praying that Arran's judgment of sails and timber was sounder than his ability to keep himself out of trouble. The prayers continued through the uneasy night. Megrithe was certain that she could hear the shrieking cries of the Siheldi mixed with the yowling wind.

She clutched her covers close and her red iron pendant closer, drifting into fitful, broken sleep that somehow carried her through to the morning.

But there was no golden dawn to greet her groggy eyes that day, nor even the day after. The storm raged for countless hours, sheathing them in black, driving downpour and bitterly angry squalls. She had lost count of how many times Nikko had come to empty the sloshing bucket by her side, but she was continually amazed at how often her sore stomach still saw fit to fill it.

It was damp, miserable, dark, and dreary, and she wished for nothing more than a moment of stillness on solid land and legs that didn't wobble every time she tried to stand up straight. Like most of her wishes, however, it was not about to come true: the tossing continued for at least three days, her apprehension and fretfulness reaching a sharpness that not even her sickness could blunt as the maelstrom raged on.

On the fourth morning, the endless dripping of water through the planks finally slowed, the towering surf calmed, and the clouds began to clear. In the pearly, weeping sky, there were no more signs of whispery plumes of smoke to the north. In fact, when she finally ventured out of her cabin to stand on her toes and lean over the rail, the squat dome of the island had disappeared entirely.

"We seem to have lost our destination. Will we not reach the island this morning?" she said to Durville when he stumped by, seemingly intent on not speaking to her. She could walk more quickly than he could with his wooden foot, however, and she did not let him escape until he turned to answer her question.

"No, we will not reach the island this morning," he replied gruffly, jerking his chin upwards. "Nor any other damn morning if the gods have anything to say about it."

She followed his gaze to the mainmast. "It's broken," she said, peering between the tangles of ropes. She knew little about ships, but even she could see that the rigging was somewhat more disordered than she was used to, and the bulk of the timber sat jaggedly askew, nearly touching its neighbor.

"Aye. Well broken, at that. I've seen green fire storms come up unnatural before. Ain't no good in 'em for me or my crew."

"Green fire storms?"

Durville pointed to the split in the great spar, where the beam was charred and disfigured. "Spirit fire. Burns clean through wood and iron, but will leave your skin untouched. It's the devil's work. The Siheldi were toying with us."

Megrithe felt her shivers return. "How soon can you fix it?"

"Soon as we get back to Paderborn, miss. I'll have my lads rig up something workable in the meanwhile. The rudder is just about as knackered, too, but we'll be off home by midday, I hope."

"I beg your pardon?"

"Ain't no one wants us on that isle, miss," Durville said, scratching at his beard. "Spirit fire is clear enough a sign of that."

"Your captain - your *friend* is out there," she protested. "And I hired you to -"

"I don't remember any gold coming into my hand," Durville said sharply. "I remember some long days in a crowded prison and some high words from an inspector with no right to be so prim and proper after all she's done.

"I came here as a courtesy that's extended long past what's owed you, and I've got naught but grief for it. We've had nothing but storms and spirits from there to here, and I ain't losing this ship in addition to what's gone already."

"But Arran -"

"Arran is my friend, to be sure, but he's a man of the sea first," Durville said. "He knows when it's right to save a livelihood instead of losing it all to try to help one gone soul. He's made the decision himself when he's had to. That's what it comes down to when you own a hundred lives. There's no point in losing the investment when the man is probably long dead."

"That's horrible," she snapped. "You don't know that at all. Don't you trust the *callawif?* She said he was alive."

"And you said he put a knife in his own gut. Am I not to trust you over a cold-hearted ghost? How about trusting my friend to do what he puts his mind to? I've seen him do what it takes to get out of a tight spot, even when it ain't pretty. He's damn good at what he does when he needs to do it. You don't survive going up against someone like him, Miss Prinsthorpe. What makes you think he would survive himself?"

"He's not dead," she said, feeling tears pricking at her eyes. "And I can't believe you'd come all the way within sight of land just to turn around again. It's not fair, and it's not right."

"It ain't fair to expect my crew to drown for a captain who left them," Durville replied, gesturing to the men who had gathered around to listen to the row. "I could try for a week to get closer to that island, and I will wager you my weight in silver that every time we turn north, there will be a storm to stop us. If it ain't the Siheldi causing it, then it's the *neneckt.* You don't know how many times I've already stopped these lads from throwing your little fellow over."

A wave of agreement swept through the crowd of sailors. They had had enough, and it was clear that Nikko was a particularly sore spot for skins already scraped rough by the ceaseless seas.

"You can't do that," Megrithe said, looking around nervously, wondering why she couldn't seem to muster up the authority that she draped around her like a velvet cape when she had been speaking on behalf of the Guild. "He has done nothing to you. No one has done anything."

"And if you want to keep it that way, you won't argue when we make our way south," Durville said. "It don't please me, Miss Prinsthorpe, but I won't be losing my life for a dead man today."

"Then give me a boat," she said when she had taken in the blank, stony faces and crossed arms that surrounded her. "I'll go myself."

The sailors started laughing. "It's fifteen miles, miss," Durville said. "Your arms would fall off before you made it a quarter."

"I will take her," Leofric said, moving up to stand next to Megrithe. "And Nikko will come with us. Would that not solve your problem? You'd be rid of all of us, and then you could do as you please."

"Begging your pardon, sir, but you don't got no more experience on the open water than the lady," Durville said in a somewhat less condescending tone. "The currents are too strong for a longboat as small as we have. You'd never make it to land."

"I suggest you let us try," said Leofric.

"Is that really a good idea?" Megrithe whispered as Durville considered, consulting with his helmsman for a moment.

"Nikko will take care of it," Leofric told her.

Megrithe turned to look at the *neneckt*, who was standing quietly off to one side, and Nikko winked at her.

"I can't say that I'd be willing to stop you, sir," Durville said slowly when he seemed to have taken the measure of his men's minds. "But I can't recommend it, neither."

"I think you already have," Leofric said. "You want us gone, and we want to get gone. Let's not delay any further. Miss Prinsthorpe, I suggest you collect your baggage."

The sailors were already readying the longboat before Megrithe had made it back to her cabin to grab her knapsack. It didn't really seem like a good idea to jump into an open boat with nothing but unsettled waves from horizon to horizon, but she had brought Leofric with her to help her solve problems, and he seemed fairly confident about this one. The only other option was to turn around, a prisoner of Durville's sense of self-preservation, and that she simply would not do.

"Ready," she said to Leofric as Durville silently handed him a canvas bag filled with enough bread and water to last them a few days, just in case the tugging currents and stormy seas turned into more than they could handle. Nikko was already in the boat, which was bobbing alarmingly next to the ship's patched side, and Megrithe swallowed hard as she realized that she would have to climb down the vessel's flank with nothing more than a few shallow wooden ledges to serve as steps and a fraying rope to guide her.

"Thank you for taking us this far," she managed to say as Durville saw them off. "When I see Mister Swinn, shall I tell him that you have decided to take sole possession of his ship?"

Durville snorted a laugh. "You think I'm stealing from him?"

"It certainly has that appearance."

The sailing master shook his head. "When you see him, you can ask him about what happened on Kittling Island if you want to put your mind at rest."

"What does that mean?"

"It means I've known him for much longer than you have, miss, and a great deal better, too. If you think I've given up on him just so I can take his tub for a ride, you're mistaken. I'd be overjoyed to give it back to him, and I hope I'll be able to. I just think his luck ran out the day he met you."

Megrithe tried to make herself as small as possible in the boat as Leofric took up the oars and pushed them away from the *Tortoise's* side. It seemed much colder so close to the gray surface of the angry water, and there was nothing to impede the wind. She listened to the echo of Durville's voice giving the orders that would turn the ship back towards Paderborn as they slowly pulled away from each other, the sailing master's last words lingering in her mind like a bee sting.

It was only a few moments before she looked up from her clasped hands in her lap, but the *Tortoise* already seemed miles away, half-swallowed by the sea as it slipped gently over the curve of the earth. Nikko was standing up in the bows, complaining loudly as he took off his jacket and started to undo the laces of his shirt.

"I cannot believe you're making me do this," he said as Leofric watched with half a smile on his lips. "This is humiliating."

"Shut up and take your clothes off," Leofric replied, putting his chin in his hand, the oars abandoned.

"What on earth are you doing?" Megrithe cried as Nikko started to step out of his breeches.

"Saving the prince here some much-needed hard labor," Nikko said, now entirely naked as Megrithe turned scarlet and covered her eyes. "There he sits, growing fatter by the second, as I do all the work."

"You can't have thought I'd be rowing us all the way to the harbor," Leofric said as Nikko put his foot on the rail and launched himself over the side of the boat, disappearing instantly into the water. "He'll pull us."

Megrithe let out a little yelp as the boat suddenly accelerated, gripping the bench while the vessel leveled off at a clip that would seem respectable to a well-bred coach and four.

"We'll be there in an hour or so," Leofric said, sitting back and closing his eyes as the breeze washed over him. "And I'll only have to handle a week of his moaning afterward."

Ordinarily, she would have found the experience enchanting. She was quite fond of horses, and rode in the Guild hunt every year, out in the rolling countryside behind the city's limits, chasing deer or boar at a flying gallop through the hedges and forests, competing not just for the prize, but for the gamesmanship of the ride.

But as they hurtled towards the island, the stiff wind now laden with the scent of green land, she couldn't shake the memory of the blank opposition and stubborn superstition that had lingered among Durville and his crew. The game she was playing now was against powers more terrifying than any wild animal, and the stakes were much higher than the temporary pique of a missed arrow or the inconvenience of a lost horseshoe.

The feeling of speed was unsettling as the boat skimmed over the tops of the tossing waves, and she felt as if her stomach was about to start its complaining again. Megrithe tried to ignore it as she kept her eyes firmly on the sky, worried that they were too low to the water to see a new bank of clouds rolling in until it was too late. The rowboat was a smaller target than the *Tortoise*, but she didn't think that it was small enough to escape Tiaraku's wrath.

It took closer to two hours, in fact, both of which were long and chilly, dashed by spray and whipped by the icy stirrings of the air, but eventually the island appeared in front of them, its dark cliffs looming like a monument to some long-forgotten war. The swooping slope of the stony formations guided them towards the harbor plainly enough, but Nikko slowed them down while they were still beyond the view of the island's lookouts, not wishing to attract undue attention with their curious flight.

"Thank you," Leofric said to him when he had gotten back in the boat, shaking out his curly hair like a dog before giving his partner a kiss. "I've always said you are a marvel."

"You could stand to say it more often," Nikko replied, reaching for his trousers as Megrithe stared steadily over the stern until he had dressed himself. "You didn't get seasick again, dear, did you?" he asked Megrithe as Leofric took up the oars in earnest this time. "You look a bit unwell."

"No, I'm fine," she said, doing her best to smile. "That really was wonderful of you."

"The sooner we get there, the sooner we can leave," he said, yawning and stretching as Leofric steadied them on their course again.

Soon enough, the current took over the task of pulling them towards Niheba's shores, leaving Leofric with little to do but steer the fragile craft away from the bigger ships that sat in the port, huddled down against the storm that had kept them idle.

Megrithe could smell the smoke again, and part of her

imagined that the tension in the tautly furled sails and slapping of the water on pitch-covered hulls was due to more than just the wild weather.

"Why isn't there anyone about?" she asked Nikko when she had figured out what was wrong. The harbor was as quiet as a graveyard.

"Maybe it wasn't a warehouse," he said, looking closely at the shore as he tucked the cuffs of his trousers into his boots. "Maybe there were deaths in the city."

"The rain would have washed the smell away if it was something small," Leofric agreed as they sidled up to a low dock. "Jump up and throw me that rope, will you?" he directed towards Nikko, who nodded and sprang onto the planks without any of his usual tart comments.

A few moments later, Leofric had handed Megrithe onto the dry land that she had craved, only to find that her legs weren't anywhere near as prepared to make the adjustment as her mind wished them to be. It took her some time before she could walk without wobbling: long enough for Leofric to secure the boat, remove their baggage, and start guiding her with a firm hand on her elbow towards the district's main thoroughfare.

It was eerily silent. A few dockhands hurried to their tasks in a tight group, neither speaking nor looking around at the newcomers, let alone hurling their typical flurry of jokes and insults amongst themselves or towards strangers they didn't fancy. Megrithe was used to being the subject of jeers or catcalls from such people, and while she didn't typically like it, the absence of any jocularity at all from the harbor folk was jarring and unsettling, only adding to the sense of oppression that had been building in her mind.

"Something is very wrong," she said quietly to Leofric,

who nodded, his hand resting near the hilt of his sword the whole time.

"Why don't I meet you two somewhere a bit later?" Nikko said. "The Spearman, perhaps?"

"Good idea," said Leofric. "Just be careful."

"Where is he going?" Megrithe asked when Nikko took a sudden detour down a different street without even saying goodbye.

"I've got my friends and he's got his," Leofric told her. "I don't know what has happened, but I do know it's almost never a good idea to be in mixed company when something goes wrong on Niheba. We'll join up again tonight."

"I'd like to see if I can find some of my own contacts," she said. "There are agents of the Guild all over the island. I just don't have names."

"I have one. But you may not wish to come with me when I see him."

"Why?"

Leofric actually looked embarrassed, which Megrithe hadn't really thought possible. "It's my uncle. He can be a bit...impolite."

"Andrus?"

"Yes."

"Andrus Gunhilde is here? I thought he was in some Paderborn gutter –" she started, clamping her mouth shut before she could finish the whole thought.

"Can't say he hasn't been, on occasion," Leofric replied with a shrug. "But he straightened up a bit after he got married again. A good woman will do that for some fellows. He never could quite leave the Guild behind, so he found a place where the Guild doesn't quite exist. It's turned out well for him – and, I hope, for us."

"He knew my father. If you don't mind, I'd like to see him. He was never unkind to me."

"If you wish."

Leofric led her into the center of the city, where the coiled, watchful atmosphere seemed only to deepen. Anyone who had to be out in the streets was keeping to themselves, hoods up or goods clutched tightly to chests, children held close and their questions constantly hushed. It didn't seem to matter whether they were human or *neneckt*. No one wanted to mingle, not even with their own kind, as if a single word or greeting would set off a wildfire.

Megrithe was expecting Leofric to take her into some unsavory corner of the town, where Andrus would be holed up in a dark den cluttered with empty bottles of liquor, but they ended up ringing the bell of a perfectly respectable little house, covered in whitewashed clapboard and sandwiched between two taller blocks of flats that looked like older brothers muscling their way onto the street.

"Well, look who it is," Andrus said, surprised but pleased when he answered the door. "What are you doing here, Leofric? I haven't seen you for an age."

"I'm just here for some business, Uncle," Leofric said, shaking his hand. "I believe you're acquainted with Miss Prinsthorpe?"

"Is that our little Meg?" Andrus cried. "I don't believe it."

"It's nice to see you again, Mister Gunhilde," she said while he shook her hand, too, before leaning in to give her a peck on the cheek.

"All grown up and making a hell of a name for

yourself, from what I've heard. How's your mother?"

"Passed on, I'm afraid," Megrithe said, laughing nervously as she tried to recover herself. Andrus was a big man, tall and broad, and while he seemed perfectly sober and the gesture was a chaste as could be, she hadn't expected the close proximity. "Just last year."

"I'm sorry to hear it. Very sorry, indeed. She was a fine woman. Come inside and have a cup. Of tea," he added. "I don't touch a drop of anything stronger anymore. The lady wouldn't stand for it, and I ain't about to blame her. Leofric, I don't know if you've even met my missus."

"Not in person, no."

"Hilda, put on the kettle," Andrus called, ushering them into the parlor. "We've got guests."

"Hilda Gunhilde?" Megrithe whispered, trying to stop another laugh as Leofric stepped aside to let her get to the settee.

"Gunhilda Gunhilde, actually," he whispered back with a smile. "Poor soul. At least he knows she must really love him."

After a series of familiar tea-related noises from the kitchen, Hilda emerged to greet the company. She was a youngish woman, with pretty chestnut hair and an engaging smile, who had absolutely no compunction about laughing at her own married name as she introduced herself.

"It's terrible, isn't it?" she said, punching her husband playfully on the arm as he beamed at her. "I will blame him forever. But I'm so glad to finally meet you, Leofric. Andrus hardly talks of anyone else."

"I hope that's not true," his nephew replied. "You must be terribly bored of me already."

"Nonsense. Will you be on the island long? Do you need a place to stay? We have a guest room. Or two, in a pinch," she added, looking questioningly at Megrithe.

"We'll be staying at an inn, thank you," Leofric told her. "I was actually hoping to talk a little politics, Uncle, if it's possible."

"A dangerous topic, these days," Andrus said. "Will you see if there are any cakes, love?" he asked Hilda, who nodded as if she was well aware of her cue before she retreated back to the other room. "What do you know already?"

"Just that there's a dark mood about," Leofric replied. "We only just arrived."

"Tiaraku has put his foot in it good this time," Andrus said. "Or at least I think he has. There have been more than a few rumors flying about."

"Rumors about what?" Megrithe asked.

"One of my contacts was killed a few days ago, and so was her friend on the *neneckt* side. I don't rightly know what she was into – she didn't come to me with it – but it can't have been something good. Some people are saying that it was a counterfeiting deal gone south, with someone named Faidal at the helm, but I don't think so. I think it –"

"Faidal?" Megrithe broke in. "Where is he? Do you know?"

"Now, Meg. Don't you go interrupting your elders," Andrus said sternly, in the tone he had used with her when she was just a girl and too eager for her own good. "I ain't finished."

"Yes, sir. Sorry, sir," she said automatically, silencing herself before she could even wonder why she still instantly obeyed. It was too late now, however. He was talking again.

"I don't think it was this Faidal at all, in any case. I think it was a right bastard I know called Habur. Tiaraku's favorite thug. It's got his signature all over it, and that's what most people who know any damn thing about it agree with."

"But Faidal – where does he come into it?" Megrithe asked when Andrus took a drink from his teacup. "It's important."

"I don't rightly know. I've never heard of him, and I don't think Agnise had, either. She wasn't responsible for anything too grand. She usually monitored some of the petty contraband headed to Paderborn in sailors' pockets. It was easy from her position."

"Who was the *neneckt* who was killed?" Leofric asked.

"Fellow called Genedi. He was a friend to the Guild, when the gold was right."

Leofric fell silent for a moment. "I think our job just got a lot more complicated," he said to Megrithe eventually.

"What job is that?" his uncle asked.

"I know Faidal," she told him. "I've been looking for him – that's why we're here. I need to know everything about Agnise and what she was investigating. Any connection she might have with Tiaraku's palace, and anything you've ever heard about Faidal. Everything."

"I can take you to her tavern," Andrus said, "but I'll have no flashing about of cards or titles. Everything we do here is unofficial. Do you understand?"

"That won't be a problem," Megrithe replied, ducking her head a bit. She didn't particularly want him to find out that *all* her business related to the Guild would be unofficial from now on. It would be a bit like telling her father she had turned her back on the livelihood that connected them through his life and after his death, and she wasn't prepared for that.

Leofric made no mention of the change in circumstances either, for which she was profoundly grateful. Instead, he took her arm protectively as they left the Gunhilde house and Andrus led them towards the waterfront again.

Agnise's tavern was one of those nameless, ancient establishments that sailors always seemed find with the help of some undeclared sixth sense. There were plenty of similar places in Paderborn that made ideal waypoints for smugglers and those with other illegal dealings on their minds, and Megrithe was used to the level of caution required when entering a hall of such low repute. There were few people in the common room, and most of them looked well into their cups already, but she took her time to mark out the one or two patrons who appeared most like to stir up trouble all the same.

"Kitty, can I see you for a moment?" Andrus asked the barmaid, who was wedged in a corner behind a stack of wooden pallets that obviously didn't belong there.

The girl nodded and slipped from her station, heading straight to the back room that passed for an office and storehouse. Andrus beckoned them to follow.

"Oh, dear," Megrithe said when Kitty opened the door to the empty room, a powerful stench hitting her like a thrown brick.

"I'm sorry, miss," the girl said. "There isn't no windows back here to clear the air. I did the best I could with vinegar and soda, but..."

"It's all right, I understand," Megrithe replied when

Kitty trailed off with a hitch to her voice. So much blood soaking into the worn, unvarnished wood of the floorboards and the plaster walls would be absolutely impossible to clean without sanding everything down. "There was just one death here?" she asked Andrus, who nodded.

"As I said, it's Habur's style. He likes to make sure his message is clear."

"Kitty, did you see anyone?" she asked the barmaid, but the girl just shook her head.

"No, miss. I found her in the morning when I came to open up."

"Has a *neneckt* called Faidal ever come here?"

"Don't know, miss. Never heard of him before they all started saying he did it. Wouldn't know him from looks, but then again, I don't know none of them when they can change so quick."

"Of course. Do you know anyone who might, though? A regular, maybe. Someone who talked with Agnise often, even if it seemed like nothing important."

Kitty paused and looked down. "Don't know, miss."

"You can tell her, sweetheart," Andrus prompted gently. "This is a good friend of mine, and haven't I always done right by you?"

"Yes, sir. I just – well, there's my young man, but – that is, he isn't mine, exactly," she stammered, her cheeks going almost as red as the rusty stains splashed on the walls. "But he comes round often and always has a kind word. A proper gentleman. Always a nice word for me," she repeated, and Megrithe tried not to roll her eyes. She knew the look on the maid's face all too well. "Agnise took a shine to him, too."

"What's his name?" Megrithe asked.

"Jairus," the girl replied. "Jairus Lanque. But he hasn't come round in a few days. He was real upset about it all."

"I'm sure he was," Andrus said soothingly, patting the girl on the shoulder as she started to well up. "We all are."

"I know, sir. I'm sorry. We just don't know what we're going to do now. Raliph has been doing the books and such, but he don't have no right to the title, and I'll be out my job if Mister Basset closes down the place. I got my little ones to feed, sir. I don't know what we'll do."

"I'll sort it out with Basset," Andrus told her. "And if he ain't willing to listen, I'll find you another good position. Why don't you tell me a little more about this Jairus fellow in the meantime? Isn't he the one who won the tourney last year?"

Despite the fact that everyone seemed to know his name, Jairus turned out to be a difficult person to find. His most obvious distinguishing characteristic was first on everyone's lips, but that was all anyone was willing to say for certain.

Megrithe was told to ask the rice merchants – the rice merchants said he was very polite and always paid in full, but not even a few minutes of hard thought could help them recall if he ever spoke about what he was doing with all that grain or where his cart went once it left the loading yard.

They sent her to their friends who sold wheat, and the wheat sellers told her that the butchers probably knew more. The butchers shook their heads and told her that no one would risk speaking out of turn about Mister

Lanque, whose impressive qualities – or perhaps his deep pockets – seemed to inspire such loyalty across such a large swathe of Niheba's human community.

There were rumors that he belonged to the Divided, of course, but those rumors followed every blind, penniless beggar that held out a withered hand on the edge of a curb. Leofric told her it was mostly meaningless: a reflexive habit that helped settle the minds of well-to-do passers-by who convinced themselves that the street folk were nothing more than devils in disguise and didn't deserve their patronage.

Jairus didn't sound anything like a beggar, and he didn't seem much like a devil from the way he inspired respect among the subjects of her interrogations. But there was no telling anything for certain unless Megrithe found him – and there was no finding him by the time the sun was slipping golden sheets between the edges of buildings and deep into the clear, ornamental pools.

"I'd like to go catch up with Nikko, if it's all right with you," Leofric said eventually, glancing up at the sunset. Andrus had gone back to his home an hour ago, and even Megrithe was beginning to realize that there was nothing more that could be done before nightfall.

"Yes, I agree," she sighed. "Another day wasted."

"I don't think it was wasted," Leofric said. "We have more information than we started with. Tomorrow we can approach it from the other side. Genedi's associates may be easier to find."

"I do hope so."

The Spearman was a sprawling public house that catered to the types of merchants and minor diplomats who demanded good food and passable liquor, but were content with little else from their rented rooms and service for hire. It was comfortable enough, but it was not a place where anything but coin was met with interest, which was perfectly suited to their current needs.

Nikko was waiting for them in the taproom with a tall, thin glass of clear spirits by his elbow as he browsed one of the monthly harbor papers that collected in musty stacks on the end tables. He flashed his bright smile when he saw Leofric, and Megrithe heard her companion breathe an audible sigh of relief.

"I thought you might find yourself in trouble," he said when they had joined the *neneckt*, who raised his eyebrows in amusement at his partner's worry.

"Trouble found me, instead," Nikko said, his eyes darting to the bar, picking out a young man whose back was turned towards them. "That fellow seems to think you're looking for him."

"That must be our Jairus," Leofric said when the stranger turned around. It was obvious even from across the room that there was something very different about him, but it wasn't until he came a little closer, one hand holding his drink, the other barely trailing out a bit to the front, that the firelight reflected the strange scarring inside his eyes.

"May I presume you are Mister Gunhilde, sir?" Jairus said with a perfectly polite bow, no hostility evident in the action. He appeared unarmed. "And Miss Prinsthorpe, of course."

"Inspector Prinsthorpe," Leofric cut in, shooting Megrithe a look. She supposed it didn't hurt to establish herself as someone who would be missed if something happened to her.

"Yes, indeed. My apologies. How do you do, Inspector?"

"How do you do," she replied carefully.

"Quite well, now that we have caught up with each other," Jairus said with a smile. "I was told you were interested in speaking with me. I think I can probably guess the topic."

"You knew Agnise," Megrithe said, trying not to let her tone reveal that she was finding the stranger somewhat more appealing than she had expected. He was younger than she thought he might be, and taller, too. It always made her sound more interested than she should be when her lesser senses took over.

"I did, gods rest her soul. She was a good friend, but I'm afraid I have no information about her death to share with you. It took me by surprise as well."

"I'm not sure much takes you by surprise, Mister Lanque," Leofric said, cautiously sitting down near Nikko.

Jairus smiled again. "No, sir. Not much," he said, finding a seat of his own and placing his mug on the table next to it without hesitation. Megrithe wondered if maybe he did have some sight, after all. She immediately lowered her eyes – if he could see that she had been staring at him, she would be mortified.

"I have actually been asked to keep an eye out, so to speak, for Miss Prinsthorpe," he said, inclining his head towards her. "We have a mutual acquaintance who is interested in her welfare."

"Arran?" Megrithe asked, the name little more than a squeak of surprise and hope before it turned into a hiss of condemnation at her own stupidity. She had just freely volunteered information he might not have known. A foolish, amateur mistake.

"No, Inspector. I have heard something about him,

but I have not have the pleasure of a meeting. Our acquaintance has, however. He would like to discuss the matter with you at your earliest convenience."

"Who is he?"

"I'm afraid I have not been given permission to say, miss," he told her as Megrithe's face compressed into a scowl. "I understand that you are wary, and rightly so," he said as if he could read her thoughts. "But I do believe it would be worth your time."

"I'm sure you do," she replied tartly.

Jairus stood up, and both Leofric and Nikko matched the movement. Leofric's hand hovered over his sword again.

"Please, gentlemen. I swear on my gods and yours that I mean you no harm," the blind man said. "I will return at sunrise to collect you, should you wish to come with me. If not, I'm afraid the person in question might send someone who does, in fact, have a desire to hurt you. I shouldn't like to see that happen."

"That is not much of a choice," Megrithe said.

"Everything is a choice, Miss Prinsthorpe," Jairus replied, bowing again before he left the room.

"And I think we should choose to trust him," Nikko said when he had gone, settling back into his seat and picking up his glass. "Or at least to use him. The man he is working for calls himself Bartolo. Is that not the name you've been wanting to hear?"

"It is," Megrithe said. "But how do you know Jairus will bring us to him?"

"Because Jairus is not quite as crafty as he may believe himself to be. Or at least I am craftier," Nikko told her. "You can tell many things from a first meeting with a man. He is Paderborn-raised, by his speech, and not from too high a place. How many paths are there to winning tourneys for a blind man with no fortune? The attention of some society patron, perhaps. But such a man seeking fame for his charity would not go to great lengths to hide his name, I suspect.

"The Guild or the Divided are more likely to train a misfit like that for their own needs. Jairus has been purchasing large quantities of food and supplies, which naturally leads us to the cult. And the cult leads me to plenty of sea-folk willing to spread gossip about a group of sorcerers who are not very well liked."

"We tried all that," Megrithe said. "No one could tell us anything."

"You didn't ask in Emyer-Ekvori," Nikko said. "The *neneckt* don't have the same fears of recognition that your humans do. It took me less than an hour to find someone who recalled him, and hardly more than that to find a quiet little apartment by the harbor with a talkative young woman stationed on the corner. She was glad enough to tell me the owner, after I fed her a few coins.

"I don't know what you two were doing that took you all afternoon," Nikko said, failing to hide a rather self-satisfied smirk, "but I was glad enough to have some time to spend in my favorite tea house before meeting you here."

"Tea house, indeed," Leofric sniffed, nettled by Nikko's success. "I know exactly where you were, and I don't want to hear any more about it."

"I'd have been happy enough for you to join me, love," Nikko grinned.

Megrithe didn't know what they were talking about, but she didn't care. If she could make her way to Bartolo, she would be more than half way towards her ultimate goal: finding out what had happened to Arran, and what Tiaraku was really up to, and how to stop all of it.

"I'm going with him tomorrow," Megrithe said.

"Not alone, you aren't," Leofric said. "I will come with you, at least. Though Nikko might be too busy at the tea house."

"Oh, stop," the *neneckt* said. "All I did was spend an hour in the steam baths. After so long on that horrid ship, I needed to relax. There wasn't even anyone interesting there. It was nothing."

"It's always nothing," Leofric said under his breath.

Nikko sighed again and handed his glass to Leofric as a peace offering. A sip seemed to settle his hackles, and he turned his attention back to the problems at hand.

"What is this tourney everyone is talking about?" Megrithe asked, trying to change the subject. "I've never heard of it."

"A competition among the locals," Leofric explained. "Very bloody, and very difficult to win."

"So he's dangerous?"

"Extremely, I should think. If he is playing the nice one, I can only imagine that someone like Habur is Bartolo's insurance. It might not be wise to go tomorrow, but I don't think it would be any wiser to be forced into it."

"I'm going," she repeated firmly. "I have to. Bartolo is the key to everything."

"Then we will go, too," Nikko said. "And maybe they will be surprised to learn a thing or two about who's dangerous."

Halfway through a night filled with dreams of invisible

talons clawing at her throat and the echoes of terrified screams doused by spurts of searing fire, Megrithe gave up on the notion of sleep and wandered over to the window. The cold air quickly wicked away the sweat on her brow as she opened the shutters and then the pane, desperate to clear away the remnants of her disturbed imaginings.

There was no moon and few stars, just the soft swishing of little waves against the buttressed shore and the muted night noises that attended any large city: a lone cart rumbling over the cobbles; a flock of sleepy pigeons cooing to themselves under the eaves. Her window faced the hulking bulk of Tiaraku's palace, and there was a bell in one of the towers that was barely swaying after its last exercise of the evening, the clapper nosing up against the ringing side to waft a memory of sound over the rooftops.

Despite its peaceful contribution to the resting dark, Megrithe felt her stomach turn in revulsion and fear every time she caught sight of the shadowed gables of the *neneckt* fortress. Nothing but death dwelt in that house, and it had come for her once already. It would be coming again as soon as the sun rose, she was nearly sure, and she could not master her fear of it.

"May I have a whisky, please?" she asked the man behind the bar downstairs in the common room, who was using the quiet time after most people had turned in to take stock of the barrels and bottles that remained after the day. But he wasn't about to turn down a customer, even in the small hours of the night, and he paused his tasks to pour her a generous serving. "Thank you."

The fire in the hearth had mostly gone out, but the ashes were still warm enough to attract her. She curled up in a deep, wide leather couch with her shawl tightly tucked around her, cradling her drink and thinking aimlessly about what she might say to Bartolo should she encounter him the following day.

The next thing she knew, Nikko was taking the glass from her hands, startling her bolt upright with his touch.

"It's only me," he said, placing the cup on the table beside her. "You nodded off and were going to drop it."

"Oh. You can't sleep, either?" she asked as she settled down again.

"Not very much. I am used to sharing a bed. It feels wrong when I am on my own. But Leofric thought it best."

Megrithe nodded and fell silent for a while, fidgeting with the fringe on her wrap as she tried to bring some order to her exhausted, melancholy thoughts.

"Nikko, I don't know what I'm doing," she said eventually, her shoulders sagging under the crushing weight of her uncertainty.

"There now," he said softly, taking her hand, giving her a bit of a reassuring squeeze as a little sob escaped, followed soon by a modest flood of tears as Nikko made meaningless, soothing noises while he stroked her hair.

"You have a shadow in your heart," he said, turning to look into her eyes as she sniffled to a halt. "No one could face the Siheldi like you did and survive it without damage. You have been trying so hard to pretend it didn't happen – you are trying to convince yourself that finding Arran will help you close that wound before you have to face the truth of it. Am I wrong?"

"You're not wrong," she whispered.

"Then that's what you are doing," Nikko replied simply. "It is not for me to say whether or not you are being wise."

"I can't be wrong about this," she said, wiping at her cheeks. "An *callawif* can't lie. She told me that he is alive and that I need to find him, so that's what I must do. Even if it means facing Bartolo," she added, her nose wrinkling in disgust. "I am not afraid of what he or anyone else can do to me. I'm not afraid of the shadows."

"That's my brave little liar," Nikko laughed, hugging her tight again for a moment.

Megrithe tried to smile. "It doesn't help to tell myself what I want to hear. I know it's all false."

"Maybe you are too smart for your own good, then. But do you know what my people say about land-dwellers who have been touched by the Siheldi?"

"What?"

"That if they have the strength of spirit to survive such a thing, they have the power of will to make anything they dream come true."

"What do they say about children born of an *callawif's* bargain?" she asked after she had thought for a while. "Do their dreams also come true?"

"We say they are *beschk-ekch'hlott*," he told her, a lilting hitch to the foreign sound making it both intriguing and harsh. "They are divided in two. They are what those Siheldi worshippers wish they could be, which is why they call themselves after the name. But those brought to the world by an *callawif's* spell are closer to that darkness than any other man or beast – even the *neneckt*, who are kindred of the Siheldi from ages ago."

"The – the *besh...*"

"*Beschk-ekch'hlott.*"

"Yes. Are they evil?"

"Not by nature. But when the Siheldi get inside the heart of one, like they got inside of you...there will always be sorrow following. There will be great power, but there will always be death."

"Arran is an *callawif* child," she said quietly.

"How do you know that?"

"His mother told me."

"But you didn't tell us," Nikko said, a shade of upset in his voice.

"I'm sorry. It seemed like her secret – and his. Does it change anything?"

"Everything. It makes it even more important to find him. An *callawif* will always protect her children, even if that means keeping them alive when, by all rights, they should die. If what you say is true, then I have fewer doubts that we will find him living. But if the Siheldi have breathed their spirit into him, or scoured his soul away, then his remaining life may do nothing more than hasten the unwinnable war that you fear."

"But he doesn't want that."

"He *didn't* want that," Nikko corrected her. "He may not be capable of wanting anything of his own will anymore."

"I don't believe that. I can't. He is a damn bloody fool, but he isn't a weakling or a coward. He will fight them until I find him. He has to."

"I hope you're right. But I must tell you, Megrithe, that if he is nothing more than an empty husk doing the bidding of the Siheldi, and if that puts you or Leofric or anyone I love in danger, then it will be my duty to put an end to him and any designs that the Siheldi might wish to work through him. I won't want to, but I can do it and I will. Do you understand?"

"It won't come to that," she said. "I know it won't."

"But do you understand?" he persisted, and eventually she nodded.

"Yes. I do."

CHAPTER SEVEN

From the number of times Arran had drifted in and out of sleep, he thought several days must have passed. He hoped they had. If it took so long just to crawl through a couple of hours, he was sure he would die of boredom long before the slow decay of his flesh could claim him.

He didn't feel like he had gotten much better, but neither did he think it was worse. He had gingerly tried to explore the crusted, scabbing edges of his wound, which crackled and oozed under even the lightest of touches when he slipped his fingers under the bandages, now so sodden as to be irrelevant. It didn't take long for him to leave the site alone, focusing instead on rest, stillness, and trying to parse meaning from his convoluted dreams.

He knew that was probably a hopeless task, but the image of his weeping mother haunted him whether his eyes were open or closed. The Siheldi who had spoken to him – the only time it had spoken to him – had told him that there was a reason for the heartbreaking vision, and he was determined to find out what it was.

Was it simply a reflection of her lifelong sorrow, magnified by his own? Someone had told him once that dreams were the gods' way of touching human minds, but that not all the gods had good intentions when they did so. Perhaps Kashni, the trickster, was merely toying with him. It would not surprise him. He was beginning to feel like his entire life was nothing more than a token caught up in someone else's game.

At some point during the endless night, he woke up from a blank slumber with his heart suddenly pounding, like he did when he felt a change in the seas during the long middle watch. He opened his eyes, but that hardly helped. It wasn't until he heard the groan of the stone slab moving backwards and the shuffle of feet in the dust above him that he realized he was no longer alone under the silent Siheldi's watchful gaze.

"Arran? Are you awake?" a voice called.

"Faidal?"

"Yes. Wait just a moment," the *neneckt* said, dropping over the side to land nimbly near Arran's head. "Are you well?"

"That is a very stupid question."

"Well, you're better, at least, if you're sassing me again," she said, feeling his forehead for fever before opening the tin door of an oil lantern, flooding the space with a dazzling light that reflected strangely from the smooth, cream-colored walls.

"Where did you go?" Arran asked, shutting his eyes quickly as the blaze burned through them.

"To get you this," she replied, taking a bottle out of a leather bag slung around her shoulder. "It should help."

"What is it? And why didn't you take me with you?"

"Medicine. Here. Drink it," she said, holding it near his mouth and waiting for him to open up, which he didn't. "Arran, do you think I would willingly come back to this place if I was trying to poison you?" she asked patiently. "I could have left you to the Siheldi in a heartbeat, and yet here I am."

"What is it?" he said again, sullenly.

"*Neneckt* medicine. From an *oughon* I know. It will help you heal quickly enough to get out before they –"

"Before they what?"

"Just drink," Faidal urged as she glanced upward at the pale speck of light hovering on the pit's edge.

Arran did as he was told, certain that if he resisted, the *neneckt* would simply overpowered him. It was deeply, bitterly unpleasant, like a rotted lemon doused in salt and vinegar, but the only thing he could do was swallow it with a garbled noise of disgust as Faidal firmly ensured that he drank it all.

"Now this one," she said, pushing a smaller vial at him.

"No," he groaned, but his protests went unheeded. It was not quite as bad, and tasted much more like the salty, vaguely sweet drink she had given him before his first foray into Emyer-Ekvori.

"Now go to sleep," she said when the potion had settled in his sloshing stomach. "Sleep through it. It will be all right."

"I don't want to sleep. I want to – oh," he said, changing the thought before he could finish it. A sudden, leaden exhaustion washed over him at the same moment that a sharp, silver ache bloomed in the region of his ribs.

It hurt like a brush fire, enough to make him scream, but even before he could express his pain, he had tumbled into oblivion and had never been more thankful for it.

He didn't dream, but when a trace of the lantern's glow gently reappeared in front of him, ages and ages later, there was barely any strength left in him to pull him back up into the world.

"What did you do?" he mumbled as his sluggish thoughts caught up with the notion that he was meant to open his eyes.

Faidal didn't answer, and Arran started to panic a little, afraid he had been left alone again. The thought propelled him into a higher degree of wakefulness, and he realized that the *neneckt* hadn't gone anywhere: she was just asleep herself, pressed up against the curving walls of the pit, which cast a dim shadow in front of her, as if the light was coming from the stone itself instead of the lantern at her feet.

He relaxed again and drifted for a while, waking again with a slightly greater clarity of mind. Faidal was still at rest, and he turned himself slightly so he could study her unfamiliar face.

Arran had never, to his knowledge, spent time with a single *neneckt* that cloaked itself in multiple guises. It seemed a bit odd that there would be some sort of shared thread between them that he could see in her plain but approachable features – an indefinable essence that marked her as the same individual as before. Perhaps she had done it on purpose for him.

She looked tired and sad, he thought, without the animation of her waking mind to mask her emotions. She looked as raw and frightened and weary as he felt. She looked lonely.

She had told him that she was Tiaraku's slave, and for the first time since he met her, he could see that sorrow graven deeply inside her, the watchfulness of her coiled posture making it look like she was expecting a blow at any moment. It didn't make him want to forgive her for her treachery towards him, but he wondered if it wouldn't, eventually, help him to understand it.

"Faidal?" he whispered when she started to stir, and she smiled sleepily when she saw him.

"You survived."

"I think so, yes. What exactly did you do?"

"Something I didn't think would work," she said, scooting over to his side and pulling back his bandages. He didn't want to risk moving too much, but he craned his head to look the best he could.

There was a puckering, wickedly red slash and a deep, throbbing tenderness when Faidal gently pushed on the spot, as if the surface had healed but the damage inside still remained. He flinched away when she pressed a little harder, but she just nodded and looked perfectly satisfied.

"It will do for now," she said. "Rodnei will be thrilled that it actually works. He had not been able to try it on a real human before."

"That's...not very comforting," he said, wincing as he tried to sit up for the first time.

"Carefully, if you must," she said, helping him to move against the wall, stuffing his pillow behind the small of his back to support him. "There wasn't enough to heal you wholly. You will still bleed to death if you strain yourself."

"I want to get out of here," he said when he had caught his breath. "How did you leave?"

"I climbed. Very far."

"Did you tell anyone where I am? Is help coming?"

"No," Faidal said, not meeting his eye.

"Why the hell not?"

"There is trouble on the surface," she said. "Niheba is in an uproar, and there are riots. They are looking for me. I think I am probably safer down here, to be honest."

"Well, I'm not."

"I think you are. They cannot touch you here. They are confused about you, and they don't know what to do. You have red iron in you. It will keep you safe until we can figure out what to do. You need more time to heal."

"Never mind that," Arran said, making an enormous effort to clamber to his feet, stymied by the slippery walls that gave his sweaty palms no purchase. "I'm getting the hell out of here."

"Stop, please," she begged, trying to keep him still as he battled to get his feet to stay under him. "You don't understand. Just sit down."

His efforts were getting him nowhere, and he sank back down to the floor without much resistance. "Fine. But only because you owe me an explanation," he panted.

"Like I said, they are confused," she told him, handing him the water skin and watching with more than a little smugness on her face as he gulped from it. The medicine she had given him might have closed the wound, but it didn't seem to have replaced his lost blood or made up for the days and days he had been lying motionless on the cold, hard ground.

"They wanted me and the gemstones," he said after he had slaked his thirst, and she nodded.

"I don't know what they have done with the stones. That is a concern."

"You said I was safe here. Why would I be?"

"Because there's red iron in you," she explained again. "From your pendant. I gave it to you before I brought you here."

"About that," he said sharply. "What on earth made

you think coming here was a good idea?"

"Because I knew the Siheldi had the ability to prevent your death. Or at least I hoped they did. It was the only chance you had."

"It doesn't seem like a very good one."

"But it was the only one. Do you see this?" she asked, stroking the lining of the prison with her fingertips. "It is called *bezhaka.* Sorcerers use it to make their words more powerful. Like the bell of a horn that throws the sound far across the room, yes?"

"All right," he said, glancing at the walls.

"They need your breath to make the sound," she said. "And the stone will amplify it. The gemstones – the ones you carried here – I think they are..." she paused, waving her hand in the air as she searched for the right word. "A compass? Perhaps more like a tuning ring."

"I don't know what that is."

"For music," she said. "You don't know anything about music?"

"Not really."

"You strike it on a surface and it makes a pure note to guide a singer. I suppose it is not a thing that has gotten up to Paderborn yet."

"You don't have to say it like that," Arran told her, a little offended by the condescending tone of her voice. "It probably has. I just don't know about it."

"Maybe," she said doubtfully.

"So what will these gems be making me sing?"

"I don't know. But somehow I don't think the Siheldi intend it to be a beautiful song."

"Why do they need me, though? If the gems are the key, can't they use anyone? Can't they use you, or any human they find off the street?"

"I don't think so," she said, looking at the ground again. "I think they have had you marked out from the very beginning. I think a lot of people have. You are something special to them, Arran."

"Then why didn't you let me die?" he said dully, the words bringing back the form of his despairing mother to his thoughts.

"Because there will be a war either way," she said. "Tiaraku is not content with ruling the seas, and he wants more than Niheba. From what I saw when I was on the island, the fight may already have begun.

"The *neneckt* are very strong, Arran, and we are not very nice. Your people think there are rules to combat, but we don't follow them. I think we would win if we fought you. And I don't think that's a world anyone wants to live in."

"Isn't that a matter for King Malveisin?"

"I don't put much faith in kings," Faidal said. "Do you?"

"I've never really had a reason to think about it."

"Niheba is nothing but a pot of coins to the men in Paderborn," said Faidal. "And the *neneckt* are nothing but foreign devils who are only useful to keep the pot stocked. Malveisin underestimates us. You all do. It will be your downfall."

"I think that's probably true," he said, putting a hand to his sore stomach to try to quiet the pain as he shifted to a more comfortable position. He had certainly changed his opinions about the sea people as his dealings with them became more complicated, and the opinion hadn't changed for the better. "But what am I supposed to do about it from here?"

"Nothing. I think we need to find those gemstones

and get out. There are people on the surface - people like Rodnei, and others - who have a better understanding of the situation. Maybe they know how the Divided are involved, too."

"The Divided? I thought they were just an old nanny's tale."

"They aren't. Your friend Bartolo is one of them. And he knows more about the Siheldi than he ever bothered to tell me. People in the city were saying that he has disappeared, which means Tiaraku can't have been pleased with him for letting you out of his sight. That's a good thing. It means Tiaraku wants you alive, too."

"Seems to be more and more evidence for slitting my throat," Arran said.

"No. It means there is something you can accomplish that's important. It could be important to us, too."

"Us?" he said incredulously. "Which 'us' do you mean, exactly?"

Faidal was quiet for a long time. "I know you can't trust me."

"Damn right. You are a liar and a would-be murderer, not to mention a kidnapper and a thief."

"But I've saved your life. More than once. I came back here for you even though I could have run and left you far behind. I've told you everything I know, and I'm going to try to get you out of here. What more can I do to prove myself to you?"

She looked sincere, but a *neneckt* could look like anything. He didn't *like* thinking of her that way, and it was true that she had, in fact, kept him alive against all the odds. That had to count for something. But for how much? She had never told him a truth that didn't have another lie behind it. He couldn't be sure she wasn't still lying to him now.

"Tell me your name," he said after thinking for a while.

"What?"

"Your real name. That means everything to your kind, doesn't it? Like a blood oath. Then I'll trust you."

"I'm not going to tell you my name," she said dismissively, but she looked a little frightened.

"How can I believe you when I don't even know who you are?"

"I'm this," she said, gesturing to herself. "I really am."

"Prove it."

"I - I can't," she said, on the edge of tears as he refused to relent. "Please don't make me. Please."

"I'm not going to make you," he said. "Then it wouldn't mean anything. It's up to you. But that is the price of my trust. I think it's only fair."

"You have no idea what's fair. You don't know what you're asking."

"I'm asking you for a truth you can't lie your way out of."

"No. I won't. You won't take that from me. Not again. Not after they - I won't do that again."

Arran shrugged. "Fine. Then don't expect me to believe another word you say. If I'm safe down here, then here is where I'll stay."

"I'm the one who told you that, too, you idiot," she snapped. "You'll believe that, but not the rest of it?"

"Yes," Arran said, trying not to show that she had caught him out a bit.

"I should have let you choke," she muttered, turning away.

"Would have been fine with me."

She spat something at him in the *neneckt* language, which sounded like water steaming over piping hot coals. He didn't understand the words, but the sentiment was clear enough as she turned her back to him and hunkered over like she had been shot with a poison dart.

Arran just shook his head and leaned back against the wall, trying to get comfortable before closing his eyes again. He wasn't going to get anything else out of her now that he had made her angry, so he figured he might as well try to sleep. He wondered if he would ever stop being tired.

The vibration that rang through his skull as the prison's lid opened again jolted him out of a doze, and the sudden movement of his muscles produced a searing ache in his chest that made the wound feel fresh again as he hissed in pain.

Come, said the voice of the Siheldi, stern but distant, making him crane his head upward as it refused to approach the lantern light. *Now.*

Arran looked at Faidal for a moment. "No?" he said.

You will obey, the spirit commanded, but it came no closer.

"I think I'm fine where I am, thank you."

"Don't make it angry," Faidal whispered.

"Why? What's it going to do?"

"Stop feeding us? Stop letting me into the storeroom?"

"What's in the storeroom?" Arran asked.

"Human things. The lantern and the blankets and the water skins. Things that you need to survive down here."

"The Siheldi can carry objects?"

"Apparently," Faidal said. "Either that or –"

"What?" he prompted when she suddenly paused, thinking.

"Or the Divided are much more involved and much more powerful than we knew."

"The Divided brought supplies down here?"

"There was – the items were arranged in a strange manner," Faidal explained. "Like a face. A blinded face. I don't know why the Siheldi would have done that on their own."

Do you want to find out? the spirit said. *I will tell you. I will tell you what the Warden of the Divided has said. He will betray his people, and it will be glorious. I will tell you, but you must come.*

"No," Arran repeated. "My curiosity has gotten me into enough trouble. I'm staying here."

"I'll come," Faidal said, standing up. A ladder made of knotted rope instantly dropped down into the pit, and she grasped the bottom rung to pull herself skyward.

"Are you mad?" Arran said.

"I've been up and down before. They haven't hurt me," she replied.

"Because they wanted you to fix me. Now they don't need you anymore. Stay put."

"I'll do as I please," she retorted. "It's kept you alive so far, hasn't it?"

"And I'd like to stay that way. It's stupid to go out there."

"It's stupid to stay here with you."

"Faidal –"

"That's not my name," she snapped.

"Well you won't tell me your real one!"

She growled at him, deep in her throat like a dog

getting ready to bite, and he closed his mouth. She was going to do whatever she wanted. She was going to do it just to spite him, because he had pushed her.

"Fine," he said. "You're insane, but I guess that's your business."

"Getting you out of this place is my business," Faidal said over her shoulder as she started to shimmy up the ladder. "Every time I have left this ditch, I have come back in a better position to get you to the surface. I'd be insane if I *stopped* trying."

In a moment, her feet had disappeared over the lip of the pit. Arran wasn't particularly keen on the idea of being alone again, but neither was he prepared to indulge his inquisitiveness.

It would take something more than a hint at information to get him to budge from what seemed like the safest place he could be – and the blood-curdling shriek of pain and terror that suddenly echoed above him was good enough.

He sat up as straight as he could, alert and wide awake, as the scream faded. He had heard the Siheldi calling to each other in the darkness, and it didn't sound like that. It sounded like it had to be Faidal.

They must be killing her, he thought as another cry pierced the blackness, followed soon by the triumphant howls of the Siheldi themselves. It was stupid that she had trusted them, but that wasn't what he wanted. He had told her to stay. He had tried – no, he hadn't tried. But he didn't want her to die like that. He didn't think anyone should.

"Arran! Please!" Faidal screamed, the sound of his name distorted by the winding tunnels. "Please!"

It was a trick. It had to be. They knew they couldn't

get him out of his refuge on their own. Faidal was helping them. Faidal was lying again. It had to be a trick.

"Oh, gods, please," she cried, as if they were tearing her body in two, and Arran couldn't help himself.

"You stupid bastard," he said through gritted teeth as he crawled over to the ladder and grasped the swinging rope, the runners and rungs not taut enough to climb without significant effort. "You idiot, stupid – ow," he gasped, as the force required to pull himself up sent shocks through his middle. "Don't do this. You're so stupid."

Ropes and rigging had never posed an impossible challenge for him, however, and slowly, achingly slowly, he managed to put aside the pain and climb. It wasn't that high, but it felt like forever, and he was desperately trying to suck in enough breath to sustain him by the time he collapsed onto the solid ground.

"Faidal? Where are you?" he called, cursing at himself for forgetting to swing the lantern over his wrist before he made his ascent. It was as black as a piece of coal rolled in a bucket of pitch, and he didn't know where any of the tunnels led. "Tell me where you are."

Another helpless scream ripped through the corridor, and he stumbled forward towards the sound. The ground was as smooth and level as the best of Paderborn's stonework, but that didn't make it any easier to move quickly. He couldn't run – he was trying to, but there wasn't enough air; there wasn't enough blood left in him as he shuffled forward with his hand pressed against one wall to guide him and to hold him upright.

It didn't do him much good to rely on the pressure when the wall suddenly dropped away, and he barely had time to gasp in surprise before he was tumbling forward, thrown off balance and unable to keep himself standing on his own. There was a space where everything was painful knocking and bumping against his head and knees and elbows and bruising shoulders as he rolled down a slope, eventually coming to a halt as the floor evened out again.

"Shitting hell," he hissed as he grasped at a throbbing, twisted wrist. He didn't know where he was. He felt a sense of wide open space, as if he had tumbled into a vast cavern, but he didn't know if his battered mind was playing yet another trick.

The screaming was silenced. Everything was silence, and as he slowly pushed himself to his knees, and then to his feet, his wrist forgotten as the familiar agony in his gut took hold, the only sound he could hear was the ragged raking of his breath as he tried and tried to catch it.

"Faidal?" he whispered. The sound bounced and skipped off the walls around him – not around him, he realized, but very far away. His head hurt.

"Arran, is that you?" the *neneckt* responded faintly.

"Where are you?"

"Don't," she said, her voice stretched with pain. "Don't come closer. I'm sorry. I shouldn't have – just don't come closer."

"I don't know which direction would be closer."

"Then don't move at all."

"All right," he said uncertainly. "What have they done?"

"Just stay right there. Don't cross into the circle," Faidal told him, but Arran was starting to get used to the acoustics of the strange place, and thought he could pick out which way to go. He took a hesitant step, sweeping his foot carefully for obstacles before putting it down, and

Faidal cried out again.

"Don't! She can –"

The *neneckt* may have finished the thought, but Arran never heard it. He didn't know exactly what it was that came whistling towards the back of his head, only that he turned around to face it just in time for it to slam into his temple, knocking him backwards and down to the ground, his skull bouncing hard off the stone, an explosion of false light consuming his vision until a half a heartbeat later he was as dead to the world as he ever had been.

* * *

Jairus waited quietly, if not calmly, in front of the Warden's desk as his superior finished writing his letter. It was warm in the room, bordering on stuffy, and he didn't want to be waiting in idle discomfort for so long that the Warden might mistake his honest perspiration for the scent of fear.

He knew the Warden did it on purpose. Few of the Divided had anyone to write to, and most preferred to pay a sighted scribe to take a dictation when necessary. But the Warden had a perfectly legible hand – or at least that's what he told his subordinates – and he was always working on something. He could be scribbling nonsense, for all anyone knew, just to make himself seem that much more mysterious and powerful, keeping his supplicants off balance as they waited to speak their piece or take their reprimands.

Jairus wondered if any of the other Divided thought like that, or if his lack of devotion just made him more than ordinarily cynical. He could not bring himself to be a true believer, not even after witnessing the Warden's very real powers of sorcery on more than one occasion. He had seen a Siheldi summoned from the thin air and trapped in a circle of blood, where the Warden had conversed with it as easily as the ancient prophets of the Namarja claimed to speak with the angels.

A little shiver ran through him at the memory of the spirit hissing and spitting with anger at the stink of the butchered goat, restrained by powerful symbols painted red on the ground; burning entrails filling the chamber with thick, choking smoke. The slight motion of his discomfort made the leather chair underneath him squeak in protest, and the Warden put down his pen.

"I can put my tasks on hold if you're impatient," the Warden said.

"I'm sorry, sir. Please take no account of me."

"You have made me lose my thought," the Warden replied, pushing the paper away slightly. "Has the girl arrived yet?"

"Yes, sir. I spoke with her this evening. I think she will go see Bartolo tomorrow."

"Good. That will be the perfect opportunity for you."

"For me to do what, sir?"

"To get rid of her," the Warden said, as if it was obvious.

"I'm sorry, sir? I'm not sure I follow."

"I don't want her to see Bartolo. If the two of them come together, my plans will be in jeopardy. I want you to kill her and put an end to it."

"I'm afraid that won't be easy," Jairus said slowly. "She has protection."

"Who?"

"Leofric Gunhilde. And a *neneckt* I'm not familiar

with. He calls himself Nikko."

"Gunhilde is nothing," the Warden said dismissively. "Malveisin's pet with a pin in his hand. He will not be a challenge for you, I'm sure."

"Perhaps not, sir, but the Prinsthorpe girl is a member of the Guild," Jairus tried. "Is it wise to upset them further when the city is already on edge?"

"Are you questioning my wisdom?" the Warden asked, his chair creaking as he leaned forward.

"I would never, sir. Forgive me. I am just too ignorant to understand."

"What is your objection?" the Warden asked, ignoring the false apology. "You have killed for me before. Is this woman special to you, perhaps?"

"I only met her for a moment," Jairus said, hoping he was keeping his voice steady enough for the tightness to escape the Warden's hearing. "She is nothing to me. I simply believe that the city would erupt at the news of it."

"And what makes you think that isn't my plan?"

"I don't claim to know your plans, sir," he said. "If it is what you wish, then I will do it."

"Good. I expect you back here with the news by noon tomorrow."

"Yes, sir. Thank you, sir."

"And Jairus," the Warden called when he had stood up to leave, a hint of taunting in his voice. "I will be watching you."

It took a great deal of self-control not to slam the door on his way out, but he managed to keep his fury locked inside until he was a long way away. He almost went back to his room, where he could give a sound thrashing to his pillow, already worn thin at the seams from such treatment. He didn't know how many more setbacks it could take before he was on his hands and knees scooping feathers off the floor.

Instead, he ended up in the cavern that served as a training ground, where he spent an hour pointlessly scowling at anyone who came near him while he threw daggers at the heart of a straw man.

The Warden should not have brought up the fact that he was a killer. It was the truth, but it was one he hated. He had been nearly as surprised and dismayed as the woman in question to find his blade buried in her ribs and her lifeblood boiling over his hands as he held her wilting corpse, unable to give her the satisfaction of looking her murderer in the eye.

She had been a traitor, a thief, and a menace to the people of Niheba, and in her own right she had been very dangerous. The Warden had asked Jairus to find her, much like he was now asking him to find Megrithe. It was one of the first times the cult had tested his commitment to their cause, and he had intended to pass. He had not planned to kill her, only to capture her and turn her over to whomever the Warden wished, but the altercation had simply escalated out of his control. He had been required to defend himself.

No one else in the world had mourned her passing. In fact, many people had rejoiced. But even though he had left that encounter with enough wounds of his own to justify the action, the few dreams he could ever remember were filled with the sound of her last breath and the feel of her blood dripping from his shaking fingers.

It made him feel foolish to be so shy of killing when all of his highly honed skills were intended for that very purpose. He enjoyed a good fight – he enjoyed it more than nearly anything else – but it had always been practice, or friendly sparring, or wagered contests that were not supposed to end in death. He may be a spy, but he was no soldier, and the wars he wished to fight were ultimately matters of the mind, not the body.

The Warden didn't see the difference. He had not drawn those careful lines between life and death, because he had never done anything other than give the orders. He was a scholar by origin, and a politician. He had the luxury of using his pawns as he saw fit instead of getting dirty himself.

The Warden trusted Jairus to be one of those pawns, and that trust was vital for his larger mission. He had to keep up the illusion of faithfulness if he was to continue to have access to Bartolo, and eventually, hopefully, to the cache of counterfeit iron that was surely hidden somewhere within the unsavory fellow's purview. Jairus was nearly convinced that Faidal was just a phantom invented by Bartolo to hide his own involvement in the counterfeiting ring, but he didn't have proof yet.

He needed to follow it through. He needed to what he was told. Megrithe had been trained by the Guild, and she would likely do the same thing herself if she was required. She would have encountered hidden agents in her work before, and she would know what they sometimes had to do in order to remain undetected.

She would understand the need, he told himself. At least, she probably would, if he gave her a chance to realize what was happening. But he wouldn't. He would be quick, and it would be painless, and it had to be done. He knew that it did.

The dawning sun meant nothing to him except that it

was time to damn his soul to one of the less pleasant hells. He had spent more of the night than he should have at the training grounds. After tiring of his target practice, he had been more than willing to try to leech the anger from his thoughts by beating on his fellows with padded wooden swords. It hadn't been much of a challenge, but the sweat and action, followed by a good measure of wine, had helped him catch a bit of sleep.

But now it was the morning, and he had to make a decision. As far as he knew, Megrithe had done nothing wrong since her arrival on the island. He didn't quite like the fact that she had indirectly linked him to the Guild by identifying him as a friend of Agnise, but he didn't think she would betray him to anyone who could do him harm.

He kept thinking about their meeting. Her voice had sounded tired, maybe even a bit brittle, as if she was determined to keep her emotions stowed away but was struggling to do so. All women seemed taught from birth how to confuse men with their feelings, and those in the Guild were given additional training that made them absolutely inscrutable, in his experience. If such a studied and sturdy façade was cracking, she must be under a truly enormous amount of pressure. He was familiar with the feeling.

It didn't take him long to find her when he reached the Spearman. There were few people about so early in the morning, and none of them were quite as tense as Megrithe and her companions. He could feel their trepidation from across the common room, like a hawk sensing out the minute shuffling of a frightened mouse hiding in the leaf litter. He put the notion out of his mind immediately. He didn't want to think of her as his prey.

"Good morning, Miss Prinsthorpe," he said. "Sirs. May I assume you will be joining us?"

"Yes," Leofric said.

"Very well. I suppose there is no point to insisting that you leave your weapons here."

"Not in the least," said Leofric. "Besides, Nikko doesn't need any."

"I am quite aware," Jairus said. Even the young or the infirm among the sea people could overwhelm an average human, and the *neneckt* could rarely be killed by anything except the special coral glass weaponry produced by their own priests.

Nikko was neither a child nor a weakling, and Jairus was only armed with ordinary blades. He was not looking forward to testing the *neneckt's* loyalty to his friends. He would need to catch Megrithe when Nikko was off his guard.

"Where are we going?" Megrithe asked, oblivious to his thoughts.

"The harbor side," Jairus said as cheerfully as he could. "And a lovely day for it, too. It's very warm."

"This is not a jaunt in the park for pleasure, sir," she replied with a sharp edge to her words.

"No, miss," he acknowledged. "It certainly isn't."

He usually tried to render himself as agreeable as possible when he was with new people, as a general rule. But this time, he could hardly think of a thing to say to any of them. They didn't seem to mind the silence as he led them down Cherry Street and through one of the nicer market squares, though no one stopped to admire the stalls of jewelry and glasswork attended by bustling artisans primping and preparing their wares for the day.

He could do it at any moment. Leofric was hovering

by her side, and Nikko was walking in front of her, so it might be tricky to get around him, but there was a sharp, slim knife up his cuff that could slip into his hand and through the air at a moment's notice. He wouldn't miss. Her protectors might bring him down, eventually, but the job would be done. A simple job. A stupid one. A test that he couldn't fail.

"This way, please," he said, turning a corner that would give him the perfect opportunity to catch her unawares. He could feel the shoulder of his throwing arm tensing, but the knife stayed hidden in its place until they reached the last turning before the tall brick construction that served as Bartolo's lair.

"I don't suppose I could speak to Miss Prinsthorpe privately for a moment, could I?" he asked her bodyguards before they started down the lane.

"Whatever you want to say to me, you can say in front of them," Megrithe told him.

"If that were true, miss, I wouldn't have asked to speak to you alone."

Megrithe hesitated, and even if Jairus couldn't see the looks that passed between them, he was sure the men were warning her against granting the request. He didn't blame them.

"Very well," she said eventually. "They will take a few steps back."

"Thank you." Jairus said, then waited until he heard the reluctant shuffle of boots. "What I'm about to say will alarm you," he continued in a quieter voice, "but I would be much obliged if you didn't make a scene until you hear me out."

"I'm not sure I can promise that. But I will try."

"Well, the fact of the matter is, Miss Prinsthorpe, that

if I had any courage whatsoever, you would be dead right now."

"I beg your pardon?"

"I have been asked to kill you."

She fell silent, clearly taken aback, but he was pleased that she didn't scream or run or try to hit him. She was thinking calmly about his words, assessing the impact of them, and that raised his opinion of her so much that he knew that there was nothing in the world that could now change his mind about what he had just done.

"Who asked you?" she said. "Was it Bartolo?"

"No, miss. He really does want to see you. I serve many masters at the moment, and he is actually the least of my concerns."

"You are one of the Divided."

"In a manner of speaking. But in truth, I am working for the Guild. Like you."

"Then I'm sure you are familiar with the statue in the Guild House," she said suspiciously.

"The king cloaked in blue?" he asked, playing along with the standard series of questions and answers that would separate him from an impostor. The color of the fictional cloak and other items included in the code changed according to a complicated cycle of Guild-related holidays and other secret dates that were hardly common knowledge.

"Yes. But I can't remember the inscription."

"For the glory of the light out of the darkness," he recited, picking the right words carefully, "and the call of day to the old red crow."

"You worked with Agnise," she said after a moment, and he breathed a sigh of relief at getting the sequence correct. "You were her informant."

"Yes, Inspector. The Guild Master – well, my physician Doctor Cloche, really – thought that my situation might help investigate the Divided. There was some thought, originally, that the stream of counterfeit coming from Niheba was related to them."

"And is it?" she asked innocently.

"No. Not at all. But I know for certain that Bartolo is involved, and I have more than a guess that Tiaraku himself is behind it all. I am doing Bartolo's bidding so he will lead me closer."

"There's no point in that. I've seen the iron works, but the counterfeit is hardly the most dangerous thing Bartolo and Tiaraku are doing. Why do the Divided want me dead?"

"I don't rightly know. The Warden said you must not work with Bartolo if his plans were to succeed. That's all he told me."

"I don't plan to work *with* Bartolo at all," she said. "I plan to leave him begging to tell me everything he knows about Arran, and then I plan to slit his bloody throat."

"I'm afraid I cannot allow that, miss," he said, trying not to smile at her stern conviction. "But I confess that he's a bit of an arrogant prick, if you'll excuse my language."

"Indeed," she replied. "If you wish me to trust you, Mister Lanque, I suggest you tell the Gunhildes exactly what you told me."

"If you will vouch for me, then I would be glad to."

"I am well acquainted with Doctor Cloche," she said. "He is a goodly soul and was kind to me when I was a child. I remember a blind boy he used to read to when he had finished his duties. Was that you?"

"Yes, Inspector. It was."

"Then on his name you will swear to Leofric and Nikko that you mean us no harm."

"Very well. I swear it."

Megrithe nodded and beckoned her friends forward, trying to explain the new development to them. Jairus could tell that the two men did not trust him an inch, even after Megrithe endorsed him. But neither of them tried to make a move against him, which was acceptance enough for the moment. There would be time later, he hoped, to convince them. There would be time enough for many things, if the Warden didn't discover his disobedience first.

* * *

Despite Megrithe's generally strong sense of will, she was not entirely immune to the shock of being told that the person standing inches from her face had been asked to take her life. He had responded correctly to her inqueries, and his inaction during a fine opportunity to execute his duty was certainly welcome proof that he meant what he had said to her.

Nonetheless, it was with a buzzing lightness in her head that she climbed the steps to Bartolo's apartments, keeping her face half-turned towards her would-be assassin, every movement that he made sparking a jerking contraction of her muscles as her brain wrestled with the urge to flee.

Leofric and Nikko hadn't believed a word of it. She didn't blame them. Guild passcodes meant nothing to them, and even she had to admit that they were not a foolproof way of securing trust in someone's intentions.

If the name of Doctor Cloche hadn't triggered a

memory that had been meaningless at the time – a cut on her finger during a visit with her father that had sent her to the infirmary, where a frail, pasty child who looked destined to die was lying rigidly in bed, his whole body straining to take in, to greedily remember, to live through the words that the kindly physician slowly read out – she would not have thought twice about running for her life.

The man in front of her seemed in no danger of losing himself to ill health, and the solid breadth of his shoulders spoke of anything but frailty. But there was something about his expression, curiously muted by the blank, directionless stare, which reminded her exactly of the eagerness and attentiveness of that studious child, desperate to be taken seriously in a world too quick to dismiss him, and immediately helped her identify the face as belonging to the same person.

But Nikko and Leofric didn't have the benefit of half-stirred childhood experience to anchor a passing thought, and they had only grudgingly accepted the situation. They had closed ranks around her as if she was some high royal at risk of harm from an angry peasantry, frowning at Jairus like he carried some deadly plague.

"This is an even worse idea than it was ten minutes ago," Leofric said under his breath as Jairus fumbled momentarily with which way the key should go in the door. "This is foolish. We can't trust him. He could be leading us into a trap."

"If he wanted me dead, he could have killed me the instant you stepped away," Megrithe whispered back. "He didn't."

"That doesn't mean he won't."

"Maybe, but that's not the most important thing right now," she replied as Jairus opened the door just as

Bartolo's serving man came to do the same. Her fingernails pressed angry crescents into the soft skin of her palm as she found her fists clenched at her side without her knowledge.

They did not stay there when Bartolo showed his pinched and scheming face as he wandered in from the other room. Before Leofric or Jairus or even Nikko could stop her, she had crossed the floor, drawn back her arm, and let Bartolo feel the full force of her fury with a blow so powerful that her own father would have been proud to have delivered it.

Bartolo flew backwards with an unmanly shriek, a fountain of bright blood spurting from his broken nose as he sprawled on the floor.

"You stubid *pitch*," he shouted as he pinched his nostrils shut to stop the flow. "Johan, get me a rag. Now, you idiot!"

The birdlike bones in her hand had barely started to throb before Leofric was by her side, ready to prevent her from striking again as Bartolo moaned and swore at his servant, who looked rather pleased with the unexpected development as he hurried away to fetch a cloth.

"That was for Arran," she spat, shaking off Leofric's grip. "You better hope I don't get a chance to give you what's coming from me."

"Keep her away from me," Bartolo snapped as he dragged himself onto the couch and tilted his head back to press the moist towel to his wounded face.

"Perhaps you'd like to sit over here, Miss Prinsthorpe," Jairus said, motioning to a chair on the other side of the room. Like the servant, he was struggling to keep a straight face, and had done nothing but stand quietly to the side as his patron suffered her assault. Nikko was nearly laughing outright, barely hidden with a pretend cough into his sleeve, as she sat ramrod straight on the edge of the chair, her heart racing with pleasure, excitement, and rage, ignoring the growing twinge in her knuckles. She always bruised after hitting someone. It had never been more worth it.

"Now. Where is Arran, and how do I get there?" she said calmly, putting on her Guild inspector's voice.

Bartolo was trapped like a rat in a baited flour sack without a single soul in the room on his side. She would have her information and be on her way in a half hour at the worst. For the first time since leaving Paderborn, she felt like she was in control not only of her mission, but of herself. It was a good feeling. It was the best feeling, and she knew how to use it.

"I don't know," Bartolo said.

"You have one chance to change that answer," she said steadily.

"I really don't," he repeated, lowering the rag to glare at her. The circles under his eyes were already puffing up, she noticed with satisfaction. He would be in pain for days. She smiled.

"I'm afraid that wasn't the right thing to say," she told him, and made to stand up. He flinched.

"If you will listen for one goddamn minute," he cried, holding up the cloth like a bloodied white flag. "Just listen. I want him back as much as you do. But I don't know the answers. If I did, I'd have him already."

"Continue," she said, sitting down again.

"The Siheldi have him. I can only assume, from their inaction on the surface lately, that they are either working out what to do with him or starting the process already.

If they had succeeded, we would know, because we would all be dead."

"Succeeded with what, exactly?"

"Arran is...special," Bartolo said carefully.

"I know. He is an *callawil's* child," she said, and he looked surprised.

"How -"

"Please," she scoffed. "Do not treat me like an idiot, or I will treat you to another wallop. There is something about him that the Siheldi want."

"Yes. And they will squeeze him like a ripe grape to get it."

"And you wanted to be the one turning the winepress," Megrithe guessed.

"More like collecting the end result. If I could doctor that wine as the Siheldi consumed it, they would be entirely under my control."

"Under Tiaraku's control, you mean," Nikko put in. "He is behind this."

"He is financing it," Bartolo acknowledged.

"But you plan to betray him," said Nikko.

"That is a strong word."

"But an accurate one," Megrithe added. "No?"

"I think that's really beside the point. My plans are irrelevant if I cannot prevent the Siheldi from breaking through the only prison that has held them this long."

"Prison?"

"Sind Heofonne - what you might call *Fyrendor* - is not just an entrance to their world. It is a gateway that has been locked and guarded for many, many centuries. As I understand it, the Siheldi wish to use Arran as a prism, focusing his power on the keyhole, so to speak. At least, that's what I think. If they do this, the Siheldi

Queen would be unbound. She could do as she pleases to humankind. Which is why I need him back. For the good of all of us."

"You only want him back in your control," Leofric said. "You don't want to keep the Queen in her prison. You want her to break out, but only so you can have her as a pet."

"Is that not better than allowing her to roam entirely free?" Bartolo asked with a brazen innocence that raised Megrithe's hackles again. "Either way, Arran must be recovered, and it must happen soon. I saw Faidal take Arran through the gateway. I know that's where they are – Tiaraku's mirrors do not lie. What I don't know is what sort of state Arran may be in – he wounded himself quite severely before being taken – but I believe he still is alive, and that is dangerous for us all."

"And how do the Divided enter into all of this?" Megrithe asked, turning to Jairus.

"As far as I know, the Divided are in agreement with Bartolo," he said. "I am not privy to such important information, Miss Prinsthorpe. I only do as I'm told."

"The Warden has asked for your cooperation," Bartolo told Megrithe. "He specifically said that I should meet with you and obtain your help."

"Is that so? And how do you suppose I help you if neither one of us knows where Arran is?"

"Because he does," he said, pointing right at Nikko, who looked uncharacteristically discomfited by the attention as everyone else turned towards him.

"I have no idea what you are talking about," he said. "What do I have to do with it?"

"You're the Daggertooth."

"I'm *a* Daggertooth," Nikko corrected. "So?"

"So you know how to reach Sind Heofonne."

"What is he talking about, Nikko?" Megrithe asked when the *neneckt* scowled and slumped in his seat, arms crossed and brows lowered. Leofric put a hand on his shoulder, but Nikko shook it off.

"He's confusing me with someone else," Nikko said. "There are a lot of Daggertooths. Or at least there used to be. Before Tiaraku."

"And whose fault was that?" Bartolo said.

"You're Nikodelmus Daggertooth?" Jairus said suddenly, as if he had just made a connection. "Really?"

"No," Nikko said. "I'm not. That's a stupid human name and it doesn't belong to me."

Megrithe felt like things were slipping from her grasp a little, and she didn't like it. She didn't know what was happening to make Nikko so uncomfortable, but she wanted it to stop. "Explain," she said sternly to Bartolo.

"Do they teach you no history at the inspector's school?" he asked.

"Suppose that they don't."

"Your little friend here nearly ended up on the throne – before Tiaraku got the best of him. A pretender that everyone decided to believe was real," Bartolo said with a smirk. "Of course, Tiaraku had no more of a claim to it, but he did have the strength and the fire. It was hardly a contest, when it came down to it."

"Tiaraku had mercenaries who slaughtered their own people without remorse," Nikko said. "It is no failing of character to try to preserve lives."

"It is if you lose," Bartolo said.

"There are other things to break along with your nose," the *neneckt* growled, but Bartolo just ignored the threat.

"Regardless of the politics, you are no stranger to the mountain of fire. You know where it is. You could take your friends there. I am certain you could even take them under."

"My brothers were the ones who held those secrets," Nikko said, all the fight suddenly draining from him as if someone had pulled the plug from a tub. "And they are dead."

"Enough of this," Leofric finally said as Nikko withdrew into himself even further. "This is pointless. You haven't given us any answers, or any reason why we shouldn't tie you up and bring you back to Paderborn to hang."

"You have had the answer with you already," Bartolo said. "Let the Daggertooth take you to the mountain. I will lend you Jairus, if you wish. The darkness will not hinder him. You will be as well equipped as anyone to find Arran, assuming he can be found."

Megrithe hesitated. She wasn't opposed to the idea of bringing as much protection as possible with her, but taking Jairus would mean leaving Bartolo free to pursue whatever plans he had in motion. And it would give Jairus plenty of chances if he did feel like changing his mind about killing her.

"I would be happy to accompany you, miss," Jairus said. "I do have some experience with the Siheldi which may be helpful to you."

"Are you certain that's a good idea?"

"Yes, miss," he said, but he couldn't see her face, and she didn't know how to communicate her misgivings about Bartolo to him in any other way.

"I can't get you inside Sind Heofonne," Nikko insisted. "It is sealed. There's no point in going there."

"Do you know how to get to the mountain, at least?" Megrithe asked.

"Yes," he replied reluctantly. She didn't blame him for being reticent. He should have told her before. He had wasted so much of her time – after being cross with her for withholding some of her own information, too – and she wasn't sure just how angry she was about it.

"Then that's a good enough start," she said firmly, putting the thought aside for the moment. She stood up, and everyone but Bartolo followed suit. "Thank you for the exercise," she said to him, flexing her sore hand. "I hope we can do it again sometime."

Megrithe turned and left the room without a single look back, not even to see Bartolo's face, and simply expected everyone else to follow her. They did, and they kept on following her without a word as she marched purposefully down the street and turned several corners, leaving the block of flats far out of view before she stopped to take a few deep breaths.

"I presume you would like me to send a message to my uncle about this," Leofric said.

"Yes, please. I would like the Guild to keep watch over him. I don't think it would be wise to take him into custody just yet, though I would be perfectly thrilled to pull the lever of his gallows when the time comes."

"As would I," said Leofric. "But Andrus should question him, at the very least."

"I would prefer if he didn't, sir," Jairus put in. "As far as I'm aware, Tiaraku does not know where Bartolo is hiding, which means he doesn't know that you have been visiting him. If you want to get to Sind Heofonne unmolested, I suggest we keep our travels a secret for as long as possible. Watch him, by all means, especially since I won't be able to, but I cannot advise further action at this time."

"I am still not all that convinced that your advice is much worth following," Leofric said. "What is your game here? Is the Warden trying to double-cross Bartolo, or are you trying to get the better of them both with that story you told to Megrithe? I swear to all that is holy, if you lay a finger on her –"

"On my honor, sir, I mean Miss Prinsthorpe no harm," Jairus protested, but Leofric just shook his head.

"Your honor? What does that mean to me? I don't know you, and I don't think I care to."

"It should mean a great deal if Miss Prinsthorpe believes it, sir."

"Miss Prinsthorpe is entitled to her opinion, but I am entitled to mine. Guessing a few colors does not make you trustworthy."

"I have taken no action today that would indicate I am anything but sincere," Jairus said, but Leofric was unwilling to hear it.

Megrithe sighed, turning to Nikko with the expectation that he would intervene, but she was surprised to see he was no longer with them. He had wandered a half block away, seating himself on the lip of a pool, turning his head so he could stare into its depths. Megrithe left Jairus and Leofric quarreling with each other and went towards him.

"I suppose we must let them have it out, as long as they don't come to blows," she said, trying to sound cheerful. He didn't respond, but neither did he object when she perched beside him on the stonework.

"I didn't lie to you," he said after a while. "Not intentionally."

"I don't think you lied. But I wish you had told me you knew how to get to the mountain so I didn't have to waste so much time."

"I don't want to go there."

"Neither do I. But you know I have to. You're the one who told me that."

"I fear that you will die there, Megrithe," he told her, raising his head to look into her eyes. "I fear that I will, too. I hoped that you would find another way before it came to that. I was just – I was just hoping there was another answer. I am sorry."

"I'm not angry," she said. "I'm just not sure I understand. Is it true, what Bartolo said? About who you are?" she asked, but trailed off as he hunched his shoulders again.

"It was so long ago," he said quietly, but then he stopped.

"I suppose I'm not the only one with shadows in my heart that I'd rather forget."

Nikko sighed. "No, you're not. I left Niheba to follow the sun," he said, looking over at Leofric, who was still bickering with Jairus. "But in my heart, the night always returns."

"And so will the light," she said. "Eventually."

He smiled faintly. "We will not find any in Sind Heofonne."

"You said you had brothers," she prompted after some time.

"Yes. Two of them were *oughon*, with interests in the Siheldi. They were very well respected, and they even advised our previous king. The third of my brothers was not trained in any arts – he was just a plain fool, arguing with the old men and the radicals in the streets of

Niheba, quarreling over history that couldn't be changed.

"It was all an accident, really. He did not like our practice of choosing a ruler, which is far too complex to explain to you, if you'll forgive me. It seemed random to many of my own people, too, and it irked my brother deeply.

"One day, he used me as an example during a rally to say that any stranger off the beach was as good as whom the the *oughon* picked, and unfortunately, I decided to play to the crowd. You know I can hardly ever turn down a spot of fun. It was just some theater to make them laugh. I thought that's all it was, and I hardly even remembered it the next day.

"But not everyone was so forgetful, and it all got rather complicated very quickly. There was a great deal of discontent among the *neneckt* – this was before the Treaty of Libourg, and old Eormi Stoneclaw was not the best of kings. His weakness let us slide back into being loyal to our clans ahead of our nation. There were so many petty little wars brewing between the tribes, and we had let ourselves be carried by that current far too many times before.

"No one wanted a return to that bloody way of life. They wanted something different, and I suppose a young mason's apprentice who charmed them with jokes and courted them with fresh ambitions was about as different as it could get.

"I let myself be turned into a figurehead, brought along to a war that had nothing to do with me," Nikko said. "And I can't say I didn't love every moment of it, before everything went wrong."

"Tiaraku saw the weakness in your people, too," Megrithe guessed when Nikko paused.

"Yes, and he was not slow to exploit it. Tiaraku was a bully and a bastard. A violent, greedy, horrible choice, but he promised strength and unity. He brought us all together, for a time, but it was in opposition to the humans instead of in harmony with ourselves. Not even the *oughon* really wanted to choose him as king, but they said the Sea Father's signs all pointed his way.

"There were a great many protests against Tiaraku when he took the throne. When my *oughon* brothers broke ranks with their fellows to lend me their support, suddenly there were no rules anymore.

"I wanted to be what the people wanted, and I really did try. But I wasn't willing to take the crown by force. When it came down to it, I just couldn't outmatch Tiaraku. I didn't have the fortitude to do what was required when there would be so much death because of it. Bartolo was right about me."

"Bartolo isn't right about anything," Megrithe said. "Don't you ever think differently."

"Tiaraku killed them all," he said bleakly. "My brothers, my parents, my clan. Many other clans. Anyone who stood against him. The Black Salts, the Fan Sharks, the Hawkfish...so many families obliterated. It was the worst war we've ever had. And I don't think the humans even knew it was happening."

"There were storms," Megrithe said. "My father remembered. He said there was a year where it rained almost every day and the sea was impassable for months at a time. Trying to go to Niheba was a death sentence."

Nikko nodded. "There were fewer humans on the island back then, but the Siheldi cannot resist the call of strife. Their work was very bloody, and I think that's where Tiaraku must have gotten his ideas. My brothers took me to the mountain once, to show me what Tiaraku would do to us if he won. They showed me the Siheldi so that I would fight with my eyes open, they said. And I really tried to. And I still lost."

"But you're still here. Tiaraku hasn't defeated you yet."

"He thought I was so small of a threat that there was no point in killing me," Nikko said bitterly. "I amused him. He traded me away as part of the Treaty of Libourg, after I had spent enough time in prison. As much as I love that it led me to Leofric, sometimes I wish Tiaraku had changed his mind and killed me instead."

"Don't say that. It isn't fair."

"It isn't fair for you to ask me to do something I can't do," he replied. "I can't open the gateway. I don't know how."

"If Faidal could find a way, then so can we."

"That's right," Jairus said, coming towards them. "And as a last resort, we can have the lady knock her way through with her fists."

"Where did Leofric go?" Megrithe asked, smiling vaguely at the joke.

"To see Andrus. I think we have come to a very tentative agreement," he said before putting out his hand to help Megrithe stand up. "We will not kill each other unless one of us gives the other a good reason. He is an impressively tough nut, that one."

"And tougher if you betray him," said Nikko.

"I have no intention of it. Bartolo's red iron may be important to me, but there is nothing I hate worse than the Siheldi. I would like to put an end to all this before it gets out of hand, if you'll have me. I would simply like to help."

"Very well," Nikko shrugged. "If he is willing to trust you, then I suppose I am, too. We can leave tonight."

"Why wait that long?" Megrithe said.

"You must take your medicine first," Nikko told her. "Remember?"

"Oh. Oh, no. You don't mean that awful stuff, do you? It made me so sick."

"What made you sick?" asked Jairus, picking up on her distress at the thought of drinking *ychauyad* again.

Nikko just smiled, a shade of his usual self returning at the prospect of enjoying his friends' discomfort. "Let's go find out, shall we?"

CHAPTER EIGHT

The Warden sat quietly with his hands stretched out in front of him, palms flat on his desk. There was an itch above his eye – a tiny fly had been buzzing around for half an hour, brushing up against his skin – but he didn't reach up to scratch it. Instead, he ignored the sensation the best he could, letting himself float free of his familiar surroundings and upwards towards the city that trundled obliviously over his head.

"Damn and blast it," he muttered eventually, raising one of his hands to erase the annoyance with the edge of his fingernail, sighing at the unconquerable weakness of the flesh.

His own master, two High Wardens prior, had always beaten him over the head with a switch when he broke his meditations in such a way. It was supposed to instill good discipline, but he had found that the new bruises and petulant disgruntlement of his soul only added to the likelihood that he would fail to concentrate. That had never stopped him from doing the same thing to his students now, however, and they would do the same to theirs, in time – if the Divided continued to exist beyond his rule.

There was a serious risk that they wouldn't. Bartolo's meddling had sent the Warden's delicately balanced plans careening wildly off course. The thought of that fool and his arrogant dabbling made the Warden remove his hands from the table once and for all. His contemplations, and the far-ranging sight that came with them, would have to wait. He was too anxious, and there were plenty of other things he could be doing instead.

The Siheldi needed baiting again. A little leather curricle had floated free of some boat in the harbor and ended up on the craggy beach beneath his caverns. The curved timber joints and iron bolts would make a nice little puzzle for the spirits, who seemed to enjoy dismantling human engineering almost as much as they liked taking apart the humans themselves.

Not only did engaging them with such toys and games secure their good will, such as it was, but they also gave the Warden the chance to observe their intelligence, so different from that of their prey.

They were fascinating creatures. They squabbled over their worthless prizes like children, or perhaps like feral dogs, competing for brightly colored objects that both attracted and repulsed them. Light was their enemy, and for the most part it could not be borne, yet smoothly polished silver or colored glass were trophies of the highest value, to be clutched tight and hidden away and marveled over when they thought no one else was looking. It appeared that they took a certain pleasure in the pain of the forbidden, and in that sense they were no different from humans at all.

The Warden picked up a small bell on his desk and shook it back and forth to call for Guthrin.

"I am going to the island," he said. "I want to bring that boat. Fill it with something that will please them."

"At once, sir."

"Has there been any news from the surface?"

"Some. Jairus has joined with the Guild woman and

her friends. He is going with them to try to find the mountain."

"Excellent," the Warden nodded. "I'm sure he will make certain they will arrive safely, and then he will no longer be my concern. I want you to follow their progress and send word immediately when they have reached Sind Heofonne."

"Yes, sir."

"And get someone else to ferret out a few more Guild contacts and kill them the *neneckt* way," the Warden added. "Paro and Briggs, perhaps. Make a scene. The city is taking too long to crack itself open. And Liment should gather some men outside the palace and cause as much of a fuss as they can. I want Tiaraku to know we're serious."

"Immediately, sir," Guthrin said, his respectful bow failing to hide his wolfish smile. The Warden nodded. This was exactly the sort of charade that the old man loved.

Tiaraku had largely ignored the riot that had swept through the city of Niheba after the death of Agnise. The fervor had settled down again once it was clear there would be no results, but he didn't want the *neneckt* king to feel like he could dismiss his unhappy residents forever.

The Divided would continue to fan the flames of human discontent as long as necessary to make Tiaraku start feeling truly uncomfortable. As soon as he reacted against the humans' concerns, the city would explode into a violence that would be impossible to control.

That would give the Warden the opening he had been looking for. Ruling the island was not exactly in the cult's original charter, but survival in difficult circumstances demanded new tactics. Niheba was a golden peach ripe for the picking – the perfect fortress from which the Warden could act at will to conquer his main concerns.

Tiaraku would have to work harder if he wanted to keep hold of his kingdom. The *neneckt* king had pinned his hopes on having the Siheldi Queen to help him, but he did not know that the Divided had been taming the spirits, slowly but surely, for close to a thousand years. Tiaraku's first mistake had been trusting to Bartolo's half-baked schemes. Underestimating the reach and ambitions of the Divided would surely be his last.

There was a meeting spot on an unmarked, rocky atoll a few miles off shore, where the Siheldi flocked like eager gulls when plied with baubles. There was nothing pleasant about the little knob of jagged basalt that stuck up from the ocean like the raw end of a giant's nose. There was hardly even a landing site worth approaching consistently, so the boatman judged the best location based on the winds and tides, often leaving the Warden with wet feet and skinned knuckles as he dashed across the unforgiving stones.

The waters were relatively calm this time, and he was able to get ashore with little trouble. The curricle followed, handed up to him along with several small sacks of various goods. The boatman then backed his vessel away from the speck of land to take refuge in safer waters, promising to return as soon as the Warden called.

"I bring gifts," he said loudly to the empty, windswept knoll. He opened up the first of the sacks to feel what his men had provided for him. "Copper and slate," he said, sifting through some broken bits of roof tile and green, corroded gutter fittings. "Wood and iron," he continued, opening another bag that contained short planks with old nails of various sizes driven through at random, "and good strong cowhide," he finished, gesturing to the round boat next to him.

The Warden was used to having to wait in these situations. The Siheldi didn't congregate on the little stump of land, and only came when they sensed the warm blood of a potential meal. It could take some time for that to happen, especially if they were distracted, and he knew for certain that their attention was much taken up with Swinn and the *neneckt* slave.

He had seen the prisoners curled up in the bottom of a ditch lined with *bezhaka* stone. He had seen them where no others could direct their sight. Tiaraku was blind to what happened underneath the ocean's floor, but the Divided's gifts had unlocked many secrets the sea people had yet to learn.

The Warden hadn't told anyone that he had seen Arran Swinn alive, nor that he had traced Faidal's movements back to the surface, into the slums of Niheba and through the door of an *oughon* known as a healer. He had kept to himself that he was familiar with the strange properties of the medicine Faidal had given his friend, and how quickly the dying man recovered after drinking it. He had watched in silence as the Siheldi lured the *neneckt* from its safety, and as Arran groped helplessly in the dark for his fallen companion while the Queen stirred from her rest, tasting the tang of his blood in the air.

"I bring gifts," he called again after nearly an hour had passed, repeating his litany to entice the spirits to show themselves, and shaking the metal pieces in their sack like the bell on his desk to summon them.

Eventually, as the boatman made several wide circles around the island and the sun crept slowly across the sky, making the Warden break out in a sticky sweat, he felt the first stirrings of another presence. It was a Siheldi: a single spirit braving the harsh daylight for a glimpse of the Warden's presents, trying to snatch the best items for itself before the day cooled enough to attract any rivals.

"Greetings, my friend," the Warden said, taking a step back from the heap of objects. He may be intrigued by the demons' behavior, but he had no desire to be touched by one.

The Siheldi ignored him. It was true that not all of them wasted their energy on human speech, especially when the sun was glaring and they needed to conserve all their strength just to survive. It would exhaust itself by carrying even the smallest trinket back to its lair, but apparently it felt like the effort was worth it.

"I can offer you shade," he said, when the spirit barely shifted around a few of the pieces on display, unable to do much more. He lifted the curricle and propped up one edge with a length of scrap wood, forming a shelter that he would have been happy to occupy himself. "Please, take your rest and speak with me."

It was dark and cooler under the boat, and the Warden felt the Siheldi hiss in relief as it scuttled into the shade.

I want it, the Siheldi said after some time.

"What do you desire, friend?"

It sparkles.

The Warden made a slight noise of displeasure. For all his foresight that allowed him to glimpse the workings of the world, past, present, and future, he couldn't see what the Siheldi wanted even though it was no more than two feet away from him. "The metal?"

Golden, the Siheldi whispered, and the Warden nodded.

There must be a piece of copper that wasn't covered in dull green scale. He could feel out the difference, and he could talk while he was doing it.

"Your brethren are busy underground," he said, getting down on his knees to sift through the gutter parts. "I have not seen any of you for some days."

They are preparing.

"That is good. When will they be ready?"

Soon.

The Warden kept groping through the scrap metal, grimacing at the grit and dirt that was coating his hands. "Soon?"

When our Queen is strong enough to take the iron from him. Soon.

The Warden nodded again. That was the problem that they couldn't solve. But the Siheldi hadn't been out hunting for days – he wondered how the Queen planned to prepare for the difficult task without feeding herself first.

"Does the Queen require food? I can arrange for some. She would not have to distract herself."

The Siheldi spat at him. *She has fed. She does not need your aid,* it sneered.

"Indeed not," the Warden agreed, reminding himself to check the ship registries to see which vessel never made it to shore. "Golden," he said, finally closing his fingers on a smooth piece of metal, offering it to the spirit by placing it very close to the limits of the circle of shade. "For you."

He heard the object, a short, slim piece of piping, roll

slowly under the curricle. It was not a heavy thing that would be unduly burdensome even to a spirit parched by the sharp, sucking heat, and the Warden half expected the Siheldi to flit off with the object within a few moments.

But it stayed there, pushing the pipe back and forth along a little depression in the stone, listening to the noise it made. Perhaps it wasn't finished talking, the Warden thought. Perhaps this one would give him more than he had expected.

"It has been a troublesome process, but it will surely lead you to glory," he said eventually.

You know nothing of either.

"Oh, I know trouble. The man you have in your possession certainly fits the description. I wouldn't mind meeting him, in fact. It would be such a great honor to witness the Queen's triumph."

To steal triumph for yourself, scoffed the Siheldi.

"To help," the Warden countered. "I have never been anything but a faithful friend, and I have the most fervent desire to continue to serve you. Please, if there is any way I can aid you, I beg you to allow me the privilege. After all, you would not have either of them without me."

Leave this place, the voice said after a long pause during which the pipe kept shifting back and forth, back and forth, the copper ringing dully. *Train your sight upon the Queen when you arrive at your home. Your reward for your friendship will be to witness her victory.*

"And a better reward I could never imagine," the Warden said, smiling broadly and bowing to the darkness under the boat. "Thank you."

The Siheldi made no reply. The sound of the rolling

metal stopped suddenly, and the Warden felt the spirit withdraw, the curricle collapsing to the ground as it went.

"Perfect," he said to no one in particular, then started to walk around the island, waving his arms, trying to attract the attention of the boatman, wherever he was in his circuit.

It didn't take long for the skiff to come inshore, and the Warden gratefully accepted a skin of water, pouring some out into his hand to wipe on his face after he had quenched his thirst. The gifts could stay, to be collected that night by the more timid members of the tribe. They were of no value anymore. The piece of copper pipe, which had cost less than a shilling, had bought him everything that he could possibly need.

The journey home was far too long for his liking, and he kept urging the boatman to greater speeds despite the fact that the wind was barely sighing past the sail and there was nothing more either of them could do about it.

It took ages – there wasn't even any room on the tight deck to pace out his anxiety – but eventually they fell under the shadow of the cliffs. He didn't mind getting his feet wet this time as he leapt onto the pebbly beach before the sailor even had a chance to tie up.

He practically ran back to his rooms, restraining himself only when passing one of his subordinates in the hall. The High Warden couldn't be seen to skip towards his quarters like a schoolboy at the start of his holidays, no matter how much he felt like one.

"I am not to be disturbed for any reason, Guthrin," he commanded sternly to the old man who was waiting to tell him how his preparations in the city had gotten on. "For any reason whatsoever."

He slammed the door in Guthrin's face before he

could say a word, turning the key in the lock and dashing over to his desk. He would have to concentrate this time, excitement or no. Laying his hands flat on the surface again, he pressed down as hard as he could to stop the tiny tremor in his fingers from spreading.

"No," he whispered, jumping up again and moving over to a bookshelf, where a heavy volume was laid crosswise on top of shorter tomes, their thick bindings marked with embossed characters that he could feel with his fingers. He had commissioned the books from the engravers in Paderborn, gathering the expensive collection one and two at a time to indulge his interest in the sciences, undimmed even after he had relinquished his sight.

But he wasn't trying to read about the movements of the stars or tides in the large book, which didn't want to dislodge itself. He had to struggle to get a grip on its edges before it tumbled free, sending him staggering backward half a step before he recovered himself enough to open it up. Instead of carefully printed letters on sturdy vellum, traced over backwards with a blunt awl to produce raised letters, there was nothing but a hollow carved from a few dozen pages: a secret spot where he kept a polished nacre box.

He held the container close to his ear as he delicately pushed the edges of a series of miniscule wheels upward with his finger, waiting until he heard the tiniest of clicks before moving on to the next.

When the last tumbler slotted into place, he lifted the lid, running his fingers along the bottom of the case. There was water inside. He scooped the pair of gemstones from the liquid, patting them dry with the corner of his robe before closing the box again and stowing it back into its compartment.

He would always cherish being able to call Bartolo a fool to his face, but the priggish little upstart would never know how stupid he truly was. There were more treasures in the world than such a narrow man could ever hope to learn about, and the Warden had two of them clutched tightly in his hands.

Bartolo had been operating under the assumption that there had only ever been two of the gemstones, but he was wrong. They had been created by the Siheldi out of a special type of *bezhaka* stone with a magic lost to the secrets of eternity, and cherished by the night spirits until the ancestors of the *neneckt* stole them away.

The stones had been fought over, recovered, lost again, taken into hiding, separated, forgotten, and disguised for thousands of years. Some of them had faded into legend; others had been destroyed; many of them had been burned up during dark rituals, made as hollow and useless as glass when their power had been drained dry.

The Warden had spent many years tracking down the two he held, and just as much time ensuring that he could account for any others still in existence, even if they were in rival hands. It would not be work wasted as he pursued the unearthing of what had been buried under the sea, so very long ago before the first *neneckt* broke apart into feuding clans and petty kingships, diminishing themselves with pointless conflicts when they could have had everything within their grasp.

There was so much in the world that few men remembered and more wished to forget, but the Warden was not one of those men. His bespoke books held only a fraction of the knowledge he craved, and with the gems pressed firmly into his flesh, his sightless eyes trained on the Siheldi caverns and the Queen prepared to strike, the Warden began to sing.

* * *

Arran was getting plenty tired of waking up in strange, dark places, groggy and in pain. His forehead felt like it had been split in two, and the rank, sticky wetness that engulfed his left temple was becoming far too familiar for comfort. He had been hit hard – hard enough for the resulting gash to leave a notable scar if he lived long enough for it to heal, and he couldn't even wipe the blood from his stiff, swollen face because his hands were tied tightly above his head.

"Faidal, you son of a bitch," he groaned, the sound scraping across his ears like a rusty saw. "Why does this always happen to me whenever I follow you?"

"I didn't do it," Faidal said, sounding small and scared nearby. "I'm sorry. I didn't do it."

Arran tried to turn his head, but his eye was bruised shut and he couldn't see her. "What happened?"

"Just – just don't draw attention. Be quiet."

"I think it's a little late not to draw attention," he said, trying to move his fingers and search out the nature of his bonds. Rope. Thick, old rope tied in constrictor knots. Doubled, he thought glumly as he tried to bend his wrists around. He would not be able to pick them apart. And this time, the *callawif* was under no obligation to suddenly appear with a knife to help him.

"Shh," the *neneckt* whispered at him as he muttered a curse to himself. "Stop making noise."

Arran ignored her. His feet were on the ground, and

there was a post at his back. If he could just get a little higher, maybe he could see what the rope was attached to. He stood on his toes and tried to inch his spine upward, his fingertips straining to grab onto the ropes that disappeared above him.

"You'll never get free," Faidal said.

"Oh, what do you know about it?"

"I tied the knots," she told him.

"What? You lying little -"

"They made me. I'm sorry. They were - they were going to kill me. I'm sorry. It hurt so much."

Arran grimaced, but shut his mouth. She sounded terrified, and he hadn't even asked if she was all right. Of course she must have tied him up. The Siheldi still couldn't touch him.

"It's fine," he mumbled, trying to focus again on his task. He knew exactly what they had put her through. She hadn't had a choice. He probably deserved it.

She watched in silence as he succeeded in hauling himself about six inches off the ground, his breath held in anticipatory triumph, before his arms simply gave way, firing sparks in front of his eyes and sending him heavily back to the ground gasping in pain.

Something laughed at him from the darkness, and he froze. *You think rope is the only thing holding you here?*

"I was rather hoping so, yes," he replied. He thought he saw something shifting in the distance.

Foolish boy. So bright. So full of light...but not for long.

"You can't touch me," he said nervously. "You can't."

The Siheldi was silent, and Arran couldn't see it, but he knew as a certainty that if the thing had a face, it would be grinning at him like a butcher about to take apart a carcass.

"You can't..." he said again, less sure of himself. "Faidal?"

"I'm sorry, Arran. I didn't know what they wanted. I didn't know."

"Didn't – what do they want? What –"

There was a rush of movement, of cold, cold wind blasting him backward, the bones of his shoulders grinding into the rough wood, and an unholy shriek of carrion triumph split the frigid air.

Arran felt his heart stop. He couldn't breathe, he couldn't see, and there was nothing, nothing in the whole entire world except the terror of the Queen's sudden presence, so much stronger and deeper and more loathsome than it had been when she had tried to reach through the gateway under the smoking mountain to grab him and drag him downwards.

Do you think a pinch of red iron dust will stop me from obtaining what I desire? the Queen breathed. *I have rested and I have fed, and I am not to be denied.*

"Please, don't," he tried to say, but his throat was tied in tighter knots than the ones that held his straining arms suspended. He was afraid. Not of death, necessarily, but of the pain that would come before it. He didn't want that to be the last thing he ever knew. "Please."

The word turned into a wild shriek as she struck at him, like a runaway log in a raging river slamming into his chest. He didn't know what was happening, and he didn't care. He just wanted it to stop.

Not even his locked jaw, grinding his teeth together, could stop him from screaming when the tender scar across his middle cracked and burst, a flood of blood and yellowing pus running down his side, thick and gritty with specks of rusting red iron pulled from the fibers of his innards. He was sobbing in agony, no thoughts in his head beside the wooden repetition of a long-forgotten prayer he had never believed in, graven into some lost corner of his mind by his mother's fervent belief.

Even the prayer faded under the Queen's deadly hand, and as he numbly slumped over, shaking like an autumn leaf, the Siheldi laughed.

Through the cloud of tears that clustered in his eyes, Arran could see the glowing outline of a thin, elegant hand cupping a jewel that seemed to impart its light into the ghostly flesh. He could not flinch away as the Queen pressed the gem against his lowered forehead, the smooth stone sliding on the slick of sweat that had gathered on his skin, boring like a stone drill beneath the bones and into the soft matter of his brain, searing itself into the core of his being as some secret flame crackled through him.

Pain was not something that typically bothered him. He couldn't remember who had said it to him – a grizzled bunkmate, maybe, amused by the innocence of a wide-eyed boy on his first voyage away from the mainland – but he had once been told that the root of all courage was the ability to separate what hurt from what had to be done anyway.

He had always thought he had done rather a good job of it. Cuts and scrapes and the occasional broken finger were hazards of any occupation that required a man to do more than sit behind a shopkeeper's counter, and he had gotten used to ignoring the twinge of an achy joint or swollen bruise as he went about his usual business, certain in the knowledge that such little inconveniences could be borne without his body meaningfully betraying him.

Even on the rare occasions when he fell into the clutches of Paderborn's surgeons, he had drunk his rum and bitten down and blinked back his tears with the best of them, before dusting himself off and limping away to scratch at his stitches in silence when no one was looking.

But this was not the ordinary unpleasantness of a lingering sprain, or even the deep, gasping agony of being snipped and tugged and teased apart from the inside by a physician's clumsy tools. This was not even the racing, heightened fright of sensing the presence of a night spirit on the prowl for its supper, or even the heart-stopping terror of feeling the brush of invisible fingers across the hairs on the back of his neck.

This was the Queen of all despair and she was inside him, burning her way through the feeble guard of what his bravery thought it could muster, to scrape a hollow from the core of him and plant the seed of his death.

It was more than courage could expect of any soul, and he felt himself screaming without the slightest shade of restraint. He felt the shame of it, which only made him beg her to stop, which only made her laugh again. For what was mortal man, bowed and betrayed, beaten thin and brittle – what use was the notion of fortitude in the face of such madness?

He didn't know how long the Queen kept her touch upon him. It must have been no more than a fraction of a moment – his helpless wailing was still echoing in his ears when he half-saw a flash of dim movement next to him, drawing him for a moment out of his torment. Faidal.

The *neneckt* didn't have to untie knots in order to free herself. She just ripped right through them, terror and anger adding to her strength. She climbed, like a cat vaulting up a tree, to the top of the post that held Arran bound.

Before the Queen could straighten up to stop her, she had pulled Arran free, the gemstone slipping from his head before he had a chance to understand what had been done to him as his skull seemed to burst into a boil.

A sudden blaze of light filled the cavern, blinding him as surely as the dark had done. He crumpled bonelessly onto the floor as the Queen howled amidst the acrid stench of burning black powder.

Faidal scooped him up, throwing him over her shoulder as she sprinted away, his ear bumping against her back as her breath ran raw with the effort.

He closed his eyes and let whatever was happening keep happening. There wasn't anything else he could do. There was something burning inside his head, something sharp and sinister that was spreading its creeping tendrils deep into his flesh, and the Queen's laughter was following him like a swarm of angry wasps.

More than laughter was following. Faidal was running as fast as she could, but her legs only worked as well as a human's. There were Siheldi behind them, and they were not encumbered by muscle and bone.

"Where are you going?" Arran said, the words barely stumbling out of his mouth, but she didn't respond. There was nowhere to hide from the Siheldi. Not in their very own home. It was dark, and they were at their fittest, and the Queen had done more than feed on him. She had done something worse, and the fizzing pressure building in his brain felt like a moneychanger's lead weight settled into the space between his eyes.

"*Hkcka, osh, ninda, nibka,*" Faidal breathed as she

darted this way and that.

She was counting, he realized, marking off twists and turns that she must have traveled before in order to reach the surface. Maybe she really could find a way out, he thought, his hope rising for a miniscule moment before the slashing, crushing pain in his head blotted it out.

Time passed, somehow, as he jostled and moaned and bled across her shoulder. He may have lost his consciousness when the pounding and jolting became too much, but he found it again when she lowered him to the ground, panting with exhaustion, and shook him to get him to waken.

"Can you climb?"

"Climb?"

"Up. Here. Put your hands here," she coaxed, pulling his arm towards a shallow little divot in a sheer rock face. "Climb."

"Are you mad?"

"Hurry up," she said, pulling something out of her pocket. Flints. A packet of something wrapped in crinkling butcher's paper. "Get up above me."

"I can't."

"You can. You have to. Go."

Arran tried to shake his head, but it wouldn't move. Nothing would. He could hardly feel his legs. The only thing he could feel was the throbbing, insistent beat of his blood galloping thinly through his heart, through the aching mass of bruises and ruined skin, through the place where the gemstone had been and something else now was. He couldn't climb. He couldn't do anything.

"This will only burn for ten minutes," Faidal said, striking her flints together to catch a spark on the paper's edge. "That will be enough time if we hurry."

"I – I can't, Faidal," he whispered. "Please. I can't."

The cracking sound of the flint and steel was replaced by another stark light, a terrifyingly bright fire that filled the space and gave Arran his first chance to look at exactly what Faidal was asking him to do.

Climb? How could he climb the steepest cliff he had ever seen? They were sitting at the bottom of a circular shaft that rose straight up, carved by an ancient spurt of steaming rock and capped by unidentifiable murkiness long before it came to an end.

They could be miles underground, for all he knew. It could be days, and there was nothing to help them but a few crudely hewn handholds all along its terrifying length. He couldn't do it. He would fall to his death as surely as anything.

"Seven hells, Arran," Faidal said, nudging the burning packet of powder away from her with her foot so that it would fill the entire tunnel with a light that the Siheldi would not cross willingly. Her face was drawn and dirty – there was blood on her, too, and he didn't think it was his own. She was hurting, she was flagging, and she was willing to give everything she had for the slightest chance to save him.

"Faidal, I'm sorry," he told her, not even able to care that he was weeping like a child. "I can't."

"Will you stop calling me that, you fool?" she said softly as she picked him up, wrapping his hands firmly around her neck like a harness, shushing him as he whimpered in distress. She dug her toes into the first little ledge and hoisted herself upward. "My name is Nievfaya."

* * *

Megrithe tried not to let the queasy lurching of her stomach overtake her as she sat very still, eyes closed, on the chair in Leofric's room at the Spearman. Nikko had given her a goodly dose of his people's medicine, and she had been regretting it ever since. The sweetly salty taste was muted by a hiccup that brought up a bubble of bile into her throat, and she moaned quietly as Jairus made a similarly unhappy noise beside her, breathing deeply and slowly in and out through his nose.

Leofric had taken the draught so many times that he no longer felt ill afterwards, and Megrithe could tell that he was impatient to be on his way, even though Nikko insisted on giving the two novices a space to recuperate. The pair of them were sitting together, talking seriously, Leofric holding both of Nikko's hands clasped in front of him, no doubt trying to bolster his spirits after the revelation of his secret.

Megrithe tried not to eavesdrop. It was none of her business. Nikko had looked so dejected after telling her about his past that she had resolved to forget it all immediately and keep her mind on what was really important: her own immediate future.

"This is horrible," Jairus said, breaking into her increasingly worrisome thoughts as she faced the idea of returning to Sind Heofonne.

"Yes, it is."

"You've done this before?"

"Someone hit me, thankfully, and I escaped the worst of it."

"Feel free," he said, tilting his chin towards her, and she laughed.

"I'm not really – all of that with Bartolo – I'm not

really like that," she said sheepishly. "I don't go around knocking people to the ground everywhere I go."

"That's a shame. I did so admire you for it."

"Really?" she asked, then ducked her head as the flush crept up from her throat. "I mean, of course you didn't. Don't be silly."

"I most certainly did. He had it coming to him. And don't I wish I could add to his discomfort right about now."

"I think there's enough discomfort to go around already, at present," she said, fighting down another wave of dizziness. "I feel awful."

"Does it go away?"

"Eventually," she said, and they both sat in silence again for a little while, Leofric's whispers half-heard above their swimming heads.

"Nikko is very upset," Jairus said eventually.

"Don't listen in," she scolded. "It isn't right."

"I can't help it."

"Cover your ears, then."

Jairus shook his head. "I need something to work properly, at least. No eyes, no ears...I'd be completely useless."

"You're not useless at all," she said, and the flush crept higher. "That is – you seem to do all right. You thought you'd be able to kill me, right?" she offered as a consolation thought, even if it was a strange one.

"I *could* kill you," he said. "But I don't want to."

"You're going to be in an awful lot of trouble," she said awkwardly.

"Yes. Which is why I think it might be time for us to be going. As clever as the Warden is, I don't think he can follow me a thousand feet under the sea."

"But you'll have to come back up again."

"I hope so," Jairus said. "But I can deal with it then. Maybe I'll go back to Paderborn and start over again."

"Really?"

"I have some friends there. And the Guild may still have some use for me."

"Of course they will," she replied. "They don't just throw inspectors aside."

"I'm not an inspector. Not yet."

"Oh. I beg your pardon."

"That's all right. I could never take the tests, and they didn't see fit to try to accommodate me."

"I'm sorry," she said. "That isn't right of them."

"It's their prerogative," Jairus said mildly. "I don't deserve special treatment when there are a dozen men more capable to fill the place."

The Guild used a variety of codes to communicate with its agents, many of which were written or based on the colors and patterns of coats, kerchiefs, or shoes. While there were certainly enough spoken passwords or other methods to compensate for someone who couldn't manage to read or see, the inspector's school considered its tests an ancient and immutable tradition. Megrithe had seen fellow students fail and face expulsion for something as simple as smudging a bit of ink when drawing a symbol or hesitating when reciting the correct phase of the moon during an exchange.

"They only took me up from the list when they did because I was keen but expendable," he said. "They didn't think I would last very long in the Divided."

"But you've done well, it seems."

"I'm not done yet. I wish you would tell me about the red iron you found."

"It seems rather a small piece of all of this," she said.

"Yes, but it's an important one."

Megrithe didn't reply. For the Guild, the forges she had found on the palace's grounds during her pursuit of Arran were critical. That was the secret she had come to Niheba to ferret out, and she had succeeded.

But what would the Guild do about a few vats of red dye if Tiaraku had the Siheldi in his pocket? It wasn't important at all, and she found herself getting ever so slightly irritated at Jairus for believing it still mattered.

"I will when this is finished," she said. "I just need to concentrate."

"I understand. I've just been hoping – well, maybe the tests won't matter so much if I came back with something like that."

Megrithe smiled a little. "It's my discovery, you know. What makes you think I'll share the glory with the likes of you?"

"Nothing. I suppose I didn't really do anything for you yet. But I hope to," he said seriously. "We didn't get off to the best start, but I've made my decision to help you will whatever you need. I don't have a choice anymore, now that I've defied the Warden. And if we make it to this mountain and find your friend, you won't have a choice but to vouch for me with the Guild Master," he said, teasing a little, but she furrowed her brow. "Or not," he added lightly.

"No, of course I would. It's just..."

"I wasn't ever really going to hurt you," he said carefully. "I wasn't."

"I believe you. I'm just – I'm not an inspector either," she blurted out, feeling her head start to spin even more severely as her shame and disappointment welled up into her eyes.

"You aren't?"

She shook her head. "I was, but I resigned before I came back here. I had to. The Guild Master was not very pleased."

"You resigned before you told him about the counterfeit?" Jairus asked, a little shocked that she would ever give up such an incredible opportunity.

"It didn't come up."

Jairus just stared at her – turned his face towards her, at least, and would have been staring had he been able to. Even though he couldn't see her, she still ducked her head and didn't look up again for quite a while.

She knew the single-minded intensity it took to pursue an inspector's position. She had lived that life herself for so long that she had thought there wasn't any other way to be. It was all she had ever wanted.

Jairus was still pursuing that dream, even in spite of his difficulties. How could she ever make him comprehend that there was something more important? He would think she had lost her mind, just like she had thought the drop-outs and failures of her own schooling days were pitiful, lazy, unworthy creatures.

To resign from the Guild willingly, without any pressing evidence of wrongdoing, was nearly unheard of. She had not found religion and fled to a convent, nor had she fallen pregnant out of wedlock or decided to give up her career in favor of that blessed union with a man who could support and satisfy her.

The real reason – the *callawil's* bargain for her life – felt too private to share with him. It still hurt, and she didn't want to tell someone who couldn't understand the wounds that had led her to accept her unenviable fate.

Arran would understand, she thought. But that was different. He had fought the Siheldi, too. He was different, and he wasn't there.

"I just needed to be free to come back here," she said when he didn't see fit to break the silence. "I didn't want to be bound by the Guild's rules."

"That makes perfect sense," he told her, although she could tell that he didn't really think so. "But –"

"Nikko, I think we can go," she called instead of letting him finish. She stood up far too quickly, gasping a little as her sense of balance deserted her before recovering well enough to launch herself forward towards the door.

The harbor front smelled like algae and bird droppings. The tide was at its lowest, revealing the greenish-brown scum that clung to the wooden structures under the waterline, peppered with barnacles and tight-lipped mussels that huddled in the safety of their dark shells.

It was not a pleasant place to be for someone suffering the lingering effects of a dose of *ychauyad,* and even though Nikko seemed to find a great deal of amusement in the plight of his human charges, he didn't do anything that would cause them to linger in the stomach-churning air.

Instead, he hurried them away from the sloping bowl of earth that held the commercial docks and most of the city, taking them uphill along a wandering street that ended abruptly at the edge of the island's sheer cliffs with nothing but a rusted iron rail to stop a cart or incautious pedestrian from plummeting down into the water.

"Up and over," Nikko said as Megrithe hung back

from the disturbing sight of the deadly, crashing waves below them. There were sharp boulders in the shallow surf, crumbled off the rock faces during storms or shakings of the earth, and if Nikko meant for her to jump from such a height, he would be seriously disappointed.

"There are stairs," he told her. "Look."

Leofric held onto her arm as she cautiously peered over the railing, seeing to her great relief that the stone actually extended into a comfortable shelf only a foot or so below the fencing. The landing led towards a set of steps, wide and shallowly twisting through a deep channel cut into the edifice, a sturdy rope acting as a handhold and a barrier on the outside edge between safety and the sea.

"That isn't so bad," she said, trying to smile. The steps were large enough for two to walk abreast, if they were brave enough, and they seemed sufficiently sheltered from the worst of the wind. "Can someone else go first, though?"

Nikko did the honors, disappearing from sight almost immediately as Leofric carefully handed Megrithe over the railing. Heights had never been a strong point for her, and it took a great deal of concentration not to start trembling as her dizziness intensified. She immediately moved towards the inside of the stairs, one hand against the solid stone as the breeze, now unimpeded by buildings or trees, whipped through her hair and caught at her skirt, threatening to carry her away.

Jairus followed, seeming as surefooted as Nikko, but Megrithe decided to keep her attention focused on carefully placing one foot in front of the other, winding downwards and downwards towards the growing rumble of the ocean and the crash of spray that gently shivered the island, slowly wearing down the land's resistance to the water's inevitable embrace.

There was a little inlet at the bottom of the staircase where the ocean poked a calm and clear finger into the island's side. Around the open grotto was a pebbly beach, just big enough for the four travelers to stand on as they gazed upwards at the heights they had just traversed.

"What does it say?" Megrithe asked, staring at a line of enormous letters in the *neneckt* tongue carved into a smoothed-over portion of the cliff, plain to see from the ocean but invisible from land.

"It's an old proverb," Nikko told her. "Roughly speaking it says, 'He who keeps his love to the sea need not discover the unworth of men.'"

"Oh," Megrithe said after thinking about it for a while. "That's not a very nice thing to put plain on a mountain, is it?"

"The old ways did not so much encourage friendship with humans," Nikko said. "Three hundred years ago, a *neneckt* would never have dreamt of leaving Niheba for any reason. And a good rule it was, too. Humans cannot be trusted. A right bunch of bastards to the very last."

Leofric cuffed him lightly on the shoulder, producing Nikko's first real smile since meeting with Bartolo. "Can we get this over with?" he asked, and Nikko nodded.

"Make sure you're all holding tight," he said, giving Megrithe one of his hands and Leofric the other. "Just take hers," he said to Jairus, and Megrithe tentatively offered him her fingers.

The water was cold as they waded in, but it wasn't overly unpleasant. It took a bit of effort to convince herself to duck her head under – and even more to make herself try to breathe when she could hold it in no longer – but the strain was all in her own mind.

The water floated around her without truly touching her, as if she had simply wrapped herself in a cloak on a wet and rainy day, no bubbles rising from her nose or mouth and no stinging salt preventing her from keeping her eyes open. It was simultaneously delightfully odd and profoundly unnerving. She tried to keep her gaze anchored upon the steady, unyielding horizon as Nikko guided them down the steep shelf of the ocean floor into deeper water.

Once she got used to the sensation of rushing headlong through the water with nothing more than Nikko's grip to keep her from floating away, the journey was relatively monotonous. The flat, gray stone and drifts of buff sand produced little to attract her attention, the surprising sameness broken only by the occasional flash of a silvery fish darting into a hiding place.

Nikko was not bringing them towards Emyer-Ekvori, where they would be instantly spotted and stopped. He was taking them instead along a wide arc that skirted the city, its outlying villages, and its tall, green fields of edible kelp that helped feed the underwater populace. They had started early in the morning, but the circuitous route would take much of the day to complete, which gave her plenty of time to think about what was awaiting her at their destination. None of the thoughts were anything remotely cheerful.

Not even the notion of finding Arran alive at the other end of the journey could do much to lift her spirits. She started to wonder if she even really believed there was a chance to succeed.

What if Durville had been right to say that Arran

couldn't have survived what he had done to himself? It would all be for nothing, and she would simply be hurtling headlong into her own death. The Queen would be there. The Siheldi would surround them, and she would die screaming. She would be leading her friends to their end, and the world would burn into darkness and dust because she had not been quick enough or keen enough or strong enough to stop it.

"It will be fine, you know," Jairus said quietly, shifting his fingers in her too-tight grasp. She tried not to pinch as much as she smiled weakly and kept her eyes forward without answering him. She was aware that he meant well, but she had had enough of people who acted like they knew the future. They didn't, and she had never liked the lie of pointless platitudes, no matter how well intentioned.

Eventually, the mountain rose into view over the willowy curves of the dunes. Megrithe didn't know when her heart had started kicking so furiously against the walls of her chest, but she felt her breath shorten in response as a knot grew in her middle. She squeezed her eyes shut and refused to look at the craggy peak, cloaked in ash and misery, hung with a wreath of shimmering, steaming water that roiled black and sooty around the shoulders of the grumbling giant.

You know what I want with you, the Queen had said, and moments later there had been nothing but Megrithe's hollow screams. Arran had shouted – he had tried, but there was no way to stop it, and Megrithe grew as cold as ice as she thought back to the all-consuming terror, the unbearable, unbreakable dread of dead fingers and a flicking tongue, of feeling the Siheldi supping on her soul like a bowl of cold soup, gorging itself on the haggard remnants of her desperation to live.

She felt a little despondent mew escaping her clenched lips as she opened her eyes again and the mountain filled her vision, tall and serene and brimming with death. She wanted to let go of Nikko's hand and float away – she almost hoped that she would plummet straight down to shatter on the rugged slopes. She almost felt like she would splinter apart anyway.

But as soon as Nikko set them down carefully on a relatively flat prominence close to the mountain's head, the fear abruptly converted itself into anger. She would not let terror get the best of her. She would *not*.

The Guild had never bowed to shadows before – it was the Guild's sole purpose to keep them at bay – and whether or not she still held an inspector's badge, she had been trained to the highest abilities of her kind. She had faced the Queen and survived it, and she would not bend her knee to powerless memories and empty shades of faded trepidation.

"Megrithe?" Jairus asked carefully, placing a hand on her shoulder as she stood there as rigidly as an iron post, and she sagged under his touch like a deflating pudding taken out of the oven too soon.

"Don't make me go," she wailed, too late to bite her tongue, the fingers she clasped over her mouth unable to shovel the words back inside. She despised herself instantly.

He tried to put his arm around her in a gesture of friendly comfort, but she shrugged him off, crumpling in on herself, squatting down with her head on her knees when she realized there was no room to run.

"Leave me alone," she sobbed into her skirt, helplessly mortified and even angrier now than she had been before.

The three of them just stood there, watching her silently, bewildered and confused. They had not been there. How could they know? Only Arran had seen her – she hated that he had seen her in her worst moment, but the truth was that he had. That strange, fleeting connection was the only thing that had kept driving her towards a truth she wasn't sure she wanted to uncover, and now they were probably standing on top of his grave.

At that moment, she wanted to go home more than she wanted to bring Arran home – more than she wanted to stop the brewing chaos that she didn't understand and couldn't control; the actions of kings and sorcerers and the terrors of the night that had reigned supremely for centuries despite the best intentions of men far braver than she would ever be.

She fumbled in her pocket for a handkerchief she didn't have, which brought her back to her morose visit with Elspeth Swinn.

If there was a grave to be found, or a body in need of one, Arran's mother deserved to know about it. She deserved the truth, and Megrithe had as good as promised that she would find it for her.

She couldn't save the world, maybe, or even save her own soul from what was waiting for her, but she could try, at least, to soothe the grief of one poor widow waiting for news of a son lost to the seas.

"I'm sorry," she said a moment later, standing up again in one swift motion, pulling her tears back inside her like she had done after each of a thousand nights of hidden, despairing sorrow after her father had died. This was no different. She would *make* it no different. They would not see her cry again. Not Jairus, not Arran, not the *callawif* – not anyone. "We can go."

In any other circumstance, she might have strode away to hide her face from her companions, but on the bare outcropping of rock, there wasn't anywhere to stride. She just had to wait patiently, keeping her eyes down and her shoulders squared, as Nikko ducked around the edge of the platform, one foot on the lip of rock and the other searching for something on the other side, the solid shape he had managed to maintain while underwater shimmering and fading for a moment as his concentration shifted elsewhere.

But when he vanished entirely, it wasn't because he had let his physical form dissipate. He had wiggled his way past a jutting boulder and into what must be an entrance to the mountain's labyrinth. Leofric beckoned Megrithe to take her turn, and she glanced uneasily back at Jairus.

"I'll help him if he needs it," Leofric said in her ear. She touched her hidden medallion of red iron, just to make sure it was still there, before turning her attention to placing her foot in a crumbled pocket in the stone, crossing the other leg over as soon as she saw the mouth of a tunnel.

There was nothing to hold onto as the rock bulged outwards, hundreds of feet above the sea floor. She drew a deep breath as she remembered Arran plummeting to the ground when Faidal pushed him off the wall of their prison cell, the water providing no cushion for his painful fall.

"Steady," Leofric said, gripping the fabric at the shoulder of her dress to hold her in case she couldn't make it around.

The part of her that was still enraged at herself

resented the notion that he thought she needed help, but the sensible piece of her mind was more than a little relieved when a shower of scree slipped from under her heel and she froze in mid-motion, hugging the boulder with wobbling tears at the corners of her eyes as she remembered throwing her arms around the wide bulk of her father's barrel-like chest, unable to make her half-grown arms clasp together on the other side.

She pushed the memory aside. Why were her thoughts drifting so far away? She had not let such things touch her for many years, but now she felt unable to flee from the pictures of her younger life, before the pain of loss, before ambition – before anything bad had ever happened to her.

"I'm fine," she called back around the corner when she made it to the other side, realizing immediately why Nikko hadn't just brought them there to begin with. The tunnel had an overbite, where the floor had tumbled away, and the smooth bubbles of dried magma that were left pouring out of the tube, frozen in time, were too steeply slick to stand on without Nikko's steady support from somewhere above as she scrambled, bent over like the twisted dough of a summer festival bun, into a mouth narrow enough to admit only one body at a time.

Thankfully, the tunnel opened wider just past its beginning, and she was able to stand up straight with her back pressed against the sloping wall, feeling like she had skipped into the maw of a beast that would crunch her bones for its tea.

As she stood there in the dark, waiting, she felt a sharp, aching alarm burrow its way below her fear, below her uncertainty, and underneath the thin film of madness she suspected was lurking somewhere within her, too.

The place she was standing was all wrong. She touched her pocket again, taking comfort in the hard, flat metal under the skin of cloth. Red iron was never wrong. It was the only constant in the world: the only thing as clear and comforting and true as the knowledge of a warm bed waiting at home at the end of a long journey.

But she had no home to go back to. She had traded it for the chance to do exactly what she was doing. It would all have been pointless if she turned back now.

"All right?" Leofric asked as he slipped around the bend to join her.

"Yes," she replied. "I thought you were going to help Jairus."

Leofric shrugged. "He didn't want me to."

"Stubborn fools, the lot of you," she said under her breath, but then she shook her head to clear the irritation away. Everyone had their pride. Everyone deserved to.

"I think we should strike a light," Leofric said, putting his hand in his pocket.

"Nothing will burn," she told him, but the little stone globe he took out from his coat wasn't flint or steel. It was cloudy and greenish, like the bottom of a mossy lake.

"Fire won't, but this will," he said. As soon as Leofric brought it close to his mouth and breathed warm air over it, it started to glow ever so gently: a cool, blue blush like the lanterns she had seen in Emyer-Ekvori.

"It's beautiful," she said. "How does it work?"

"The *neneckt* have more wisdom than cruelty in them," he said, wrapping a bit of twine around a shallow groove cut into the object so it could hang from his fingers and cast a stronger light. "But like so many of us, they often let their faults outweigh their cleverness."

"I already said I was sorry about the teahouse," Nikko

said, holding together a curiously muted outline of himself, the glow filtering through him like frosted glass that caught the edge of his mischievous grin.

"The very least of your transgressions," Leofric sniffed, turning away to see if Jairus had joined them. He had, seeming no worse for wear, so Leofric started to lead the way down the path, holding the soft radiance in front of him.

The light was just strong enough to make groping along in the gloom a marginally less frustrating experience, but Megrithe still felt a slow fountain of panic rising inside her the further they traveled, her fingers reaching out to brush the back of Leofric's shoulder every so often just to reassure herself that he was really there.

The tunnel started to slope steeply forward, at times so near to vertical that she wished they had brought a rope. They were forced to slither down backwards, doing their best to let their toes slide through the rough powder, trying not to tumble on top of the person in front. The plumes of dust swirled upwards in the salty water, creating hanging clouds that got up Megrithe's nose while she followed along the incline, making her cough as she scrabbled to keep her balance as the difficult descent continued.

Eventually the route flattened out again, and Nikko let them stop to take a short rest. The sphere was giving off less light now, and Megrithe was a little afraid of what would happen when it lost its power completely. She didn't want to be crawling blind under thousands of tons of immovable rock, she thought, then guiltily snuck a glance at Jairus. That's exactly what he was doing, and he didn't even have a choice.

She hadn't the faintest idea how he could tell when she was looking at him as they sat huddled in a tight circle, dusting off dirty palms and knees and catching their breath the best they could, but he always seemed to turn towards her with a smile when he felt her eyes on him.

He had a nice smile. It was kind. Almost benign. He was not a harmless man – she knew that much. He just smiled like he meant it, or maybe like he had nothing to hide. No one ever smiled like that at a Guild inspector. A smile always meant that someone wanted something from her. On Jairus, it just looked like he was enjoying the moment.

"Almost there," he said, somewhat more cheerfully than she thought was warranted, under the circumstances.

"How do you know?"

"I don't. I'm just trying to be optimistic."

"Well, stop it," she said cringing at how harsh she sounded, and his expression immediately sobered.

"I'm sorry," he said. The careful way he spoke, as if he was afraid of making her cry again, just made her more annoyed.

She clamped her mouth shut and felt her back teeth grinding hard against each other. She didn't want to say something stupid. She didn't want to say anything at all. It wasn't his fault that she was being too prickly to accept his good intentions, but now was not the time to be making friends – or whatever he thought he wanted to make of her. It was time to stay on her task. She just wanted it all to be over.

Megrithe stood up and stepped over Leofric, making him lean back so she could pass without sweeping him in the face with her dress. She wasn't going to wait around resting with such foolish thoughts in her head when she could be moving forward instead.

It was another hour, at least, until the walls started becoming warm to the touch. The vague breath of hot air brought with it a reddish light, too faint to replace the dying glow-sphere as a guide, but just enough to drip the tainted wine of apprehension into the back of her throat, making her swallow hard again and again as her feet moved of their own accord, her mind working furiously but not focusing at all, a swirl of terrible visions clouding the blackness in front of her.

"Wait," Leofric said at one point, hooking his hand around her arm and pulling her backwards.

Megrithe blinked and all of a sudden she was standing right on the edge of another steep slope, the path falling away in front of her to shoot downwards into a pit of heat that sent gentle waves shimmering up through the water. She stepped away with a grateful glance, trying to shake herself out of her miserable reverie.

"We're too high," she said, peering down the length of the tunnel to see a crescent of the massive cavern that held the mountain's heart.

"Not for long. I've got you," Nikko said, gathering them up again. "Hold on tightly."

It was a narrow fit as they slowly floated down the chute, as if they were standing in a bucket being lowered through a well – a well in which the water was nearly scalding and smelled of yellow sulfur and harbored the specter of death. The cave opened up around them as they looked down at the circle of tall, icy boulders standing like silent monks around the pit of roiling fire, locked in a centuries-long meditation unaffected by the visitors to their noxious lair.

The travelers were still nearly as high as a second-story window, drifting carefully towards the crackled ground, when Megrithe screamed. Something had pushed her hard, dislodging her grip on Nikko, and all of a sudden she was tumbling headlong to the unforgiving stone below her.

The fall was slow and leisurely, like dragging through treacle, giving her panicked mind more than ample time to contemplate the crunch of her bones and the wet splitting of her skull as she tried to bring her shoulder around to take the brunt of the blow, tried and failed to think of anything that would make her last moments any more worthwhile than the rest of them.

It took only a fraction of a second, of course – it took less time than that to realize that she was not falling alone. Jairus had slipped away, too, the fire's glow catching the silver of his wide-eyed surprise as he instinctively tried to grab onto her, whether to help her or help himself, she wasn't sure.

They hit the ground together, an elbow smashing into her cheek; her knee in his ribs before the back of her head bounced on the flat rock, a shower of sparks cascading in front of her as his solid weight crushed her, a breathless groan coming from one of them, or maybe from them both.

"Get off," she gasped, trying to push him away, but her arms had no strength in them, and she couldn't raise her head.

A string of curses eventually turned into a question. "Are you all right?" he asked, holding his stomach where she had jammed into him.

"No, I'm bloody well not all right," she replied,

putting a hand to her face. His sharp blow had opened a bleeding gash in her skin. "Get off me right this instant."

He rolled to the side, but instead of moving to help her up, the motion brought him into an alert crouch, his head cocked upward, and Megrithe became aware of a terrible racket hovering somewhere in midair.

"Who is it?" Jairus said urgently, turning first one ear and then the other towards the sound, like a bat trying to locate its supper by moonlight. "What's happening?"

"I don't -"

"What is happening?" he repeated, grabbing her arm tightly and hauling her half-upright, pointing her at the noise.

"It's a *neneckt*," she said, trying to focus on the commotion. Nothing seemed to be where it ought to – she was fairly sure the walls weren't supposed to be moving like that. "It's Nikko – and someone else. Something else. I can't – where's Leofric?"

A quick look around did not reveal him, and she turned her attention back to the point where Nikko and a strong, immense shadow were grappling in mid-air. "I don't know. It's a *neneckt*, I think. Is it Faidal?"

Jairus stood up and gave her his hand to do the same. "I need you to tell me where I have to go. How do I get up there?"

"There's no way," she said, scanning the stone for a pathway that didn't exist. "It's just a sheer cliff."

Just then, she heard Leofric shout something that echoed dully behind them, too distorted to understand. He was on the other side of the circular moat of molten rock that ran along the edge of the space – the one that she and Arran had crossed over on the slender bridge that later collapsed. There was no other way across.

Leofric was trapped.

Whatever he had shouted had caught Nikko's attention, and the two shaded figures crashed like falling stars to the earth. Jairus sprinted ahead, a pair of slim knives appearing in his hands as if by magic.

"They won't work," Megrithe muttered, swaying on her feet as crashing nausea slammed through her. Nothing could kill a *neneckt* except for coral glass. She had learned that somewhere.

She wasn't entirely sure what happened next. She thought she was falling, but then someone was lowering her gently to the ground, propped up against a pillar of stone that felt as cold as packed snow. It was Leofric, she realized, as soon as she saw his back, running away from her and towards the fight. He must have jumped the molten stream.

It wasn't Faidal fighting with Nikko, she thought blurrily as she blinked hard, vaguely wondering what was getting in her eyes before wiping away the blood. It couldn't be Faidal. This creature was huge and angry and mad as a bull, charging like a thunderhead while Nikko flitted moth-like around him, sweeping and stabbing and trying to bring the creature down to earth again, so Leofric and Jairus could help him.

It must be Habur, she realized, and the notion made her head swim. Habur liked blood. Habur liked to make a show. She shrank up as small as she could behind the boulder, but she knew there was nowhere she could truly hide. Habur would kill Nikko and then he would find her, and he would tear her limbs from her body like a rag doll.

She had to run. Somewhere. She knew there were other tunnels – she had used one to enter Sind

Heofonne the first time, when Arran had tried and failed not to peek up her skirts. But she was cut off from that exit by the river of magma, and she knew she would not be able to make the leap that Leofric had. There was only one other place to go.

The central pit of fire, with its slow, thick bubbles blobbing to the surface before popping damply with an exhalation of lethal breath, was so far away. She wasn't sure she could reach it. She wasn't sure she wanted to. But that was where Arran had gone. And if hiding was useless, she might as well try to follow him.

She tried to grasp at the smooth surface of the stone behind her as she levered herself up, but snatched her fingers away with a cry, slumping back to the ground as she stared in confusion at the blistered skin of her palm. It was cold enough to burn, leaving a strange, pale mark in the flesh, and under the creamy surface, something was moving.

"N-Nikko?" she breathed, watching the delicate darkness congeal and stiffen, as if it was a chicken's egg held up to the light with a tiny, half-formed life stirring inside.

"Leofric?" she called a little louder, panic overtaking her as she scrambled backwards on her rear end, trying to get as far away from the wrongness and the terrible, terrible fear that threatened to burst from the chrysalis.

She wasn't looking where she was going, scuttling on all fours, and bumped into something that was softer than stone, but only just. She looked up to see an outstretched arm coming down, and the *neneckt* grabbed her by the throat.

There was nothing Megrithe could do as the *neneckt* started to squeeze. Of course Habur would not have come alone to such a place. It briefly occurred to her to be angry with herself for not anticipating that, but the anger was swept away by dismay as the air drained from her lungs.

She couldn't see the others. There was noise from somewhere, maybe close by, but the whole of her attention was on the watery outline in front of her, inches from her face, staring into her bulging eyes with absolutely no expression as it wrung the life from her.

It wasn't how she wanted to die. It wasn't how she had imagined it would be, and she had thought about it a lot over the years. She had asked her mother what it was like, once, after her father's funeral, and her mother had said it was just like quietly drifting off to sleep. Megrithe had always wanted to believe that, despite all the evidence to the contrary she had experienced during her career. But now she knew better as she sagged to her knees, entirely consumed by searching, strumming agony while the soft structures of her throat crumpled under her skin.

Megrithe had closed her eyes by the time the *nencckt* let her go, throwing her to the side with a shriek like a startled kettle, as if it had suddenly realized she was poisonous to the touch. Some part of her realized that it would behoove her to start breathing again, and without much of her consent, she was gulping in great raggedy gasps of air that sawed through her in convulsive coughs, a hand weakly opening and closing in front of her, a dying spider that had been crushed by a heavy book.

There was more noise. There was more than noise: there was a chanting of voices and a cracking of stone. A man's clear, cold singing covered the cavern in unearthly music as the words took the shape of hammers, smashing the tall, shining prisons standing guard over Sind

Heofonne.

Megrithe stared in silent shock as the white boulders around her shattered under the incantation. From within each one rose a shrieking phantom made of formless smoke. Before she could even convince herself that she wasn't dreaming or already dead, they had disappeared into the scalding wreath of cloud that clothed the mountain's mantle, as quickly and completely as if they had never been there.

Megrithe raised her head and tried to understand what was happening. The echoing melody came from everywhere and nowhere, overwhelming her. A stranger's voice. A familiar song. An exhortation to madness that stopped her breath as surely as the grip of the *neneckt*, which had had fled from the music while she was preoccupied.

Much had happened in the few seconds that had passed – it was only a few seconds, she was nearly sure. But the colossal form of Habur was lying sprawled on the ground, flickering somewhat in and out of the visible realm as his life fought to stay within him. There was an ornately carved dagger sticking straight up from his breast, the edge of a salmon-colored blade just visible above the burbling gore. He was still and silent. Nikko was standing over him, staring down for a moment before reaching over to pull the weapon out with a tug of slimy resistance and tucking it in his belt.

She turned back towards the ring of boulders. There were pieces of stone scattered across the ground. She didn't know what had escaped from the shells, but she was somehow sure that the singing was like the whistle of a master to his dogs, and something sinister had heeded the call.

"Come with me," someone said in her ear, an arm around her waist, the stickiness of blood soaking through her dress as Jairus drew her close for support as she found her feet. He was hurt.

She fell again as the earth shook beneath her, and something crashed down beside them: a shard of rock, long and thin and massive, that had fallen from the ceiling. Jairus picked her up again, but he was limping, and she didn't know who was helping whom as they lurched forward and ran for safety.

But they didn't know where they would find it. The cavern was shaking and her skin was tingling with the chant that seemed to fill her bones with screaming despair. What was it? She needed to know. She craved the knowledge; she ached to follow the sound and break free from her skin and shriek into the heavens like the unknown creatures hidden for so many ages in the buried earth.

"Come on," Jairus said again, urgently, trying to push her forwards as she slowed to a halt. If she left now, she would never know. She would never understand, and she would never be able to return to finish her search for Arran. The gods of the sea were trying to seal the cavern, and she could not bear the notion of leaving him to the crushing depths of such a terrible mausoleum.

"No," she said, pulling away. "Not yet."

She stumbled back towards the crater of boiled earth, another tremor unbalancing her, knocking her to her knees, but she scrambled along like a crab for a moment until she could get her feet again. "Not without Arran."

"He isn't here," Jairus shouted after her. "You're going to get yourself killed."

"He *is* here," she said, mostly to herself, staring

downward at the gateway, a strange conviction filling her as the song pounded in her ears. She suddenly felt like she could see him, if only she could slip below the illusion of instant, fiery death. It wasn't real. It couldn't hurt her – there was something underneath. There was so much just below the surface. The song was telling her. The song was opening the way. She only had to find it. She only had to jump in. The song would open the way.

She felt like sparks would crackle off her skin if she touched anything; she felt rather than saw the scorching wall of heat that suddenly exploded in front of her, slamming her backwards as the molten core of the earth shot upwards to the ceiling of the immense heart of the mountain.

The blast triggered another quaking, strong enough to crack the cooled surface where she stood, and she nearly slipped sideways into a bottomless crevice as Jairus caught up to her, yanking her upwards, tumbling away to firmer ground before he picked her up bodily, her arms flailing and her mouth screaming curses, and ran as fast as he could towards where Nikko waited.

How he got there without falling, she had no idea. But she wasn't about to marvel at his reflexes as she tried to pull away from Nikko, his arms now wrapped as firmly as iron around her as he sprang upwards towards the tunnel they had entered only a few minutes before.

"He's here," she sobbed, her struggles slowing as they streamed through the narrow tunnel, racing the eruption, wriggling like an overgrown eel as Nikko dodged and twisted up each tight turn. "Let me go. Nikko! Let me go!"

Her protests were useless. He did not relinquish his grip on her, and she no longer had the strength to fight him. She felt a desperate flush of fever welling up inside her, burning like her hand had burned, and her consciousness was fading by the time they burst out of the slim crack in the mountain's face, the whole world shaking as plumes of ash spewed ferociously from the peak.

The water was as dark as sin for a hundred miles around as the volcano's rage breached the face of the sea with a throaty roar, blotting out the clean, sparkling light of the sun. It was abysmally hot and impossible to breathe, but Megrithe somehow found the strength to cry inconsolably as she peeked under Nikko's arm at the convulsing edifice while they shot away as quickly as they could.

She had never heard a sound louder than the volcano's final explosion, a torrent of white-hot fire spurting upward as the entire bulk of the ocean's floor slipped to one side, untold tons of bedrock shifting, cracking, crumbling, collapsing in a mushrooming of dust and grinding boulders and gritted sand, sending Nikko careening sideways when the shock pushed the water away, stampeding towards Niheba's ignorant shores, building into a wave that would sweep the harbor inland and drown half the city.

"He was there," Megrithe wept, burying her face in Nikko's shoulder as he used all his remaining stamina to try to outrun the force of nature, to warn the city what was coming, to get them somewhere safe. "Oh, gods have mercy," she whispered as she was carried along, spent and numb. "He was there."

CHAPTER NINE

The light from the packet of burning powder cast harsh shadows on the sheer rock face as Nievfaya climbed and climbed with Arran clinging weakly to her neck like a sick child, silent and barely breathing. She could feel his forehead against the crook of her neck, and where his skin met hers, it burned like smoking acid.

The Queen had touched him. She had used the gemstone in her hand to burrow deeply inside him, tucking a terror into his soul that would grow and grow and grow until it consumed the world. Arran would die, surely, but so would everyone else if the little kernel of hate and evil and dank, sweeping dusk was allowed to blossom.

There was no hope for him, she knew, trying not to cry as she placed her grasping fingers into the shallow hollows in the wall. The only thing she could do now was to ensure that the Queen couldn't feed on the nectar she was brewing in his poisoned heart by taking him as far away from her as possible.

She had a notion that perhaps her *oughon* friend Rodnei might do something – he had saved Arran's life once already, and perhaps he could do so again – but the chilling wetness that cascaded down her back, drenching her shirt and making her trousers chafe uncomfortably against her waist as she climbed, made her wonder if she could even get him to Niheba before he finally succumbed to his wounds. Without the protection of the Siheldi's *bezhaka*, he had an hour or two at the very best, she was sure.

Her calves were crying out at her, begging for rest as she planted her toes firmly before levering herself upwards, again and again. Her arms spat hatred at her, scraped knuckles and cramping fingers competing with her straining shoulders to complain the loudest. She didn't know how high she had to go. She hadn't even reached the bottom of the ocean yet. A sob hitched in her throat as she kept her eyes firmly on the stones, no more than a hair's breadth from her nose. She was strong for a human – she was strong for a *neneckt*, but there was a limit even to the endurance of the sea people, and she was fast approaching it.

There was no relief in pausing, a clinging limpet terrified to relax her grip even a little, but she did so anyway, hoping her lungs would thank her for the short respite with a renewal of their energy.

"I'm sorry, Mum," Arran whispered, the words slurred into meaninglessness for anyone who hadn't uttered the same words themselves in the small night hours when grief reigned unchallenged. Nievfaya had said such things, uncountable thousands of times, but the dead couldn't ever hear her.

"Hold on, Arran," she said. "Just a little while longer. Hold on for your mum."

His barely awake sigh shifted into a hacking cough, and Nievfaya reached up to find the next handhold. If she could just get to the water, they would be all right. Once they found the water, they would be safe – for a little while.

"Hold on," she said again. "We're almost there."

But they weren't. And even when they reached the seabed, what then? Arran had no *ychauyad* left in his stomach. As soon as the salt water hit him, he would drown. She had thought that she would be fast enough to get him to the surface in time to let him breathe, but she wasn't so sure now. She wasn't sure of anything, but she continued to climb.

Nievfaya found herself humming a tune as she let the work take over, pushing her discomfort back into a tight little ball like she used to do when laboring in the fields of her clan. The tune was more suited to the up and down motion of planting kelp seedlings, dipping into a wide canvas sack at her side, stooping down to push the roots into the sand, straightening and bending and pushing, over and over, until the waters changed from bright, sunny sapphire to a deep, smoky jade and it was time to gather at home for food and a short night's rest.

But the insistent stresses of the rhythm made her climb faster than before. Faster, but no one was fast enough to outrace fire. She heard the rumbling before she felt anything, but trying to peer down between her knees only meant that her face was exposed to the inexorable rush of scalding air that nearly dislodged her, throwing her off balance as the heat sucked all the breath out of her. She felt Arran's hands start to slip.

"No, no, no," she cried as his head rolled back, swinging her sideways. Her fingernails dug into the tiniest cracks, splitting painfully as his weight wrenched her away from the wall.

"Please," she gasped, terrified of the fall, the remnants of the black powder's light all but lost in the distance between them and the ground.

She didn't know how she managed to keep herself

clinging to the stone, but Arran's limp skull struck the nape of her neck as she arced her back and tried to shift him forward, sliding him down so she could take hold of one of his sleeves between her teeth, a last effort to keep him from tumbling into nothingness if he loosed his locked fists around her.

It was nearly impossible to breathe with only her nose free, but she kept climbing. There was nothing else to do.

"The Irithi Athdra are coming," Arran muttered, and suddenly Nievfaya stopped stock still, heedless of the debris that was raining down on her as the mountain shivered and shook in its distress.

"What did you say?"

"They are coming," he whispered. "They are free."

Nievfaya wanted to say that they couldn't be coming, because there was no such thing as the Irithi Athdra. There couldn't be. They were nothing more than a pervasive myth woven through the fabric of *neneckt* legend, linked always to the Siheldi Queen, but Nievfaya didn't know that humans had ever heard the same tales.

Arran was in no state to argue with her, much less to lie to her. He could not have known it unless he was speaking the truth – the Queen's truth – and the words struck a fear into her heart that could not be equaled.

"Sun Mother save us," she said as she redoubled her efforts, shaking pumice and ash from her hair. The stories said that the only thing worse than the Queen of the Siheldi were the broken pieces of her power, defeated and imprisoned long, long ago.

Some called them her sons; others said they were merely servants; some even said they were the remnants of a long lost consort and King. But all had celebrated the end of the Siheldi's unbridled butchery when the Irithi Athdra had been entombed in strong *bezhaka*, warded by the wisest and more powerful of the *neneckt*, wrapped around with invisible chains of deep and unbreakable sorcery time and time again to keep them from making their mother whole.

There was no prison in any realm of earth or sea that could hold back the full might of the Siheldi if the Irithi Athdra were unleashed upon a feeding ground as rich as Paderborn. The spirits would be weak, and they would need to fatten up significantly if they were to help the Queen break through the last of the seals that held her in check.

If they were smart – and Nievfaya had no doubt that they were – they would flee to the outskirts of the city where the poverty-riddled peasants had little red iron to sting them, and they would feast to their hearts' content before gaining enough strength to gorge themselves in Paderborn proper. If even half the tales were correct, Nievfaya could not think of a single thing – not even all the contents of all the Guild's vaults – that could form an effective defense against them once they were fighting fit again.

The old stories told of a champion, of course, to keep the black defeat at bay, but she had never heard of a prophesy's promises that had ever come true. She had never seen the point of putting hope in them, not as a youngling and not now. Her family had barely even been able to feed itself, and no gods or warriors or good men seemed to care. What was the use in foretelling a hero who would save the whole wideness of the world when something as simple as a full belly for a single child was always so far out of reach?

"Where are they?" she asked him.

"They are coming."

"Coming for us?" she asked, glancing down between her feet again.

"They are free."

Nievfaya bit her lip to stop herself from lashing out at him for repeating himself. He couldn't help it. It probably wasn't even Arran who was talking. His mind would not be his own for much longer, if there was any of it still left at all.

"Keep quiet," she said, giving up for the moment. "You need to conserve your strength."

Nievfaya started humming again to distract herself from the overwhelming confusion of her alarming thoughts, but the song had changed. She didn't know the new strains she was singing. She had never heard the melody before, but all of a sudden there was no other music in her head, no matter how hard she tried to wrench herself away from it.

It wasn't a *neneckt* song. It didn't sound like a human song. It was something else entirely, and it was coming out of her mouth with words she didn't understand – words that hurt her like the snap of a whip and the blow of a mallet – and they frightened her even more than Arran's mumbled phrases.

"Stop it," she said to herself, taking Arran's sleeve into her teeth again to keep her mouth clamped shut, but the song kept running past her, forcing her onward, forcing her upwards, as the mountain shook again. It was more deeply compelling than her quest for her freedom, than her urge to live, than her desire to die. It sank through the very bones of the stone colossus beneath her: a song of a world that should never exist; a song to make the giant dance.

Before long, just as Nievfaya thought she saw the faintest shimmer of daylight above her, the mountain reached the limits of its restraint. Another belch of overheated air brought with it an inverted rain of scalding dust that scoured her flesh and burnt tiny pinprick holes into the fabric of her clothes. It was impossible to think or talk or draw a breath in the middle of the maelstrom, and no matter how fast she thought she was moving upwards, her body moving jerkily forward despite her blank despair, the mirage of sunlight had disappeared, and there was nothing left but a nightmare.

"I must be free," Arran whispered urgently in her ear, but her only response was a broken whimper. She was trying to save something beyond saving. She always had been, long before she had ever met Arran Swinn.

She could just let go, if she wanted to. She could just fall, and the baking oven of burning rock would kill her before she hit the bottom. She could just let go. It would be the easiest thing she had ever done.

Nievfaya tucked her chin down to try to give her a space to breathe as another queasy tremble threatened to take the choice away from her. On her back, Arran coughed again, and she felt his arms tighten ever so slightly around her neck.

"Faidal?" he croaked, his voice little more than the shadow of a thought. It was *his* voice, though. She could tell. "You need to let me go."

"Why would I do that?" she asked, hauling herself up another few inches.

"There's something – something inside of me."

"I know."

"Please," he said, and he sounded frightened. "Please

don't let it get out."

"I can't leave you to the Queen," she said. "I'll kill you later, all right?"

"Promise?"

She didn't reply.

"Faidal –"

"That's not my name."

"Please. Promise."

"Arran, I didn't come all this way just to leave you at the top," she said firmly.

"Are we at the top?"

"I don't know. I really hope so."

Arran fell silent again as Nievfaya tried to muster the last of her willpower. She had seen the water. She really had. It was up there, and she must be getting close to it by now. She might not believe in prophecies, but she did believe in her own eyes. There was nothing else left to have faith in.

She had stopped perspiring by the time her head poked up into cold, cold wetness. There wasn't any moisture left in her after being buffeted by the desiccating heat for so long, and any tears of relief she might have cried would have been lost to the ocean waters in any case.

She crouched just below the end of the tunnel, hoping to give Arran a few more minutes to breathe before she ventured further upward. She would need to be incredibly quick if she hoped get him to the surface before he ran out of air, and she didn't know if she could manage it. The whole long climb might have been for nothing after all.

"Arran," she said, nudging him with her elbow and startling him awake. "I need you to take a very deep breath. Do you understand?"

"I can't."

"Yes, you can. There's someone on Niheba who can help you," she said, trying to give him something to hope for. "My friend Rodnei, remember? The one who made your medicine. He can help. You just need to get there. All right? Promise me."

"I –"

"Promise," she snapped, and she felt him nod. "Good. Are you ready?"

His first attempt at holding his breath ended in a painful moan as his wounds stretched and strained, but after a few agonizing moments of trying, he seemed to succeed. It was as good as it was going to get, and Nievfaya couldn't wait any longer. There was a terrible humming sound, a constant vibration of pressure that traveled through her body and continued down into the roots of the mountain. The Sea Father was ready to breathe fire.

"We need to go," she said, pausing until she felt him fill his lungs and hold the air inside. With a prayer galloping through her head and a strange crackling tingle running down her spine, she sprang through the invisible film that kept the Siheldi apart from the world above. It made sure the spirits stayed in while keeping the water out, but it couldn't keep her away from her native element.

Instead of the wildly disturbing chant that had been flowing through her during her journey, her whole being was singing with the unparalleled joy of returning to the sea after too long away. There was no time for a true celebration, let alone the common rituals of rejoining, but she let the pleasure of the swift bubbles streaming along her flanks lend her speed as she pointed her face upward, allowed her human flesh disappear, and cradled Arran close as she quickly made for the pale glint of sun.

Barely a moment later, the volcano erupted with such staggering force that it nearly deafened her. With the enormous blast ringing in her ears, she desperately dodged to and fro, narrowly avoiding collisions with smoking boulders and barely cooled clumps of lava, the leading edge blackened and smoothed before the molten rock burst into hissing droplets when the natural ordinance hit a target.

The sea was black, all of a sudden, and all her relief was gone. It was taking too long – there were bubbles coming from Arran's mouth, and she knew that he would not survive the twisting, weaving path she was being forced to take. She pushed blindly through the ashes, and the sudden, searing heat, ignoring the tormented cries of sea and stone that writhed and wrenched themselves to pieces.

She couldn't see the peak of the mountain itself – she knew the tunnel they had exited was somewhere on the lower slopes, but there was nothing visible in the murky water except brief flashes of red lightning that flickered all around her, disorienting and dim.

It took an age and a half to reach the surface, but reach it she did. Hoisting Arran's head above the water forced her to waste her energy taking the form of human flesh again, but she tilted him back and pounded on his chest to get his heart working, relieved laughter mixed with more than a few tears as he gasped and spit and coughed out red-tinted water, his eyelids barely fluttering open as he gulped the relatively pure air.

Blood instantly gathered in a ruddy pool around him,

mixing with the volcano's silt to form a thick soup of filth. Sharks were too smart to stay around when they felt the rumblings of the earth below them, but she wasn't about to tempt them into being foolish when she was too exhausted to do anything about it.

"Just lie flat," she said, making sure he could float on his back while she got her bearings. There was an immense plume of smoke and dust pouring from the ocean's surface less than a mile away, a glinting swath of smothered fish bobbing up to the surface like prizes in a children's game. They had to leave if they didn't wish to be similarly boiled alive. It would be a long way to Niheba, and she would need to stay above the water, swimming as slowly and laboriously as a land-dweller if she was to keep Arran living, ducking under for quick bursts of speed only as long as he could hold his breath.

Her fingers brushed the side of his neck as she tried to grab a hold of him, and she recoiled in pain, hissing at the touch of his skin. He was burning with a fever that had nothing to do with the temperature of his surroundings. Despite the heat inside him now, the seawater would soon start to chill him all too well. She knew how little time the humans could spend in the open ocean even if they were in the best of health – and there was so much blood trailing behind them as she started to move through the water. She would need to hurry, but it would be a long, long way.

* * *

Megrithe wanted to stop crying, but that was the one thing she just couldn't do. She had been so sure. She had *seen* him. In the bowels of the ocean the Siheldi burrowed like rats, nesting and breeding and haunting the subterranean darkness, waiting for their mother to break them free. And in the middle of it all was a little hollow, like two cupped hands holding a crystal bowl. Arran had been there, curled up at the bottom, dreaming away an impossible pain, waiting for something.

She could not flatter herself into believing that he had been waiting for her, but why else would the song have given her such a vision? She knew for certain that the sight had stemmed from the incantation. It reminded her of the *callawil's* singing: beautiful and alien and as cold as the grave.

If the image had been meant for her, then it was an exquisitely painful cruelty. She had come so close. She had felt like she could almost touch him before the mountain's tortured agonies had taken him away. She felt as if the devastating wave racing to catch them could do no more damage than had been done to her already, but her heart was not the only thing at risk.

There was Niheba, and the conviction that a few innocent people still remained on the poisoned isle. They might still be saved, and Nikko was doing his very, very best to get them back to land before the roiling surf caught the city up and plunged it into death.

Her head felt like it would split open first, spilling her brains into the ocean and leaving her empty. She almost wished it, just so the pounding agony would stop. The crying was making it worse. She wanted to be safe. She wanted to feel well. She just wanted to disappear.

No one said a word as Nikko focused all his attention on speed. They simply tried to hold on. Jairus had an arm around her, and Leofric kept the back of her collar in his tight fist, but she felt no security from either of them. She kept seeing that shape flickering underneath the surface of the milky boulders, the crest of a back flexing its muscles; the shadow of claws clenching to test their strength. A suggestion of teeth, sharp and shining, gnashing together in anticipation with the scent of supper on the air.

She wanted to vomit. Her thoughts were ticking over with things that had never been there before, and her blistered hand felt like a boiled potato. She shouldn't have touched the stone. She felt as if the action had infected her, and something had settled in her stomach like a batch of rotting fish.

"They are coming," she whispered to herself, too softly for anyone to hear. The words burned inside her, but there was no relief in saying them aloud. There would be no relief for anyone, ever again, because they were coming. There would be nowhere to hide now that they were free.

Megrithe was lost in her own half-lucid twilight by the time they reached the shallows surrounding Niheba again. The rush had been for nothing. The news had gotten to the island first.

Everyone had heard the explosion; everyone had seen the column of black smoke on the horizon, struck through with lightning, raining down chucks of stone and clouds of pulverized rock. The city was in a panic, *neneckt* and humans alike crowding the streets, pointing and praying, while the smarter residents secured their possessions and the smartest sneaked into wide open doors and secured the possessions of their neighbors.

The quays were rapidly emptying as she stumbled ashore, leaning heavily on Jairus. She was glad to see it –

there was safety away from the waterfront, she hoped. But something didn't look quite right. There were men in the harbor, but they were only submerged up to the waist as they tried to haul the smaller fishing boats, already stuck in the mud, behind the stone jetties for some sort of protection from what was about to come.

"We need to get inland," Leofric said.

"There's no height to this place," Jairus told him. "There's nowhere to be safe."

"We don't need to go up," Nikko said. "We need to go under. Follow them."

He nodded towards a stream of *neneckt* heading into the center of the city, quickly and with much greater order than the humans who tried, unsuccessfully, to follow them. The *neneckt* did not hurt them, but any land-dweller that attempted to join their exodus was firmly put aside.

Suddenly a man shouted and shoved back, and then everyone was stampeding, flooding the route the *neneckt* were taking, incensed that the sea folk were heading towards their own private safety while leaving the poor and unprotected to drown.

"Perhaps not," Nikko said, steering them in the opposite direction as the crash of broken glass and a shrill cry made Megrithe cringe. "There are other places."

"I don't – I don't feel well," she said, her words cut short as she fell to her knees, the entire island jolting beneath them as a new bellow from the mountain made the buildings sway like dancers. There was nothing in her stomach to come up when she retched into the gutter, the pounding in her head exploding into blue-green lights in front of her eyes, her face as flushed as if she had sat in front of the hearth for too long.

"She's broiling," Jairus said, his hand on her forehead as she wiped sour spittle from the corner of her mouth. He sounded scared. She hadn't heard him sound scared before, not even when he was running to fight a *neneckt* three times his size.

"They are coming," she said urgently, but he wasn't listening.

"She needs a physician," he was telling Leofric.

"Do you really think we'll find one with some spare time on his hands?" Nikko said, gesturing to the spreading chaos around them. "We have only moments to get to safety. I have seen this before. You still have *ychauyad* in you, and there are safe places under the island's center that are made for this very purpose. We have to go."

"All right," Jairus decided quickly, picking up Megrithe as easily as if she was a little girl.

"Stop that," she said, squirming feebly. "I'm fine. I can walk. Put me down. You're more hurt than I am."

"You shut up right this instant," he said, silencing her quite effectively as she gaped in astonishment at the uncharacteristic impoliteness. "We have to be quick."

While the *neneckt* had dwelt near the volcano for countless years, and had memories of its moodiness to prepare them for its outbursts, the human colonists on the island were too new to have experienced such a disaster. No one seemed to know how to react. Pockets of terror and violence almost immediately sprung up across the city's human neighborhoods, and it appeared that they would soon join and meld into one seamless riot.

"They're all going to die," Megrithe said quietly as a

group of women stood wailing in front of their homes, begging for help from gods who lived too far away to hear them. There were children there, clinging to their mothers' skirts as they stared wide-eyed at the darkening sky.

Jairus didn't answer her, but he didn't need to. His jaw was clenched and his face set stonily forward. He knew it as well as she did. There were tears in his eyes.

"The city guard will try to move them into the palace," Leofric called over his shoulder, motioning towards a small cluster of the local lawmen that were herding the women and anyone else they could find towards a long queue clogging the main boulevard. "May the gods grant that they get there."

The main roads soon became too crowded for anyone to push their way through. None of the jostling or shouting or pushing made a difference: even the side streets were impassable as hopeful humans from the other boulevards tried to sneak through alleyways to find some more promising path but found themselves stuck again, only now in narrower places.

By the time the first piercing screams rang in from the harbor, followed by the crash of snapping timbers, the hollow ring of falling bricks, and the relentless churning of hungry waters, the crush was so dense that no one, not even the *neneckt,* could move an inch.

"This way," Nikko said, putting his shoulder to the door to the nearest building and pushing them through, followed by a few strangers desperate for any outlet. It was a tall construction, three floors with a flat roof, and it was the highest point for blocks around.

As soon as they reached the rooftop, which had been turned into a potted garden for the enjoyment of its residents, the space started to fill with people. Megrithe wasn't sure how Jairus made it up all three flights without dropping her – he was breathing hard and his arms were shaking as he set her down on a carved wooden bench under the shade of a spindly fig tree. Everyone turned towards the sea.

Megrithe immediately levered herself up and pushed her way towards the rail. She had to see. She would look at what she had unleashed onto the island and its people. It was her fault, and she knew it.

She had woken the sleeping beast by following the *callawif's* instruction, and these were her deaths. She would not allow herself to flinch away from the devastated harbor: its buildings demolished, its beautiful pools and sculptures buried under fathoms of churning mud, seawater, bodies, and debris.

The gnawing flood crept inland, its initial power lost as it digested half the city, but strong enough still to destroy nearly everything that tried to stand in its way. The people had mostly fled, but there had been plenty enough of the unwilling, the unlucky, or the unbelieving to get caught up in the terrible tide.

On the street below her, the pavement was still dry, but every rooftop she could see, flat or peaked, was now densely occupied with dazed or crying faces. Though the sight was tragic enough to fill her nightmares for the rest of her life, it also brought some level of relief to see how many had escaped. There would be trials to come, of course – most of the humans were now homeless, and the tainted water would bring plague with it, which would kill many more. But for now, hundreds of them were as safe as possible, and that was something, at least.

"It isn't your fault," Leofric said, reading the

expression on her face as she finally wrenched her eyes away. "You do not control the fires of the earth."

"But I helped to stir up what does."

"I don't think you did. Did you hear the chanting? The man who sang that song is the one responsible. Not you."

"It was the Warden," Jairus said, rage making his voice tight. "I would know him anywhere."

"The Divided did this?" Megrithe asked, searching his face for any sign of a lie. "Did you know?" she demanded a moment later.

"No," he insisted. "No, I didn't. I had no part in it. I never would have allowed such a thing. You have to believe that. This is beyond everything – I could never want this."

"All right, I believe you," she said, and it was true. No one but a soulless, vile monster would be capable of planning such wanton death, and she did not think that's what Jairus was.

She didn't know what to do. She wanted to form a plan, connect the events and make sense of everything – first, she would have to find the Warden and condemn him to the worst torture she could devise – but the wheels of her mind were spinning loose and wobbly, unable to find purchase.

"All right," she said again, less certainly, rubbing her temples. Everything hurt. Inside and out, everything hurt. "We can –" she started to say, raising her head to stretch the throbbing muscles in her bruised and swollen neck, and the motion made her catch sight of someone on the street below.

Perhaps it was the blood that drew her eye, as bright as paint down the front of the man's shirt. Perhaps it was the way he was slumped over the arm of a young woman in trousers caked in mud and salt, with his face hidden by her shoulder and her eyes heavy with deep, deep weariness as she dragged him along the cobbles.

"Oh my God," she breathed, nearly tumbling over the railing as she craned to get a better look. Her legs were unable to support her, and she grasped feebly at the wrought iron as she leaned forward enough to make Nikko grab her back.

"You'll fall," he said, but she pushed him away.

"That's him," she cried, pointing, but by the time Nikko and Leofric had followed her finger, the pair had disappeared into the mulling crowds. "That's Arran. That's – I just – that was him," she stammered, scanning the throngs that had swallowed them. "I just saw him. I swear I did. Where did he go?"

"You need rest," Leofric said, sharing a glance with Nikko. It was a glance that said that she was not well in the head, and that she needed to be placated so she wouldn't hurt herself. It made her angry.

"I saw him," she said again, but now she was crying so hard that she even started to doubt herself. She hadn't seen his face, but she was sure she didn't need to. She knew him. She had felt him. Something inside her had felt its twin in the limp form stumbling along the cobbles. Something that was coming. Something that wanted to be free. "At least, I think I did..."

"No one could have survived that explosion," Leofric said gently, leading her away as she twisted her head to keep her eyes on the street for as long as she could. "Even if he ever was under the mountain. You know that. We barely made it out ourselves, and we had Nikko to help us."

"But I saw him," she sobbed, her eyes closing of their own accord as Leofric eased her gently back onto the bench, making shushing noises as she curled herself into a tight, aching ball. "I saw him," she repeated to herself before her battered body finally gave out on her, plunging her deep into a nightmarish rest.

EPILOGUE

The panic and terror that swept through Niheba appeared as little more than the jerky, mute motions of far-away dolls in Tiaraku's mirrors. Each exquisitely framed oblong showed a different quarter of the city, some of which were now nothing more than swirling whirlpools of soiled water and silt. Broken beams and pieces of trees piled up in narrow alleys, damming the smaller streets and channeling the flood inward towards the huddled masses screaming for sanctuary at the palace gates.

Tiaraku had not let them in. Even Habur thought that was disgraceful as he limped along invisibly, no longer able to hold even a basic shape underwater thanks to the serious wound that the Daggertooth had given him.

Coral glass was the only thing that could kill a *neneckt*, and his own blade, snatched from his hands by his quicker opponent, had nearly finished him. It was only by luck that Habur had survived the encounter, but he wasn't about to give Nikodelmus another chance to get it right.

"Your Majesty," he said, doing his best to bow when he reached Tiaraku's presence, but the *neneckt* king was absorbed in his mirrors, and distracted by his other guest. "Mistress," he added, bowing to the *callawif* in turn.

She did acknowledge him, with a slight nod, but then she returned her attention to the king. Habur waited, looking at the changing pictures in the gilded frames. That bastard Bartolo was in one of them, a piece of red iron clutched in his hand as he huddled with a hundred other refugees in a corridor of a building. The Warden, his scarred and pitted face smiling broadly as he sat in his sheltered cave, his hands outstretched onto the table in front of him, something bright and glittering peeking through his fingers. The darkness, dim and smoking, that had once been Sind Heofonne's pulsing heart.

"I wanted Swinn recovered, Habur," Tiaraku said eventually, and his warrior cringed. That was not a tone he ever wanted to hear from his master. "Yet here you stand, weak and empty handed."

"I was not expecting the Daggertooth, sire."

"The Daggertooth," Tiaraku mocked, spitting the name back at him. "I should have you take his place in the cells. It was a mistake to ever let him go."

Habur didn't say anything. When Tiaraku was angry, making excuses would only fan him into a blind rage.

"It matters little," the *eallawif* said to the king, her eyes locked onto one of the panes of glass, which showed a swarm of people packed into Oakwood Lane. Among them was an injured man held up by a *neneckt* in a woman's shape. "Here he is. Send soldiers for him."

"He doesn't have the gemstones," Tiaraku rumbled irritably.

"He doesn't need them anymore. Neither do you. He has been touched," she said, pressing a fingertip over his heart. "He has the seed inside him now. It will do."

"I will fetch him for you, Mistress," Habur said, studying the face closely so he would remember it. It would be easy enough. Humans couldn't change how they looked. "I will not fail again."

"Very well," Tiaraku conceded eventually. He did not have to mention the consequences of another disappointment.

"And the girl, too," the *callawif* added, a flick of her wrist changing the image to focus on a young woman, her dress smeared in blood and her skin flushed with fever, lying down on a rooftop with her eyes tightly closed, long tracks of tears cutting through the grime on her face. "I need her for myself."

"As you wish, Mistress," Habur said, storing her features away in his mind. "I will bring them both to you."

The *callawif* nodded. "It will be good to see my family again," she said, and Tiaraku barked a short laugh.

"You must be so proud of your child," he said to her.

"I am," she replied, smiling fondly as she turned back to where the sleeping woman twitched uneasily in her dreams. The *callawif* reached out to touch the glass again, stroking her cheek across the distance, and the woman sighed and quieted down. "Both of them."

GLOSSARY OF TERMS

Agnise: A Guild agent working in Niheba who uncovers an important secret.

Andrus Gunhilde: A former Guild inspector who lives in Niheba.

Arran Swinn: Captain of the *Tortoise* who is accused of smuggling by the Guild of Miners, setting him on a journey that leads him to the depths of the *neneckt* homeland. His parents are Elspeth and Giles Swinn.

Bartolo: A servant of King Tiaraku who is responsible for bringing Arran Swinn to Niheba and forcing him to comply with Tiaraku's plots.

Bay of Burlera: The expanse of ocean stretching from the western prairie lands to the northward turn of Rhior-Adril's coastline. The city of Paderborn sits on its shore.

Bezhaka: A type of white stone imbued with magical properties. It is highly sacred to the *neneckt*.

Cantrid: A small trading town to the west of Paderborn.

Divided: A cult of Siheldi worshippers who are based in caverns underneath Niheba. They are led by the Warden.

Durville: The sailing master of the *Tortoise* and a long-time friend of Arran Swinn.

Eallawif: Ancient, capricious creatures that most often takes the form of a beautiful young woman. *Eallawif* grant wishes to humans in exchange for a heavy price.

Elargwyd: A *neneckt* who seeks passage on the Tortoise from Arran Swinn. She seeks to rob him of his pendant and use him for her own gains.

Elspeth Swinn: Arran Swinn's mother, who used to run a boarding house in Paderborn.

Emyer-Ekvori: The underwater city of the *neneckt*, which extends around and through the island of Niheba.

Faidal: A *neneckt* who claims to be a Guild inspector and convinces Arran to go with him to Niheba before finding his missing pendant on the sea floor.

Fyrendor: The human word for the fiery gateway to hell in their religious myths. Many believe that the Siheldi live behind it.

Genedi: A *neneckt* functionary who finds himself on the wrong side of Tiaraku's ambitions.

Giles Swinn: Arran Swinn's deceased father, who gave his life to the Siheldi in exchange for his family's safety.

Guild of Miners: A powerful association of inspectors

and enforcers responsible for regulating the sale and trade of red iron throughout the continent. They are known for their ruthless tactics and low tolerance for smugglers.

Habur: A *neneckt* warrior who does Tiaraku's bidding.

Irithi Athdra: A group of powerful Siheldi spirits that have been released into the world by the destruction of Sind Heofonne.

Ivory Isles: A cluster of islands to the far west of Paderborn, known for their balmy weather and exotic goods.

Jairus Lanque: A Guild agent who has infiltrated the Divided and attempts to learn Bartolo's secrets.

Lanning: A black market tradesman and banker for discerning clients in Paderborn.

Leofric Gunhilde: A retired politician who agrees to help Megrithe find Arran Swinn on Niheba.

Malveisin: The king of Rhior-Adril who resides in Paderborn.

Megrithe Prinsthorpe: A Guild inspector who pursues Arran Swinn to Niheba after being informed of his purported smuggling activities.

Neneckt: A race of sea-dwelling creatures that can change their shape at will when above the water. Under the ocean, they are invisible beings of spirit.

Nievfaya: A *neneckt* slave who works for Tiaraku and Bartolo, also known as Faidal and Elargwyd. She is responsible for bring Arran to Niheba, but also tries to help him escape from the Siheldi.

Niheba: A large island to the north and east of Paderborn, where the *neneckt* live. Human trade to the island is regulated by King Tiaraku and the Treaty of Libourg.

Nikodelmus Daggertooth: Known to Megrithe as Nikko, he is a *neneckt* who lives with Leofric Gunhilde and has a complicated past in Niheba.

Norem Cloche: A physician employed by the Guild who befriended Jairus Lanque as a child.

Oughon: A member of the order of *neneckt* shaman who are both healers and keepers of rites and rituals.

Paderborn: The capital city of Rhior-Adril, a spreading metropolis that lives in constant fear of the Siheldi. King Malveisin reigns over the city, and the Guild also considers Paderborn its seat of power.

Port Ravenaught: A frontier settlement to the north of Paderborn. It is known for its rough living and as a gateway for smugglers.

Red iron: A rare and costly substance that is the only sure way to repel the Siheldi. Its production and sale is tightly controlled by the Guild of Miners.

Rhior-Adril: The mainland country that includes Paderborn, Cantrid, Port Ravenaught, and other notable cities. Its king is Malveisin and its residents are primarily human.

Siheldi: Evil spirits that feast on human souls and only emerge under the cover of darkness. They terrorize the populace and can only be repelled by the presence of genuine red iron.

Sind Heofonne: The *neneckt* term for the underwater prison that holds the Siheldi Queen.

Tiaraku: The king of the *neneckt*, whose iron-fisted rule has caused much discontent among his people. He enlists Bartolo and Faidal to help him free the Siheldi Queen and take control of the spirits himself.

Treaty of Libourg: The law governing trade between Rhior-Adril and Niheba, instituted when Tiaraku came to the throne.

Warden: The leader of the Divided who attempts to gain control of the Siheldi Queen.

Ychauyad: A *neneckt* substance that allows human beings to breathe and live underwater.

ABOUT THE AUTHOR

Jennifer Bresnick is the author of the award-winning fantasies *The Last Death of Tev Chrisini* and *The Spoil of Zanuth-Karun*. Born and raised on Long Island, NY, she now resides in the Boston area, fervently avoiding all discussions about professional sports.

When she isn't writing down the conversations in her head to give them an appearance of respectability, Jen enjoys getting bossed around by her cat and spending time at the archery range.

Please visit *www.jenniferbresnick.com* for more information on *The Dreamer's Shadow* series and exclusive details about other upcoming works.